Sunbaked

Sunbather

Sunbaked

Junie Coffey

LAKE UNION
PUBLISHING

Text copyright © 2015, 2017 by Junie Coffey

Published by Lake Union Publishing, Seattle

www.apub.com

Amazon, the Amazon logo, and Lake Union Publishing are trademarks of Amazon.com, Inc., or its affiliates.

ISBN-13: 9781477823934
ISBN-10: 147782393X

Cover design by Danielle Christopher

Printed in the United States of America

Sunbaked

Sudaheh

1

Nina bought the house off the Internet. Just like that. It was two o'clock on a cold New York morning, and she held a glass of red wine in one hand while sirens wailed in the distance and Bob Marley played on the stereo. It was exactly three months and fourteen hours since she had arrived home from teaching a class (The Mating Rituals of Canadian Snowbirds in a Florida Retirement Community) at the college and opened the door to find her soon-to-be ex-husband in flagrante delicto with his paralegal on the sofa. After a brief, undignified scene, husband and paralegal—wearing a ridiculously tight skirt—scurried out together. Nina called a locksmith to change the locks, a cleaning company to scrub every surface in her violated apartment, and a fumigator for good measure. Then she sat on the sofa looking out at the city lights.

Three months went by. Three months of long coffee breaks with her best friend, Louise, sitting across from her, nodding her head sympathetically. Nina taught her classes, walked home in the rain, and sat on her sofa, staring out the window while cups of tea went cold in her hands.

Then the Christmas lights went up around town, and things began to look more festive. Nina joined a gym. And a book club. Then the group chose *Ethan Frome* as its February selection, and she quit.

Seriously? she thought. But it was starting to stay light a little longer every day, she noticed.

One slushy March day, Nina arrived home from work after dark, shucked off her damp winter coat and heavy boots in the hall, and took her dinner of leftovers into the living room. When the news ended, she clicked off the television and surveyed her apartment from the sofa. She'd spent a lot of time choosing the curtains and arranging everything just so when they'd moved in, but now it felt more like a slightly tatty hotel room in limboland than home. She sighed and stretched. She decided to clean out the hall closet. It was getting hard to open the door without something falling on her head. Over the last few weeks, she had been methodically, drawer by drawer, ridding the apartment of any lingering remnants of Darren.

Standing on her tiptoes, she pulled wool hats, cloth shopping bags, rinds of ski wax, and other junk from the top shelf. Darren's never-used cycling gloves. Right into the garbage can. Two points. Then reaching as far back as she could, she pulled out her old green canvas duffel bag. It was pre-Darren vintage. She held it in her hands and looked at it, trying out the bestselling Japanese clutter expert's technique of deciding what should stay and what should go. The handles still bore the old, curled airline tags from her pre–married life adventures: NBO—Nairobi; NAS—Nassau; MBJ—Montego Bay. She'd hold on to it.

She started to fold it. There was something inside. She sat on the sofa and unzipped the bag. Tucked away in the bottom, she found a pair of pink flip-flops wrapped in an old red-, green-, and yellow-striped T-shirt and a faded paperback novel. She remembered reading it on the beach in Port Antonio, Jamaica, while Louise napped on the chair beside her after sampling every fruity rum cocktail on the beach-bar menu.

She walked over to the bookcase and pulled down her photo album. She turned the pages slowly, her eyes drifting over the pictures of her younger self and Louise in Lamu the summer after they graduated from college, laughing and holding up wooden carvings they'd just bought in the covered market. The two of them waving to the camera in front of the Eiffel Tower. Playing darts with some motorbike-touring accountants they'd met at a tiki bar in the Florida Keys on a weekend girls' getaway—her first freelance travel-writing gig. Then a little bit older, with different hairstyles, smiling at the camera from beach lounges in Jamaica. That was a fun trip. She was in grad school then. Still doing some travel writing on the side, when she could get the assignments and the time off school to travel to Bequia, a bed-and-breakfast in Vermont, or wherever. She was up for any adventure an editor might dangle in front of her in those days. An article on what you can do in forty-eight hours with forty-eight dollars in Little Rock? No problem.

Then the Darren era. Not so many smiles.

They'd met at a charity fund-raiser at a fancy uptown hotel, where his firm had bought a table. Nina was wearing a dress she'd bought at the Salvation Army shop and had volunteered to run the silent auction. He'd bought a pizza party for $500 and donated it back to the Boys & Girls Club, which struck her as generous and heartwarming. He was a few years older than she was. He had an aloofness she'd perceived as mysterious, combined with a high-powered career, good looks, and a grown-up lifestyle that her twenty-five-year-old self had found exotic and intriguing. It was like visiting another country.

She peered at their wedding photo, taken on the back lawn of her parents' house in Maine about a year later. Funny she'd never noticed before, but Louise's smile did not make it all the way up to her eyes in that shot. Nina turned the page. By the ocean in Big Sur, California, on their honeymoon. That had been nice. A corporate golf tournament sponsored by Darren's law firm. Weekends in the Hamptons with his friends. By that point, she had retired the duffel bag, and they were using the set of hard-sided luggage they'd received as a wedding gift. She graduated and got a "real" job teaching at the college.

She turned the page. Darren and Nina on the Caribbean cruise they'd taken as a compromise between her yen to rent a beach cottage on Eleuthera and his preference for a five-star hotel in Miami. The ship had been seven stories high. She turned the page again. There they were with a large group at the ski chalet owned by the senior partner of Darren's law firm, the year she'd reluctantly agreed to trade Christmas in Maine with her family for the invitation to Aspen that Darren had so coveted.

There they were a couple of years later, standing in front of a Mayan pyramid, wearing business casual. That was at a convention at a Las Vegas hotel, not in the Mexican jungle. She'd given up the opportunity to write a piece for a well-known magazine about cruising the Arctic on an icebreaker to go with him, making an effort to save their relationship. She hardly recognized herself.

Nina closed the album. *Maybe that's just life,* she thought. She wandered into the kitchen and poured herself a glass of red wine, then wandered back into the living room, stepping over the pile of hats, shopping bags, and half-used sticks of ski wax littering the hall floor. She plopped down on the sofa, put her feet up on the ottoman, and flipped open her laptop. She took a sip of wine and idly surfed the Internet. It was her favorite waste of time—scanning the real estate listings in the Caribbean, pretending she was in the market for a cozy little beach house on a sunny tropical island.

As she clicked through the pages, she considered the drastic change of course her life had recently taken. If she was honest with herself, she had to admit she was relieved that Darren had finally taken his numerous pairs of tasseled loafers and cleared out. Things hadn't been good between them for a long time. People do change over the course of a decade, and not always for the better.

Outside, snow began to fall in big, wet clumps, and the wind picked up, whistling in the vents. Bob Marley was singing "Stir It Up" as Nina scrolled through real estate. Pink and blue and yellow villas.

Rooms full of rattan furniture, potted palms, and tropical fabrics. The bright-blue rectangles of swimming pools and blue streaks of ocean viewed from various condominium balconies. Not really her style, and she couldn't actually afford any of them, but it was soothing to browse through the photos and daydream. She could feel the wine beginning to hit her, warming her chest and making her feel a bit light-headed.

Then she saw it: Sundrift Cottage. A little clapboard house with an expanse of brilliant turquoise sea behind it, framed by several tall, graceful coconut palms. She could almost feel the warm, gentle breeze on her neck and the soft, sun-warmed sand beneath her bare feet. The house looked a bit rough around the edges—its once-yellow paint was faded and peeling, and on the windows flanking the front door, the wooden shutters hung at odd angles. The flowering shrubs and grass on either side of the path that led to the door were shaggy and overgrown, and the white picket fence was missing a few teeth. But it was adorable!

Nina clicked through the three or four other pictures attached to the listing. It looked to be just three rooms: a small bedroom, a bathroom with aged fixtures, and a large, open kitchen/living/dining room running the length of the cottage facing the water. Big back windows filled with a vista of palm trees, vine-covered dunes, white sand, and turquoise water. A screen door swung open onto a deep veranda with a couple of steps down to the sand.

It's perfect! thought Nina. A blank canvas for a new chapter in life. She jumped up, did a few dancing steps around the room in time with the reggae beat, and took another swig of her wine. She braced herself and looked at the asking price.

"Things are looking up!" she said to the photo of her late cat, Puff, peering down at her from a bookshelf.

According to the listing, the cottage was located in the village of Coconut Cove on Pineapple Cay. "The prettiest little town in the islands, and a great place to call home," claimed the real estate website. Despite her travel-writing experience, Nina had never heard of it.

Satellite images revealed a bright emerald-green dollop in the vibrant blue Caribbean Sea. Coconut Cove looked to be the only settlement of any size on the island, a tidy grid of lanes alongside a wide, sand-rimmed cove on the west side.

The Pineapple Cay Chamber of Commerce website banner read PINEAPPLE CAY: THE GOOD LIFE IS OUR BUSINESS. The website had photos of candy-colored cottages with window boxes overflowing with tropical flowers, a group of smiling schoolchildren in their classroom, smiling fishermen hauling their catch out of the turquoise sea, a smiling woman in a bright print dress weighing produce at a busy open-air fruit-and-vegetable market, and a reggae band playing to a crowd of happy people at a beach bar with a red-and-gold sunset for a backdrop.

"Just what the doctor ordered, I'd say," Nina said to herself. Without giving herself the chance to talk herself out of it, she tapped out an e-mail to the real estate office, making an offer on Sundrift Cottage slightly below the asking price but at the top of her comfort range. She didn't want to do anything rash, after all. She paused for a moment, her fingers hovering over the keyboard, then added a postscript.

> P. S. I know it's a bit strange to make an offer on
> a house sight unseen, but I just called it quits with
> my husband of ten years, and I think Pineapple
> Cay is just the change I need. What I have been
> looking for.

It wasn't like Nina to bare her soul to an anonymous e-mail account, but it also wasn't like Nina to get drunk and try to buy a ramshackle house in the Caribbean off the Internet, like she was ordering a new blender. Then she drained the last of her wine in one gulp. What. The. Hell. She put her finger on the button and clicked "Send." Nervous energy propelled her out of her chair and sent her pacing the room, her mind racing.

She had done a couple of laps of the living room, kitchen, and dining room when she heard the ping of an incoming e-mail.

She wondered who could be writing to her at two o'clock in the morning, and then she braced herself. Maybe it was Darren with some late-night spite. Worse yet, maybe he'd had a change of heart and was pleading with her to take him back. That would be a buzzkill.

Not a chance, buddy, thought Nina. She went into the bedroom she'd shared with Darren until a few months ago and lay like a starfish diagonally across the bed, stretching her arms and legs out wide, making a snow angel on the feather duvet. She went into the kitchen and made herself a heaping pile of cheese- and salsa-smothered nachos in the microwave, spilling grated cheese all over the counter and not cleaning it up. She set the nachos on the table in the living room, poured herself another glass of wine, and took a few more steps around the room, doing some interpretive dance to the music with her wineglass in one hand. Then curiosity got the better of her. It was probably just junk mail. With some low-grade anxiety, she slid back into the chair and focused on the computer screen.

To her great surprise, she saw that the message was from Pineapple Cay Real Estate Re: Sundrift Cottage.

> Hi Nina!
> Great to get your message! YES the cottage is still available!!! Your offer is in the ballpark. I am sure we can work something out. As the listing states, the property is to be sold as is, but not to worry—with a little TLC it will be a cozy little nest again! It really is a bargain for beachfront in Coconut Cove. Attached is the offer document. Sign it, scan it, and send it back to me ASAP, OK? You are going to LOVE Pineapple Cay!!

All the best,
Pansy Gallagher
Pineapple Cay Real Estate Ltd.
"If you cannot be a poet, be the poem." —David
Carradine

Huh. A split-second reply to her query about the property in the middle of the night. Apparent acceptance of her below-asking-price offer. Eight exclamation points. An e-mail signature with an inspirational quotation from the famous American actor and martial artist David Carradine. Pansy? Maybe it all added up to a deal that was too good to be true. Nina felt her heart sink a little. Wistfully, she clicked through the photographs of Sundrift Cottage again. Maybe bouncing the idea off Louise would help. The phone went to voice mail twice before Louise finally picked up.

"Hello?" She sounded like she was still half-asleep. Nina was totally wired. She paced the room, holding the phone to her ear.

"Louise, I need your advice. I think I just did something really crazy. I'm thinking of buying a house on Pineapple Cay. What do you think?"

"What? Nina? It's . . . two o'clock in the morning. Are you OK? You don't sound OK."

"I'm feeling pretty good, actually. Free as a bird. If you can't be a poet, be the poem, right? You only live once, so better make it good. Really, why should I stay here? I mean, New York is great, but it's a big world with lots of other places in it. It's not like I'd be leaving home. I'm from Maine, after all. Already left home. You can't swim in the ocean in Maine in January. Point to Pineapple Cay. And I can work from anywhere with an Internet connection."

"Nina, have you been drinking? Do you want me to come over? I mean, I'm happy you're finally getting back on the horse, or boat, or whatever, but this feels a little sudden."

"It's late. You should get some sleep. Let's have coffee tomorrow. About eleven at the Cuppa Joe? Thanks, Louise. You've really helped me see clearly to my next move. See you tomorrow."

Nina printed, signed, scanned, and e-mailed the offer document back to Pansy Gallagher, fell on her bed, and slept like a baby. By nine o'clock the next morning she'd been to her bank and signed a few more papers. By eleven o'clock, when she met an astounded, but enthusiastic, Louise for coffee, she was the owner of Sundrift Cottage. A week later, she'd arranged a leave of absence from her teaching job on campus, lined up a few online courses to teach next term from her new home on Pineapple Cay (just to keep some money coming in), and made some calls to resuscitate her travel-writing career. She rented out the apartment, which would generate some income, too; eventually she could sell it for a sum that would buy her a lot of coconuts and sunscreen. She promised to e-mail Louise regularly so that her friend would know she hadn't been kidnapped by rum-running pirates, and then she boarded a plane to Pineapple Cay with only her green canvas duffel bag as a carry-on. New chapter in life, no excess baggage.

~

Four hours after boarding a plane in New York, Nina was winding her way through the beige-carpeted tunnel that attached the belly of the airplane to the cavernous arrivals hall at the airport on the main island. There, she joined a long, snaking queue of several hundred holidaymakers just arrived from another frozen northern city waiting to clear customs. They were all dressed for fun times in sloppy T-shirts, shorts, and new sundresses—dragging large suitcases, golf clubs, and baby strollers. The line moved briskly, and before she knew it she'd received a friendly "Welcome to the Islands" from the agent and a stamp in her passport.

Most of the passengers turned right through the doors leading to a row of waiting buses that would whisk them off to their all-inclusive resorts. Nina, however, turned left through the double swinging doors—as Pansy had told her to do—into the interisland departures terminal. It was smaller than the other side of the airport, with an airy, relaxed atmosphere and a well-used feel. The low-key crowd seemed to be made up mainly of islanders. Businesspeople with briefcases at their feet sat reading newspapers, families hugged one another hello or good-bye, and small clumps of vacationers were scattered here and there.

A counter ran along the back wall of the terminal. It was divided into kiosks for a dozen or more interisland airline companies servicing the fifteen-odd inhabited islands in the archipelago. Nina picked out the cheery yellow sign that read PINEAPPLE CAY AIR and headed over to collect her boarding pass. A few minutes later her flight was called, and she joined about twenty other passengers in following the ticket agent across the tarmac toward a small white aircraft. She felt the heat of the tropical sun on her shoulders.

It was a short half-hour hop to Pineapple Cay. In the few minutes they were airborne, Nina studied her fellow passengers. At the front of the plane, a group of casually dressed businessmen chatted among themselves, laptops on their knees. Behind them, a young mother with three small children took up an entire row. The children were dressed in their Sunday best—the boy in a clean and ironed white shirt and pressed navy-blue pants, and the two little girls in fancy party dresses, their hair done up in elaborate braids tied with brightly colored ribbons. They sat quietly on the edges of their seats, looking all around them.

A few rows ahead of Nina sat a couple who looked to be in their early twenties, both a little overweight and very pale, huddled close together and looking out of the small porthole window at the water below. *Honeymooners,* Nina thought. The young woman wore a flowered dress with a bright-pink cardigan over it and shiny, pink heeled sandals. New clothes bought for this trip, Nina guessed. The woman's new husband was dressed in blue jeans and a faded black T-shirt with a beer logo on it, a baseball cap with another corporate logo on it, and dirty white sneakers. *This was the girl's idea,* thought Nina. She probably spent hours searching for the perfect destination for her dream honeymoon. He just showed up.

Across the aisle from the young pair, a tiny white-haired couple also huddled together. They were looking at a field guide. They were probably about fifty years older than the honeymooners and were dressed in identical khaki shirts, pants, and hats, each wearing a sort of canvas fishing vest with lots of pockets. They wore similar tan walking shoes, and even the silver wire-rimmed glasses perched on similarly long, thin noses were the same. They looked like a pair of birds, twittering quietly to each other. Clearly they were birders looking to check off a few more species on their life lists. Their appearance and mannerisms were so alike, it was almost as if they had abandoned trying to be individual entities at some point and were now fused into one being.

Watching the older couple share a packet of complimentary in-flight cookies, Nina felt a small pang of—what? Regret that she wouldn't be sharing cookies with Darren in her golden years? Nostalgia for the ten lost years of her marriage? Maybe, but she also felt something else—relief. Thank God it would not be Darren and her sailing into the sunset. She was no longer responsible for his happiness or his dirty socks. She glanced over at the newlyweds. Thank her lucky stars, also, that she was not just setting out on married life with a guy who thought it was appropriate to wear a baseball cap on an airplane. Nina sniffed. She checked her emotional temperature. No, she did not regret a thing. She felt a tingle of adventure she hadn't felt in years.

The sound of the engine changed pitch, and they began to descend. Nina leaned over to look out the window. There was Pineapple Cay below them. An oval of emerald green, with steep cliffs on the Atlantic coast sloping gently down to thick, soft scallops of white sand on the other side of the island, which faced the Caribbean Sea. The water on the Atlantic side was a deep sapphire blue with a froth of white at the base of the cliffs and along the several wild strands of beach they flew over. On the Caribbean side, the water was shades of turquoise, emerald, and jade. The gorgeous jewel-colored water surrounding the island was dotted with miniature boats. A sprinkling of tiny sandy islands of various shapes trailed off the southern tip of the island.

The plane flew low over gentle green hills dotted with coconut palms, citrus fruit orchards, and large tracts of pine forest and bush. A ribbon of a creek wound its way from the interior to the coast, its many tendrils curling around clumps of mangrove and tracing channels through the sand flats along the shore. Here and there were clusters of tiny houses in sheltered coves scooped out of the coastline. At the northern end of the island, Nina saw a larger settlement fronting a wide bay rimmed with white sand and knew it was Coconut Cove. She recognized the tidy grid of lanes lined with candy-colored toy houses from the satellite image. Seconds later, the plane touched down. *Here we go,* thought Nina, taking a deep breath and slipping on her sunglasses and sandals.

Descending the rickety aluminum stairs of the plane, Nina saw a yellow stucco building the size of a large garden shed. A sign on the roof read WELCOME TO PINEAPPLE CAY. The midafternoon heat hit her full in the face, and she suddenly felt overdressed in her close-fitting black T-shirt, linen blazer, and blue jeans. There was a covered area to the right of the building where a small crowd of people was milling about. Her fellow passengers headed in that direction, and Nina followed them. She passed through a gate in the chain-link fence that separated the runway from the baggage-claim area and looked around her, wondering what she should do now. She watched an older couple with salt-and-pepper hair bend down to kiss and hug each of the three small children from the plane.

"Hello, Nina! Over here!"

Nina turned her head to follow the sound of the voice. Walking toward her quickly was a woman about her own age with long dark-red hair and bangs, bright-red lipstick, and a mile-wide smile that lit up her face. A few inches shorter than Nina and a little rounder, she was dressed in a white linen tunic, bright-blue leggings, and strappy gold sandals. She held a small sign in her hand that read NINA SPARK. As she reached Nina, she put her other hand on Nina's forearm in greeting.

"Hi, Nina! I'm Pansy Gallagher. Welcome to Pineapple Cay! How was your flight? What does your bag look like? We can pick it up over here." She gestured behind her to where passengers were collecting their bags off the baggage cart parked next to the gate.

"Hello. Thanks for meeting me. No baggage," Nina said.

Pansy looked surprised for a second. Then she said, "Gotcha," and smiled. "OK, I guess we can go. My cart is out front."

Nina shouldered her duffel bag and followed Pansy through the crowd and out to the curb, where a shiny turquoise golf cart stood. It looked like a miniature antique car, complete with doors, a pretend chrome grille, and a hood ornament.

"Hop in!" said Pansy, and Nina did. Pansy put the key in the ignition and began to drive slowly out of the congested arrivals area.

"A lot of people in Coconut Cove get around on foot or by golf cart because the island is so small," she said, glancing over at Nina. "This cart is electric—we charge it off solar panels on our roof. So! I am so glad you are here and to finally meet you in person after all those e-mails!"

"Thanks. Me, too," said Nina.

There was a commotion up ahead. Several people who'd been walking on the road ahead of Pansy's cart were suddenly jumping up onto the narrow sidewalk as the snout of a champagne-colored Mercedes convertible nosed its way in and came to a stop ten feet in front of them. The driver—a slim, balding man in his late fifties dressed in pressed khaki dress pants, a pink golf shirt, and white shoes—sprang from the car. He marched toward Pansy's golf cart holding a large placard above his head, his gold watch glinting in the sunlight. As he got closer, Nina saw that he was holding a Pineapple Cay Real Estate lawn sign with a fluorescent orange **SOLD** banner running diagonally across it. The man was livid. Pink-faced and wild-eyed.

"What is this? You sold Sundrift without consulting me? Without even telling me you were finally listing it?"

"Yes, Barry. I understand you're upset, but what can I say? The posting went up Tuesday morning, and in my role as Miss Rose's executor, I accepted the first reasonable offer I received."

The man in the white shoes threw the sign on the ground in front of Pansy and slammed his fist on the hood of her golf cart. "You knew I wanted to buy that land! I came to see you the day the old lady croaked! As soon as I heard!"

Nina flinched involuntarily as the sign clattered to the ground, but Pansy maintained her composure, sitting tall in the seat with both hands firmly gripping the steering wheel. She turned her head slightly toward him and spoke calmly and slowly, as if to a small child in the throes of a tantrum.

"Yes, I understand your position, Barry, as you have explained it to me many times. You were interested in the land. However, I was charged by Miss Rose with selling her *home*. There is a difference, which I am sad to say, it appears you cannot see. Now if you don't mind, we are blocking the road, and people are waiting to get by."

Nina looked around. A small crowd of onlookers had gathered, and three or four golf carts and a couple of cars were backed up behind Pansy's cart, their drivers and passengers straining to get a better view of the action.

Seriously? thought Nina. *I've been on Pineapple Cay for approximately ten minutes and am already engaged in an angry confrontation with a stranger and stuck in a golf-cart traffic jam. I might as well have stayed in New York.*

The man took another step toward Pansy and put his hands on his hips.

"Listen, you hippie, this is *not* over. That place is a wreck. It should be torn down and something useful done with that land. I know you'd like it to become an organic seaweed-juice commune where you could all sit around all day making jewelry out of junk you find on the beach and talking about the meaning of life, or some goddamn airy-fairy thing, but I'm here to tell you that there is no money in that. So tell all your hippie friends, change is a comin', whether they like it or not!"

He pranced around a bit as he spoke, fluttering his hands and swinging his hips, presumably mocking the airy-fairyness of hippies. Pansy rolled her eyes.

Throughout this entire exchange, a woman sat impassively in the passenger seat of the Mercedes, scrolling through text messages on her cell phone. Her eyes were hidden behind the huge dark lenses of designer sunglasses, but her posture suggested she was finding the whole thing—and maybe life in general—supremely boring. Nina gave her a quick once-over. Fake boobs, bee-stung lips, long hair an unnatural shade of chestnut brown with blonde streaks, and skin burnished to a light terra-cotta with the help of a tanning bed or a spray can. Oversize gold hoops dangled from her ears, and large rings adorned several fingers. As Barry finished his hippie speech, the woman reached a thin, tanned arm across to the steering wheel and gave three angry jabs at the car horn with her palm, bloodred-tipped talons spread flat to avoid breaking a nail.

"And that's Her Majesty heard from," said Pansy under her breath. Nina looked behind her to see if she could still get back on the plane and head back to relatively easygoing New York. It was taxiing down the runway. Nina watched it climb into the cobalt-blue sky.

"For heaven's sake, Barry," said Pansy, "you're going to make yourself ill with all that raging. Look around you. The sun is shining. The birds are singing. You have your lovely wife beside you. Go have a mango smoothie with extra fiber, and I'm sure things will start looking up."

With that, Pansy slammed her foot on the accelerator and steered the golf cart up onto the curb and around the Mercedes. As the cart pulled away, there was a smattering of applause and laughter from the crowd.

They drove in silence for about ten seconds, and then Nina found her voice. "They seem like a nice couple."

Pansy laughed, slapping the wheel with her hand a few times. "You are *so* right."

"Um, is there a problem?" asked Nina.

Pansy glanced over at her and, registering the look of concern on Nina's face, waved her hand dismissively and said, "Hey, don't worry about that. Everything is fine. I saw the lawyer this morning, and I have your deed to the cottage in my purse. It was all done as it should be, and according to Miss Rose's wishes. Old Barry just doesn't like to lose." A decidedly mischievous grin lit up Pansy's face.

"You see, Barry is our local tycoon. He rolled in here a couple of years ago from Miami with his trophy wife and built a huge monstrosity of a villa in The Enclave. The Enclave is a very upscale residential development along the coast north of town. That kept him busy for a while, ordering people around and such. When the house was finished, he immediately started looking for something else to do. He spent a few months playing pirate, looking for lost treasure. Then he hatched this scheme to develop a huge condominium-and-resort complex on the edge of town."

Playing pirate and looking for lost treasure? Nina decided to let this pass for now. At the moment, her primary concern was why the man was so angry that Pansy had sold the cottage to her and how that might complicate her new life.

"So far, Barry's managed to buy up about forty acres bordering the village," continued Pansy. "The problem is, there isn't a stretch of beach on it. It's all limestone right up to the water's edge, and a rocky bottom all the way—no good for swimming."

Pansy chuckled. "As far as Barry's concerned, the missing piece is Miss Rose Knox's property—Sundrift Cottage, with its one hundred yards of white sandy beach. He has already tried to buy Ted Matthews out, but Ted's not interested. Ted owns a fishing lodge on the point with a nice beach below it. It adjoins yours, actually. You'll be neighbors."

Pansy glanced at Nina and then continued. "Ted accesses his land by a right-of-way across Barry's property. That right-of-way has been established forever, and Barry tried to close it off and squeeze Ted out, but the judge denied his claim. So, Ted owns the point, including the beach, and Barry is left holding a useless piece of beachless scrubland behind it. After he lost his claim against Ted, Barry turned his full attention on Miss Rose."

They had left the small hubbub of the airport behind them and were now traveling along a narrow, winding paved road with no other vehicles in sight. Tall banyan trees grew on either side of the road, their broad canopies of green leaves growing together overhead to form a corridor of sun-dappled shade. Where the trees thinned out, Nina caught glimpses of the sea to her left. At regular intervals, they passed driveways that led up and over low dunes to houses, with only their roofs visible from the road. The signs on the gateposts gave them whimsical names like MERMAID HOUSE, THE FLIP-FLOP, and BOUGAINVILLEA VILLA.

Pansy continued her story. "Miss Rose's family has owned Sundrift forever. She was born in that house, and she lived there her whole life until she died two months ago at the age of ninety-three. At first, Barry tried to sweet-talk her into selling, and when that didn't work, he bullied her. She was a sweet, refined old lady, but she was no pushover. She was a schoolteacher, and anyone who can manage a classroom full of eleven-year-olds can handle Barry Bassett, no problem. She knew what he wanted to do with her land, and she wanted no part of it. Then he decided he'd just wait her out. She'd never married and had no living relatives, so he knew the property would have to be sold when she died. She directed me to sell it and give the proceeds to the local museum for children's educational programs and a scholarship, and not to let him get hold of it. He has been after me about it constantly since she died. So, when I heard he was going off-island for a few days, I bet on his not paying attention while he was gone and posted the listing at midnight. Lo and behold, two hours later, I got your e-mail! As soon as I read it, I knew it was fate! You are meant to be here, living in Miss Rose's house!"

She reached over and gave Nina a friendly and reassuring pat on the shoulder. Although Nina couldn't let go of the feeling that she'd stepped into the middle of something potentially messy, Pansy's warmth and enthusiasm made her smile as she took in her surroundings. They were entering the village. A sign on the side of the road read WELCOME TO COCONUT COVE, LARGEST SETTLEMENT ON PINEAPPLE CAY, POPULATION 3,000. Suddenly, Nina had a hankering for a piña colada.

Coconut Cove was picture-postcard perfect. Rows of colorful little houses lined both sides of the narrow lane, each with a tidy front garden enclosed by a picket fence or a low stone wall. There were coconut palms, mango trees, and waves of pink-and-orange bougainvillea blossoms tumbling over garden walls. They passed the primary school, painted bright yellow. A noisy swarm of small children dressed in white shirts and navy-blue school uniforms was climbing on the play structures under the watch of two teachers. Next door was a pristine white stucco church with a tall steeple soaring into the cloudless blue sky. Then they were in what looked like the center of town. On the water side of the road sat an imposing two-story pink stucco building with an official coat of arms above the door. Next to it was the police station, painted sea blue. A road between them led down to a wharf and a marina where boats of various sizes bobbed in the water. Wide green lawns separated these official buildings from the main street.

On the other side of the street was Pineapple Cay's main commercial district. Pansy and Nina drove slowly past a row of golf carts and pickup trucks parked diagonally in front of a couple of blocks of storefronts with striped awnings shading the sidewalk. Nina noticed a bakery with a few people sitting at tables on the sidewalk out front, a clothing and gift shop, a bank, a hardware store, and a small grocery store doing a brisk business. People were going in and out of doorways, greeting one another cheerily as they passed.

"You can get just about any basics you might need here," said Pansy, waving her arm at the shops. "There's a drugstore on the next block, as well as the public library and the museum, in case you're interested."

A few minutes later, they were on the outskirts of town again, passing clapboard houses and small bungalows spaced increasingly farther apart, until Pansy came to a stop in front of a little faded-yellow wooden cottage in the middle of a large, overgrown lot. Nina's new home— Sundrift Cottage. It was the last house on the edge of town before the village gave way to bush.

"Well, here we are at last," said Pansy. "Your new home sweet home. Let's go have a look!" She hopped out of the cart. Nina grabbed her bag and followed her through the creaking front gate and up the overgrown path. Pansy pulled out a key chain with a miniature foam flip-flop on it and unlocked the door. Then she stepped aside with a big smile on her face to let Nina enter first.

The first thing that struck Nina was the row of large windows with a wall-to-wall view of the turquoise sea. The floors throughout were rough planked wood, and the once-white walls were stained with rectangular shapes where pictures had been removed. It wasn't in perfect shape, but Nina was excited, imagining it with a fresh coat of white paint and polished wood floors. The furnishings were simple but adequate: a stove, fridge, and sink set into a countertop that ran along the wall at one end of the main room, a wooden table and four chairs set in front of it; a faded chintz sofa and a pair of easy chairs grouped around a coffee table at the other end of the room; a built-in bookcase. And in the bedroom, a wrought iron bedstead and wooden bureau filled the space.

"I thought you might not feel like going shopping as soon as you got in, so I picked up a few groceries for you," said Pansy, opening the fridge. "There's bread, cheese, butter, milk, pineapple juice, orange juice, Susie's cocoplum jam—fabulous—bananas, and, of course, a little bottle of rum to help you get in the groove."

"Pansy, that is so nice of you," said Nina. Now that she was here, the fact that she knew absolutely no one on Pineapple Cay hit home. She was grateful for Pansy's kindness.

"Not at all," said Pansy. "I've got to go collect my kids from school, and I'm sure you're eager to unpack." She looked doubtfully at Nina's single duffel, sitting on the floor by the front door. "Anyway, my husband, Andrew, said he would watch the kids tonight, so if you're up for it, I thought I'd take you out to The Redoubt for a bite and introduce you to some of the locals. Andrew just got back from a ten-day skiing trip with his buddies in Canada, so he's on duty all week."

"Um, that would be great," said Nina.

"OK," said Pansy. "Let's meet there about five thirty. You can't miss it. It's on the main drag, ten minutes' walk toward town. Just follow the music and the delicious smells. Have fun settling in!"

2

Nina watched Pansy's turquoise golf cart drive away and then took an exploratory walk through the three tiny rooms of her new home. She poked her head in the bathroom. It was worn but clean. Nothing a coat of paint couldn't fix. She turned on the tap in the tub and pulled the lever to start the shower. The pressure was OK, and the water came out nice and warm. The toilet flushed. One less worry. She wandered into the kitchen and opened a cupboard. There was a stack of plates and bowls and a few glasses and mugs. She pulled open a couple of drawers and found a tray of cutlery and some other useful cooking implements. Under the sink was a bottle of dish soap and a few dishcloths. Another thing she wouldn't have to sort out.

Nina poured herself a glass of orange juice from the carton Pansy had left, pushed open the screen door, and stepped onto the veranda. She slipped off her sandals and jacket and rolled up the cuffs of her jeans, then stepped down onto the sand. It felt divine under the soles of her feet and between her toes. Like a mini massage. A narrow, sandy path through low dunes covered in cocoplum bushes led to the beach about twenty feet away. It was shaded in places by towering palms that dwarfed the cottage. Nina picked her way along the path, onto the beach, and down to the water's edge. She walked into the gentle surf. The water was crystal clear and unexpectedly warm. In the shallows, tiny fish darted about in schools. The tide was going out. The water had receded out into the bay, uncovering inviting white sandbars in stripes and swirls. Way, way out, she could see a fisherman standing thigh deep on the flats casting a fly rod. There wasn't another soul on the beach.

To her right, the sand made a long, sweeping curve out to a point of land jutting out into the water about five hundred yards from where she stood. At the tip of the rocky point was a wooden deck with a ring of Adirondack chairs on it. About a hundred yards back from deck, Nina could see the white rooftops of several small buildings otherwise hidden from view by green foliage. A sandy path emerged from the vegetation onto the beach, where three or four motorboats were pulled up onto the sand. *That must be the fishing lodge,* thought Nina.

She swiveled her head and looked left down the beach, back toward the town center. It looked like she'd be able to walk right into town along the beach. About half a mile away, she could see the big town wharf that sat behind the police station, the marina bristling with the masts of a few dozen sailboats and fishing boats. A few larger yachts were tied to moorings farther out in the harbor. A couple of other wooden piers poked out into the water with small boats tied up to them. Based on the collection of colorful umbrellas and picnic tables on a wide wooden deck on stilts in the sand near the water, Nina guessed it was a bar. To her left, her nearest neighbor was about a hundred feet away, a modern bungalow painted periwinkle blue with a hot tub on the deck. There was a Boston Whaler moored out front, but no sign that anyone was home. She guessed it was a vacation home. She turned and made her way back up the sandy path to the cottage, thinking she would unpack and maybe have a shower.

Just as she stepped up onto the veranda, Nina heard a loud knock on her front door followed by "Yoo-hoo! Mailman!" Looking back through the tiny house, she could make out the silhouette of a man on the other side of the screen door and a red golf cart parked in the lane behind him. She walked the ten steps back through the house and opened the front door. A man in his midtwenties stood at the door, dressed in navy-blue Bermuda shorts and a crisp, white short-sleeve shirt with a pineapple crest on the breast pocket. He was deeply tanned, with shaggy dark-brown hair. A long lock of it fell over one eye. Around his wrists he wore a collection of colorful, but faded, woven friendship bracelets and leather laces strung with silver beads. He stuck out his hand, and Nina shook it.

"Hiya," he said. "Dave Jensen, Pineapple Cay Postal Service. Everyone calls me Danish. Hello, Nina Spark. I've got a letter for you." He handed her a large cardboard envelope with a registered-mail sticker on it.

"Thanks," said Nina. "Nice to meet you." She turned and started back toward the kitchen table, reading the return address as she walked. It was from Katherine, the features editor at a magazine she sometimes worked for. To her surprise, mailman Dave "Danish" Jensen followed her.

"So, you're the one who bought Miss Rose's house," he said.

"I'm the one," said Nina.

"She was one sharp old doll," he said. "Pretty free and easy with the love-life advice, too, especially for someone who was about a hundred and watched cooking shows and reruns of *Columbo* every night."

"She wasn't always a hundred. I imagine she experienced a lot in life," said Nina.

"She used to come to the door every day when I delivered her mail," said Danish the mailman. "Sometimes she'd be out in the yard picking flowers or something, and she'd always invite me in for a cookie or something and a free lecture. Nice old lady. I even miss her *pep talks*."

"Well, I hope your love life is sorted out now, because I'm not really qualified to dispense advice," said Nina.

Danish looked over her shoulder as she tried to tear open the envelope, which had been sealed with several layers of packing tape.

"Do you need a knife to open that?" he asked.

"Ah, yes. I guess I do, thanks," she replied. He produced a Swiss Army Knife from his pocket and handed it to her. She opened the envelope and read.

"So, what is it?" asked Danish the mailman.

"It's an invitation to a party at the home of Jules and Kiki Savage on Saturday night. Apparently to celebrate the donation of the *Morning Glory* emerald and other artifacts from a shipwreck to the Pineapple Cay Museum. I didn't know Jules Savage lived here. Do you know anything about this? I guess I'm being sent to write a magazine piece about it."

When Nina had called Katherine to let her know she was available for work, Katherine had mentioned a possible job once she'd arrived on Pineapple Cay—but Nina had no idea it would be the day she arrived. *Oh, well, you can't eat sunshine and sand. A puff piece on a party at the home of rock legend Jules Savage isn't exactly hard labor,* she told herself.

Suddenly, Danish was down on his knees in front of her, hands clasped beseechingly.

"Can I be your plus one? Your escort? Please, please, please, please?" She took a step back.

"Why are you so interested in a donation to the local museum?" she asked, suspicious. "Are you a big Jules Savage fan?"

"No—I mean, yes, he's a great guy, and I like his music, but no . . ." Danish hopped to his feet, turned away from her, and took a few steps toward the window, where he stood looking out at the water for a moment. Then he spun around to face her again. "I'm in love!" he said with feeling.

Nina's eyes widened.

"It's hard to be a virile man in his prime like myself on an island this small," he continued.

This can't be for real, thought Nina. She took another step back behind the kitchen table. Her mind raced, thinking of how to buy some time until she could figure out if he was crazy but harmless, or call-the-cops crazy. She said the first thing that came into her head.

24

"Let me see. Pineapple Cay has a population of about five thousand. That means roughly half of them are women—or men, whatever. So that means about twenty-five hundred women, and probably at least fifteen hundred over the age of twenty. Let's say about a quarter of those are around your age, give or take a few years: three hundred and seventy-five eligible women. Have you run through them all already?"

He continued with his speech as if she hadn't said anything. "Then just three weeks ago, into the barren wasteland of my love life walks this goddess . . . Alice Rolle!" He savored the name in his mouth. "With a name like a delicious iced pastry and supersmart and beautiful. We were made for each other! But she won't give me the time of day." His shoulders sank. Nina tried to interject, but he kept talking.

"She'll be at that party on Saturday night. She's the new curator of the museum. I need another chance to show her that I'm *the guy*. I'm done with weekend romances with the ladies of Pineapple Cay. I'm done with the predawn exits out the back doors of vacation rentals while Stephanie, Brittany, Amanda, or whomever slumbers on with a satisfied smile on her face while I trudge home alone."

Nina raised her eyebrows.

"Alice is my destiny, and I'm hers!" He collapsed onto the chintz sofa, head in his hands. Tentatively, Nina sat down beside him.

"Do you talk to her like that?" she asked. He ran his hands through his hair and raised his head to look at her, his hair now standing on end.

"I know what the problem is," he said. "Deputy Superintendent John 'Blue' Roker. The long arm of the law. I've seen him squiring her around town, taking her out to lunch at The Redoubt, showing her the sights, trying to be charming."

He stood and started pacing the room again as he spoke. "I mean, I can see why he's homed in on her. She's smart, sophisticated, and drop-dead gorgeous, with the sweetest smile I've ever seen. Everyone loves her. But what does she see in *him*? He spends all his free time in his backyard puttering around in his flower garden. Taking them out of

25

pots, putting them into pots, making dirt soup for his plants, picking bugs off the leaves one by one by one! Does that sound like a fun date to you? *Boring!*"

As a Mainer who had been living in Manhattan for the past ten years, Nina was actually pretty excited at the prospect of bringing the cottage flower garden back to its former glory. She might even put in a small kitchen garden for vegetables and herbs and hang some window boxes. She had gorged on home renovation and gardening magazines like *Martha Stewart Living* on the plane ride down, but she didn't interrupt. Danish continued his rant.

"I spent a lifetime over at Blue's house one afternoon, hanging with him and Ted, watching Mr. Tough Guy the Chief of Police *garden*. At least there was beer. OK, Blue is good-looking, I guess, or so I've been told. But he's so old! He must be about forty."

He glanced at Nina. "Sorry, no offense. Obviously, you're pretty hot for an older woman. Under other circumstances, sparks might be flying here, Nina Spark. But as it is, I'm all Alice, all the time. What am I going to do?"

Nina took a deep breath. She'd been on Pineapple Cay approximately one hour.

"Listen, Danish. First things first. Thirty-six is only *older* when you're twenty-five. For the rest of us, it's just the beginning. Secondly, you know, that kind of *intensity*, all that destiny talk, can be a bit offputting—not to mention a little scary—in the early stages of a relationship. Dial it back a little. Try kind, attentive, but . . . calmer."

Nina mulled over the implications of taking an overwrought, lovesick mailman she'd *just* met to a party at the island hideaway of a rock star she'd *never* met. Yesterday, in New York, she would have nixed the idea immediately, without a second thought. Today, on Pineapple Cay, with the future more or less a complete blank, anything was possible. She couldn't see what harm it would do. Why not give young love a chance. Maybe they'd be better at it than she was.

"OK, Danish, against my better judgment, yes, I guess you can come with me to the party, because I do need some help getting my bearings here. But *please* remember that I'll be there representing a magazine. Don't make me regret it. No shenanigans, OK?" she said, looking at him in what she hoped was a stern way.

He raised his arms above his head in a victory salute.

"Yes! Thank you. You won't regret it. No shenanigans," he said, making air quotes with his fingers as he backed out the door. "I promise. I've got to finish my route. Catch you later."

Then he was gone.

Alone at last, Nina locked the front and back doors, peeled off the tight-fitting clothes she'd been wearing since she got dressed in the dark at five o'clock that morning, and hopped in the shower. The hot water felt exquisite on her skin. Afterward, wrapped in the bath towel she'd brought from home, Nina emptied her bag onto the bed and plucked out a pair of cut-off shorts, clean undies, and a light cotton peasant blouse in dusty rose. It felt wonderful to be clean and fresh smelling and not to be wearing a heavy winter coat. Making her way back into the kitchen, she cut a chunk of fresh bread and sliced some cheese, taking a few bites to quell the hunger pangs before returning to the bedroom.

She made up the bed with the cotton sheets and the light feather duvet she'd brought. It was amazing what you could fit in a small bag if you knew how to pack. Nina had traveled a lot for her freelance gigs, and she had packing down to a science. The bedding, running shoes, and a wool sweater were the bulkiest items she'd brought. Rolled into tight balls, the shorts, T-shirts, blouses, bathing suit, socks, underwear, yoga pants, and flip-flops didn't take up much room. She'd also brought a cozy plaid flannel shirt, two light cotton summer dresses, an olive-green jersey skirt, and one little black dress with a weightless black mohair shawl and a pair of strappy black sandals that would do for a more formal event, like the Savages' dinner party. Rain pants and a waterproof jacket folded away to nothing in their own little pouches.

Along with her laptop computer, a notebook, the magazines she'd picked up on the plane, and a couple of paperbacks, that was it. She'd filled the nooks and crannies of her bag with her toiletries, including the tiny bottles of shampoo and soaps she'd collected from hotels she'd stayed in on various trips.

Nina stowed her clothes in the bureau, and her toiletries in the bathroom. In ten minutes, she was done moving in. It was four o'clock. She grabbed one of the books and mixed herself a goombay smash with the rum and juice Pansy had brought, plopping in a couple of ice cubes from the freezer. She headed out onto the veranda, where there was a white plastic chaise longue and two chairs. Nina settled herself onto the chaise longue and sighed contentedly. She opened the book, which she'd been reading in New York. It was the second in a six-volume memoir by a Norwegian writer whom all her friends had been talking about. A bleak tale of growing up and struggling to find meaning in life in a place where it always seemed to be dark and snowing. She'd been engrossed in it, curled up on her sofa in New York, nursing her own wounds through the dark winter months. She plucked out the bookmark and started reading. The hero declared his love for a beautiful woman poet. She rejected him, saying she preferred his friend. He went to his room, stared into his bathroom mirror, and proceeded to cut his face open with a broken bottle.

"OK," said Nina, slamming the book shut. Out in the distance, the fisherman was still casting, his long line making a graceful arc through the still air. She watched the slow, regular rhythm of his movements. In a couple of minutes, she was asleep.

She awoke with the sensation that she was not alone. A shadow was blocking out the sun. Nina sat up quickly. The dark silhouette of a man with his hands on his hips loomed over her. She squinted up at him, trying to make out his features.

"Hello, Miss Spark. I hope I didn't wake you. There was no answer to my knock on the front door, so I thought I'd check around back. Welcome to Pineapple Cay."

It was Barry Bassett, the angry man from the airport. He held out a fruit basket wrapped in cellophane. Nina scrambled to her feet and put a more comfortable distance between them. Then she reached out to accept the heavy basket, which she clutched in front of her. There was a pineapple and a bunch of bananas and some mangoes. All the weighty fruits. She glanced up and down the empty beach and out at the water. The fisherman way out on the flats stood motionless with his fly rod in his hand, his sun-glassed eyes looking in their direction.

"I think this is the first time I've been ambushed by the welcome wagon, but thank you," said Nina.

"Ha, ha, ha. You are most welcome. I'm glad to find you in. There's a matter I'd like to discuss with you. May I sit down?" Without waiting for an answer, he lowered himself into one of the chairs, sat back, and crossed his legs. Nina stayed where she was but put the basket down.

"Well," said Barry, "I believe you were with Ms. Gallagher when we had our little contretemps earlier today. I want you to know that I'm aware you had no knowledge of any prior discussions I have had with Ms. Gallagher related to Sundrift Cottage. You have innocently become embroiled in a situation of her creation." He paused to check Nina's reaction to his words. She said nothing, and after a moment, he continued.

"The fact remains that I have a prior interest in this property, and I intend to obtain it. I'd like to make you an offer that will earn you a tidy profit on your brief little adventure on Pineapple Cay." He smiled at her in a way she guessed he thought was charming.

"Listen, Mr. . . ." She realized he hadn't introduced himself. Should she call him Barry? Maybe better to just avoid the issue. "I've just arrived here. My intention is to stay. I'm not interested in selling the cottage. I just bought it. It was nice to meet you, and thank you for the fruit basket, but if you don't mind, I have things to do. Let me walk you out." She started walking around the side of the cottage, where a stone path led to the front yard. He stood his ground for a few seconds, but then finding himself alone on the veranda, he stood up and stalked after her.

"I was hoping you were a reasonable woman. I guess I was wrong. As I've never actually met such a woman, I guess it was too much to hope for." He walked past her, got in his Mercedes, and sped away, spraying sand. Nina walked back around the side of the house to the veranda. The fisherman had come closer to shore. He was about a hundred yards out and moving toward the beach. She looked directly at him, and he stopped walking. Then he turned away and resumed casting.

It was after five o'clock. The sun was getting low on the horizon. Time to meet Pansy at The Redoubt. Nina brushed her teeth and hair, pulled on her sweater, and tucked her wallet in her pocket. With her flip-flops hooked over a finger, she started off down the beach toward the village center. As she got closer, she heard music. The deck of the restaurant was almost full, with groups of laughing patrons enjoying beer, burgers, fries, and colorful salads at picnic tables. Climbing the wooden stairs from the beach, Nina picked a path between the tables and went inside through wide-open double glass doors.

It took a moment for her eyes to adjust to the dark. A slow reggae beat oozed out of the sound system. The interior featured exposed wooden timbers and wood-paneled walls strung with fishing nets and buoys. There were about ten tables, each covered with a blue-and-white-checked tablecloth and a candle flickering inside a storm lantern. A row of booths lined the wall on the right side of the room, and a long, polished wood bar ran almost the full length of the wall on the left side, with rows of bottles behind and polished wood stools pulled up to it on three sides. The lights above the bar cast a warm glow on the room. Nina noticed the honeymooners from the airplane tucked into one of the booths. They were holding hands across the table and sipping frosty whipped drinks.

There were a few other tables occupied but no sign of Pansy yet. Nina slipped into a seat at the bar. At the opposite end of the bar, a female bartender was mixing strawberry daiquiris for a pair of laughing middle-aged women with sunburned arms who were keeping the good times going after a day on the beach. Nina looked around the room as she waited. There was a small raised stage tucked in the corner by the glass doors and a jukebox beside it. Through the open doors to the deck, Nina watched the sun slip below the horizon. The sky was outrageous shades of salmon pink with orange-and-purple streaks.

"Hello, Nina Spark!" Nina was so startled she almost fell off her chair. Behind the bar stood Danish the mailman.

"What can I get you?" he asked, leaning forward with both hands on the bar. He had a white towel over one shoulder, and his thick, dark hair was sticking straight up, styled with beer foam.

"Danish. I thought you were the mail carrier." She glanced down the bar toward the other bartender, who had turned her attention to a tray of drinks.

"What I am, Nina Spark, is versatile. How about a bikini martini?"

"Hi, Nina! Sorry I'm late." Nina felt Pansy's hand on her shoulder. "The peas were touching the mashed potatoes, and that is a major crisis in my house."

Pansy turned to Danish. "Hi, Danish. I'll have one of those, too, please. Make it a double."

"Hi, Pansy," said Nina. "This is nice."

"Yeah. Isn't it great? Veronica has made a real welcoming spot." Pansy looked over at the other bartender, undoubtedly the owner of The Redoubt, who was serving the tray of drinks to a table of six across the room. She had the erect, no-nonsense posture of a dancer. Her hair was done up in long cornrows gathered in a silver-streaked ponytail, and she wore large, dangling silver earrings. When she was done dispensing the drinks, she swept across the room in a flowing batik skirt and snug black crewneck cashmere sweater, which showed off her sculpted biceps and triceps. She reminded Nina of Olympic sprinter Merlene Ottey.

"Why don't we grab a booth?" asked Pansy. They made their way across the floor to one of the few remaining booths. "Ah . . . it feels good to sit down," she said.

"So, how old are your kids?" asked Nina.

"Oh, Susan is six and Kevin is eight. They're good kids . . . I haven't watched a grown-up movie in eight years . . . So, how was your afternoon?"

"Here we are, ladies. Enjoy." Danish set the pink drinks down in front of them, along with a couple of menus. "I'll be back."

"I had a visitor this afternoon," said Nina. "Barry Bassett came by to give me a fruit basket and offered to buy the cottage. He was not very happy when I declined the offer."

"I'm so sorry, Nina," said Pansy. "He can be a real pain. I don't know why he wants to live here. He seems to hate just about everybody around." They opened their menus.

"This morning you mentioned that he was involved in hunting for a lost treasure. Does that have anything to do with the donation of artifacts from a shipwreck to the Pineapple Cay Museum?" asked Nina.

"Yes!" answered Pansy. "The *Morning Glory* emerald. You know how you read in the paper all the time about this Spanish galleon or that US merchant ship that went down with holds filled with gold bars and gemstones? All of them just waiting to be found. Well, there are about twenty wreck-hunting crews cruising around the islands in any given year. Most of them look for years without ever finding anything. Some spend years just waiting for permits to search the waters. Those that do find something are mostly foreign companies that sell off whatever they find for profit, usually much less than they were counting on.

"There has been a lot of local protest over the last few years about the loss of the islands' cultural heritage. The government tried to put a stop to the outflow a couple of years ago by slowing down the permitting of expeditions and putting restrictions on the sale of artifacts. Then Barry showed up last year with a permit in hand. He'd been reading about the wreck of the SS *Central America*, I guess—the guy who found thirty-million-dollars' worth of gold bars off South Carolina in 1988. The guy went on the lam with the proceeds until the police caught up with him living under an assumed name at a fancy hotel in Florida. Anyway, Barry wanted in on the action—the actual open-water pirate hijinks. Somehow, within six months his team had found the wreck of the *Morning Glory*, lying in the cut between Lizard and Wreath Cays, just south of here. People have been searching for it for two hundred years!"

Pansy paused to take a sip of her drink. "*Mmm*, that's good. The funny thing about Barry is that I really don't think it's about the money for him. It's the thrill of the hunt and the prestige. Same with the condo development. He likes to win. He could buy a nice beachfront property somewhere else and make more money, if that was really what he wanted. The scuttlebutt is he got his wrecking permit so easily because he signed an agreement to hand the whole haul over to the government. And he did. That's how the *Morning Glory* emerald, et cetera, ended up in the Pineapple Cay Museum. Now Tiffany, his wife, she's another matter. All she cares about is how much things cost and getting more of them. I can't imagine what they talk about. My guess is she was one of the things he wanted but couldn't have. And when he did get her, he lost interest. She, on the other hand, was dazzled by his money—but now she's wondering if it was worth it. She makes no secret of the fact that she wants to go back to Miami. *Civilization*, she calls it."

Danish was back and looking at them expectantly. "What will it be, ladies?" he asked.

"Oh, we haven't really looked," said Pansy. "It's been so long since I ate out with grown-ups. I'll definitely have another one of these, please. Nina, do you know what you'd like?"

Nina shook her head and picked up the menu again.

"Alrighty then," said Danish. "Here's what I am going to do for you. A nice spinach salad to start. The ladies like the salads. Makes them feel virtuous. Then the house specialty—the conch burger with a side of fresh-cut fries—not too many, of course—followed by Veronica's home-made key lime pie, because you deserve it, goddammit. Okeydokey?"

"Sounds good, Danish, except I'm a vegetarian," said Nina.

"OK. No biggie. We get your people in here all the time. A Jamaican veggie patty for the lady from New York, then. Respect. And I'll just bring a pitcher, shall I?"

"I'm not actually Rastafarian, but thanks," Nina said as he disappeared again.

Danish was just setting their salads and the pitcher of pink drinks on the table when a commotion broke out by the front door. A small group of obnoxiously loud people who looked to be in their early twenties erupted into the room. One guy was carrying a large boom box on his shoulder. It was blaring techno dance music, drowning out the subdued reggae on the sound system. The group—all of them wearing sunglasses despite the dark—danced over to a table in the middle of the room. It was obvious they were putting on a show, conscious of all eyes on them.

"The Beer Commercial," said Danish wryly. "Those idiots like to make an entrance. Makes them feel like they are living the life."

They watched Veronica walk swiftly toward the group and speak to the clean-cut, dark-haired guy with the boom box. Her hands were on her hips. The music shut off suddenly, and he looked slightly sheepish. There were three other guys and three girls, all dressed in preppy beachwear. They had draped themselves over the chairs around the table and assumed bored poses.

"The head idiot with the boom box is Lance," said Danish. "He's the tennis pro at the Plantation Inn. He came down from the States for the winter and brought all his annoying rich friends with him. They've rented a big beach villa in The Enclave. I call them the Beer Commercial because they always look like they're acting in their own movie version of what life should be like. Episode Twelve: A Fun Night Out with the Gang."

Nina thought they all looked just a little bit too old to be doing the spring-break thing all winter. Unlike her, of course. Now that they'd made their big entrance, they didn't seem to know what to do with themselves. They sat drinking beer, munching tortilla chips, and looking around the restaurant. At least they had quieted down.

The burgers arrived. Huge heaping plates Nina knew she had no hope of finishing, but delicious. The place was filling up with diners and drinkers, a mix of locals and tourists. The conversational buzz increased in volume, and the tempo of the music kicked up a notch. Nina was feeling the pink drink and was suffused with a sense of well-being, of being in just the right place at the right time, doing the right thing for the moment.

"So, Pansy, are you from here?" she asked.

"Heavens, no," said Pansy. "I'm from Winnipeg." Danish reappeared and slid into the seat beside Pansy.

"I'm on my break," he said, pouring himself a tall pink drink.

Pansy continued. "About five years ago I was standing in my driveway in Winnipeg with a snow shovel in my hand. I had just finished clearing the drive so I could get the kids to day care and get to work on time. I sold real estate up there, too. Big beige mansions in what were once wheat fields. Acres and acres of them. It was minus thirty degrees Celsius with the wind chill—that's minus twenty-two degrees Fahrenheit—at seven o'clock in the morning, and it was still pitch-dark outside. The city snowplow went by and dumped another foot of hard, crusty snow at the top of the drive. I thought I was going to lose it. I went back inside, and that morning Andrew and I made plans to move down here full-time. It took two years, but we did it! I still sell real estate, and Andrew still works at a bank, but we're happy. Our kids learned to snorkel in gym class!"

"'Though we travel the world over to find the beautiful, we must carry it within us or we find it not.' Ralph Waldo Emerson," said Danish as he helped himself to one of Nina's french fries.

"Maybe," said Pansy. "I'm sure there is a lot of truth in that. Just look at Barry and Tiffany, miserable with all their money. But you know what? It's still bloody cold in Winnipeg in February."

Nina smiled and took another sip of her drink. "So, what's the story on the *Morning Glory*? Where did it come from, and what was on it besides the emerald?" she asked.

"I don't really know much about the history," answered Pansy. "Hey! Let's ask Siri." She pulled out a big cell phone and spoke into it like a walkie-talkie. "What is the history of the wreck of the *Morning Glory*?"

Two seconds later, an electronic female voice with a British accent said, "The *Morning Glory* sank off Pineapple Cay in 1780. The ship was owned by Robert Sifton of Charleston, South Carolina."

Danish grabbed the cell phone out of Pansy's hand and held it close to his mouth. "Talk dirty to me, Siri," he whispered.

The electronic voice responded, "I am sorry. I do not understand the question. Can you rephrase?"

Pansy grabbed the phone back from Danish, wiped the screen with her sleeve, and dropped it into her purse. "You know who would be the best person to talk to about the *Morning Glory*? Alice at the museum. She's researched the whole history for the new exhibit."

"Yeah! Alice knows everything about it," said Danish, his eyes glowing. "I could introduce you."

"Thanks," said Nina. "I'll see how things go."

"OK. It's a plan! I'd better get back to work. The boss is giving me that look." He got up and headed back to the bar.

While they'd been talking and eating, several groups of people had come and gone. The Beer Commercial had slipped away without them noticing, and a group of about ten sleek-looking, silver-haired older gentlemen and a couple of well-dressed women had taken their place. They were laughing and chatting among themselves, the men nursing bottles of the local beer, the women sipping glasses of white wine. Unlike the Beer Commercial, they seemed unconcerned with making an impression on their fellow patrons, other than smiling at passersby and pulling in vacant chairs to let a waitress loaded down with two trays get by.

There was a younger sandy-haired man with them, around forty years old, Nina guessed. He had the tan of someone who spent most his time outdoors. He was dressed in a khaki shirt and khaki pants, with a pair of gold-rimmed aviator sunglasses hanging on a string around his neck. A battered broad-rimmed khaki hat sat on the table in front of him. With his dirty-blond hair and tanned skin, he was various pleasing shades of beige and brown from head to toe. Only the whites of his eyes and his teeth when he smiled provided any contrast. At the moment, he was telling a story and held the rapt attention of the entire table. Nina and Pansy were too far away to hear the punch line, but when it came, the whole group burst into laughter.

"That's Ted Matthews, your neighbor," said Pansy. She gave Nina a sideways glance. "Looks like he has a big group in this weekend." The party made a move to leave, gathering up their jackets and purses and ambling toward the door. One of the men was talking to Ted in an animated fashion, using lots of hand gestures. Ted nodded now and then as the man spoke. As he stood and put on his hat, Ted glanced in their direction. Now that he was standing, Nina could see that he was tall—over six feet. He nodded at Pansy and Nina, touching the brim of his hat with his fingertips, and then turned back to the man, who continued to talk up at him as they walked to the door. Pansy gave a little wave.

He looks like the Marlboro Man without the unhealthy nicotine habit, thought Nina. *He probably lassoes the fish.*

She took one last bite of her key lime pie and then sat back. "That was delicious. I'm going to have to learn how to make it."

"Yes, the food here is amazing," agreed Pansy. "Veronica grows most of the fruits and vegetables in her own greenhouses, and she has a big fruit orchard, too. We should go out and see it sometime. It is a pretty impressive operation. She supplies the Plantation Inn and has a farm stand, too. Let's say hi, and then I'd better take you home. I'm up way past my bedtime." They made their way over to the bar.

"Hi, Veronica!" shouted Pansy. "This place is heaving tonight! This is Nina Spark. She just moved into Miss Rose's cottage. Nina, this is Veronica Steeves, owner of The Redoubt and Smooth Harbour Farm."

Veronica smiled and extended her hand across the bar.

"Welcome, Nina. I hope you will like it here. Miss Rose was my teacher. I've got an order up, so I'd better go, but come back and talk to me sometime soon, OK?"

They made their way out of the now-crowded bar to where Pansy's golf cart was parked under a mango tree. It was a short drive back to Sundrift Cottage. Nina hopped out at the gate.

"Thanks, Pansy. That was a lot of fun. I hope you're not too tired tomorrow," said Nina.

"Oh, no," said Pansy. "It was great fun. Let's do it again some-time soon. And Saturday night is another big night out! Jules and Kiki Savages' do. Kiki told me you were invited. Can I pick you up and we'll go together? Andrew is taking the kids to a birthday party."

"That would be great," said Nina. "Um, Danish is coming, too. I said he could be my plus one."

Pansy didn't bat an eye. "Sure, no problem. I'll come by about five o'clock? There are cocktails before dinner. Don't want to miss that."

They said good night, and Nina let herself into her new house. It was dark and quiet. She flipped on the light over the kitchen sink and wandered out onto the veranda and down the sandy path to the beach. The sky was full of stars. They looked close enough to touch. The sound of the waves was hypnotic, and Nina wondered what it would sound like from her bedroom.

All of a sudden, the air exploded with the sound of loud, angry barking that got louder and louder. Nina spun around to see where it was coming from. Two large dogs sprang out of the bush in the stretch of vacant land between her cottage and the point and were churning up the beach toward her. They would be on her in seconds. She whirled around, looking for something to fend them off with. A length of green rope lay half-buried in the sand by her feet. She yanked it out and spun around to face the dogs. They had come to a halt about ten feet away from her and stood snarling and prancing, baring their big yellow teeth.

"Get back! Go on!" she shouted, snapping the green rope at them like a whip. They backed off a bit with each snap, then moved in again. She reached down with one hand, picked up two palm-size rocks, and hurled one at each of them; then she took a couple of steps toward them, snapping the rope in front of their noses in a wild frenzy.

"Go away!" They backed off but didn't leave, and their angry barking filled the night.

"Hey! Go on! Get out of here!" she heard a male voice shout. She looked toward the point and saw a man racing down the sand toward her carrying a pole in one hand. She heard a whistle coming from the vacant lot, and the dogs immediately took off in that direction. A moment later she heard an engine start, and headlights swept the trunks of several tall pines near the road. The man on the beach changed course and charged into the undergrowth toward the road. Nina stayed rooted where she was, still processing what had just happened. A few seconds later, the man emerged from the undergrowth and jogged slowly toward her. As he got closer, Nina saw that it was Ted Matthews, the owner of the fishing lodge. She recognized the pole in his hand as a fishing gaff.

"Are you all right?" he asked when he was close enough. He was breathing hard.

"I'm fine, thanks. I was running out of ideas. Thank you for coming." She hugged herself, suddenly chilled.

"Someone called off those dogs. And I know who it was." He pulled a cell phone out of his pocket and quickly stabbed in a number, watching her as it rang a couple of times.

"Blue. Ted. Bassett just sicced his dogs on the lady who bought Rose's house. Maybe you can get a patrol car to check it out." He was silent for a few seconds.

"I'm sure they weren't just potcakes. They were Bassett's Dobermans. He whistled for them, and they ran off . . . OK, thanks." He slipped the phone back in his pocket, still watching her.

"The police are going to check it out, but they probably won't get anywhere, I'm afraid. He'll be back in his compound before they get there." He paused and held out his hand. "We haven't actually met. I'm Ted Matthews. I live up there." He gestured to the point.

"Hello. I'm Nina Spark. Thank you again." She smiled wanly and shook his hand. It was warm. Her own was ice-cold.

"May I walk you to your door?" he asked. They headed toward the cottage. "Bassett is a vile character. But I believe you've already met," he said.

Of course, thought Nina. *The fisherman this afternoon.*

"That said," continued Ted, "if he really wanted those dogs to hurt you, they would have. He was just trying to scare you. Hopefully, he's gotten his disappointment out of his system. I'm just over there. If you need anything, give me a call." They had reached the veranda. He fished a notepad and pencil out of one of the many pockets in his khaki pants, scribbled his phone number on a piece of paper, and handed it to her. He looked her in the eye.

"I can't believe I'm saying this on Pineapple Cay, but you should lock your doors until this blows over. It will." He added more to himself than to her, "Somebody needs to teach that guy a lesson."

He waited while she unlocked her door. "Will you be all right now? Can I get you a cup of tea or something before I go?" he asked.

She was exhausted, and she knew she didn't have any tea. "I'll be all right, thanks. It's been a long day. I think I'll just crawl into bed."

"OK," he said. "Anyway, glad to meet you. Have a good night." He waited until she was inside and had locked the door before he turned away and headed back up the beach toward his lodge, where his guests must have been waiting for him.

She was suddenly incredibly tired, beyond worrying about Barry's next move. It was almost unfathomable that she had started this day at her apartment in New York, unaware that Danish, Ted Matthews, or Barry and Tiffany Bassett even existed. She considering sending Louise an e-mail to let her know she'd arrived safely, but even that seemed like too much work. She dragged herself into the bedroom, stripped off everything but her underwear, and crawled between the sheets. She was asleep in seconds.

3

Nina woke late, with a powerful hankering for an extralarge Cuppa Joe mocha latte. Since the nearest Cuppa Joe was about a thousand miles due north and she didn't have any coffee in the kitchen, she decided to take a walk into the village and have a look at her new hometown. She showered quickly, knotting her hair in a loose bun at the nape of her neck. She pulled on her skirt and a top and slipped on her sandals and sunglasses. She went out the door facing the street and headed along the sidewalk with her big canvas tote over her shoulder. It was only about nine o'clock, but the sun was already strong. She peeked into her neighbors' yards as she strolled along, admiring the deep, covered verandas with their gingerbread trim, the inviting porch swings, and the profusion of flowers. The air was full of birdsong, and she watched yellow bananaquits take beakfuls of sugar from an upturned coconut shell hanging from a porch post.

It was a weekday morning, and in the commercial district, people were bustling about. The mail boat was in, tied up to the town wharf. A number of men were unloading cargo while others stood around watching the action, and a steady stream of vans, trucks, and carts loaded with pallets and boxes made their way up from the dock to the various shops along the main street. There were enough people on the streets so that Nina felt the comfort of being an anonymous observer, yet she was still able to feel the small-town vibe. She followed the delicious smell of freshly baked bread to the bakery, where she bought a warm loaf of coconut bread, a mug of coffee, a healthy-ish looking muffin, and a copy of the local paper from a smiling woman in a red apron. She settled into a seat under the awning on the sidewalk, took a deeply satisfying sip of coffee, and took in the scene in front of her. A few golf carts buzzed past on the street. Beyond them were the park and bandstand, and behind them, the pink-and-blue government buildings and the bustling wharf, all set against the backdrop of the mesmerizing turquoise sea and pale-blue sky, with the low, shimmering humps of two sandy cays on the horizon, about a mile offshore.

Nina glanced down at the paper as she took another sip of her coffee. The front page was dominated by a scandal over the expense accounts of members of parliament on the main island. *Some things are the same all over,* she thought. Below the fold there was a photograph of a smiling Jules and Kiki Savage with Barry and Tiffany Bassett under the headline LOCAL BUSINESSMAN MAKES HISTORIC DONATION TO THE PINEAPPLE CAY MUSEUM. The paragraph in the paper didn't tell her anything she didn't already know, except that longtime Pineapple Cay resident Kiki Savage was the chair of the museum's board of directors, and her famous husband was a generous benefactor to the cause.

Nina looked at the photograph with curiosity, trying to glean some insight into the dynamics of their relationship from the four smiling faces. There was no sign of the famous sneer on the face of onetime rock-and-roll bad boy Jules Savage. He stood grinning amiably with one arm around his still-lovely wife and the other around a beaming Tiffany Bassett. Except for the tangled skein of chains and beads resting on his tanned chest, he could have been a well-preserved bookstore owner or a retired dentist. Barry Bassett stood slightly apart from the other three, looking intently into the camera with the pasted-on smile Nina recognized from the day before. Behind them was the roofline of the Pineapple Cay Museum. Nina made a mental note to drop in soon.

She looked at the photo for half a second longer before flipping the page to the local shipping news. What could you really tell from a photo op?

Nina spent a few more minutes perusing the newspaper, reading the birth and death announcements, the notices for bingo night at the church hall (Wednesdays), and the meeting of the Saturday-morning book club at the public library ("All those interested in participating, bring your suggestions for this month to the next meeting. Please remember, not everybody likes blood and guts. And also, it is hard to talk about a self-help book for a whole hour; we already read *The 7 Habits of Highly Effective People* last year."). There was a reminder that a drop-in yoga class takes place Mondays, Wednesdays, and Fridays at noon at the Plantation Inn. It was Friday. Nina glanced at her watch. Ten o'clock. She could make it if she did her errands now. She gathered up her newspaper and canvas bag and headed off toward the green-and-white-striped awning of the grocery store.

Inside, the shelves and coolers were fully stocked, thanks to the arrival of the mail boat. Nina filled a basket with milk and eggs and other things, not forgetting the coffee. The store was busy with local shoppers and yachters from the marina stopping in to restock. Nina didn't linger. She hoisted her bag and went next door to the hardware store. She thought she might get a start this afternoon with painting the cottage.

The hardware store was a big, old-fashioned place with floor-to-ceiling open shelving and a chandler's shop attached, stocked with marine hardware and supplies for boaters. Nina noticed, with some surprise, a large bin of fairly high-grade fireworks by the counter. Nina's father's business was Spark Pyrotechnics, "purveyors of fireworks displays to state fairs and special events throughout the northeastern United States." Really, with a name like Spark, the family business couldn't have been anything else, except maybe electrician or arsonist. Nina and her brothers had learned the trade as their father's assistants throughout high school and summer vacations. Her brothers had stayed with the business while she became a professor, but she knew how to set fireworks and sync them to music to wow an audience, and she recognized these rockets as something more than just backyard sparklers. She figured they must have been left over from some town celebration.

"What can I help you with, miss?" asked an elderly man who emerged from the dim recesses behind the long wooden counter. He helped Nina find a brush, scraper, and machete, which he assured her was the best way to the cut stubborn beach grass if she didn't have a gas mower. Also handy for opening coconuts, he added. He mixed a can of butter-yellow exterior paint for her. She hoisted a can of primer up onto the counter and paid for it all. Then with a can in each hand and her now-heavy tote over her shoulder, Nina thanked him as she headed out the door and back up the road toward her house. It was hot, and she could feel the sun boring into the tender skin on her nose. The only vehicle that passed her as she made the fifteen-minute hike back to her cottage was Barry Bassett's champagne-colored Mercedes, with Tiffany riding shotgun, fiddling with the car radio. He didn't slow down as he passed, but Nina saw his eyes looking back at her in his rearview mirror. She held his gaze, wanting him to know that she knew what he'd done. He looked away first.

An hour later, Nina was walking up the long, tree-lined drive of the Pineapple Cay Plantation Inn in her shorts and sneakers, her towel rolled under her arm. The inn was set well back from the main road on the ocean side south of the village center. Nina had walked back through the residential blocks behind the shops to get there. Two hundred years ago, the inn had been a pineapple plantation, and the main part of the inn was in the restored plantation house. It was now surrounded by sweeping green lawns shaded by tall banyan, mango, and palm trees, with a row of small beachfront bungalows on either side of the main house, separated by screens of bougainvillea and frangipani.

In the center of the circular drive that curved in front of the main entrance was a graceful fountain depicting sculpted dolphins frolicking in the water. To the right was a parking lot hidden from view behind a tall brick wall covered with flowering vines, and to the left were three tennis courts, also shielded from view by a high vine-covered chain-link fence. Nina could hear the pinging of tennis balls and the grunts of players as she passed and made her way up the steps into the lobby of the inn. It was an open, airy foyer, and she could see straight through to the veranda. A few vacationers sat on the veranda in rattan rocking chairs, looking out at the sea, which lay glittering in the sunshine at the foot of a broad expanse of manicured green lawn. The wide floorboards creaked underfoot, and several large fans turned slowly in the coffered ceiling above Nina's head. She made her way to the ornately carved and highly polished mahogany reception desk, where an elegant woman in a navy-blue suit and white blouse was typing at a computer. She looked up and smiled as Nina approached.

"May I help you?" she asked.

"I'm looking for the yoga class," said Nina.

"Yes. It's starting in a couple of minutes out in the spa pavilion," said the woman, gesturing out the veranda door. Nina paid the class fee and followed her directions across the lawn to a covered platform, where a half dozen women and a couple of men were rolling out their mats and stretching their arms and legs as they waited for class to begin. Nina joined them on the platform, then grabbed a mat from the pile by the stairs and unfurled it in an empty spot on the floor at the back of the class. She kicked off her shoes and socks and pushed them out of the way. Looking around her for the first time, she noted that Tiffany Bassett was among the women clustered at the front of the platform. Nina was briefly annoyed. Tiffany Bassett and her pushy husband were beginning to harsh her mellow, as her twenty-year-old nephew, Michael, would say. Dressed in bubblegum-pink tights and a black tank top, Tiffany was talking to a coterie of expensive-looking women who were within earshot of her.

"So, yeah. Kiki Savage is a really good friend of mine, and she said, 'I am going to throw you the best party ever, girl.' I wish I could invite you, too, but it's an intimate dinner party at their private estate. The Minister of History or whatever is coming all the way from the main island to be there and thank us personally for giving them, like, millions of dollars' worth of stuff."

Nina made a conscious effort to tune out the bimbo and sat down on her mat with her legs stretched out in front of her, breathing in deeply and reaching for her toes.

"Good afternoon, ladies and gentlemen! Let us lotus!" said a familiar voice. Nina looked up quickly. At the front of the platform, rolling out his mat and then standing to face them with his hands in the Namaste position, was Danish, the mailman slash waiter. He spotted her at the back of the class.

"Hey, Nina! Good to see you! Looking forward to our big date tomorrow night!" he called across the platform. She gave him a small wave as Tiffany Bassett snapped her head around and glared at her. A few of the other women eyed her with curiosity. Then Danish was all business, guiding them through a series of poses in a calm, soothing voice for the next hour. They finished lying on their backs with their eyes closed, listening to the sound of the waves. *He's actually very good at this,* thought Nina with surprise. When she opened her eyes, most of the participants were gone, including Tiffany. Danish was putting away his CDs and closing up the stereo cabinet. She walked over.

"So, you're a yoga instructor, too. You're everywhere," she said.

"Right on," he said. "I aim to be ubiquitous, memorable, and to have a good time at all times. Want to smoke a joint?"

"Uh, no thanks," she replied. "I thought I'd cut the lawn and maybe get started painting my house this afternoon."

"I'm up for that," he said. "My afternoon is wide-open. Alice is out of range, meeting with Kiki Savage all afternoon. Just let me get rid of this stuff, and I'll be right back." He was gone before she could reply, and back within minutes carrying a small backpack.

"OK. Let's go." They walked around the side of the inn, across the croquet lawn, and along the tennis courts. On the first court Nina saw the young honeymoon couple from the plane.

"You have to run to get the ball!" the man was yelling at the woman across the net.

"I don't feel like running. It's too hot. Why can't you just hit it to me?" she said irritably. *Uh-oh,* thought Nina.

She and Danish were rounding the corner onto the long gravel drive when they heard the snapping of twigs and rustling of leaves in the vegetation at the side of the road about fifty feet ahead of them, just between the last tennis court and the equipment shed. They walked on a few steps in silence and then saw where the noises were coming from. Half-hidden by a shrub, Tiffany Bassett was pressed up against the shed with her eyes shut, her arms around Lance, the tennis pro, with one hand down the back of his white tennis shorts, clutching his buttock. They appeared to be gnawing each other's faces off. Nina deduced that it was an amorous embrace, but it looked disturbingly like an act of mutual cannibalism. There was some moaning, and a bit too much skin was starting to show for Nina's taste. She gestured to Danish that they should cut across the parking lot to rejoin the drive farther down. Thankfully, Tiffany and Lance didn't see them before they detoured. *So much for married life,* thought Nina.

"Well, well, well," said Danish when they were out of earshot. "You don't see that every day. Or actually, you do see that every day, but with different people. That must be new. I hadn't heard about it yet. Lance is playing with fire there. Barry Bassett isn't the type who likes to share. She wanted to nibble at the Danish a while back, if you know what I mean, but I have a code."

"Unfortunately, I do know what you mean," said Nina. "I'm just going to try to forget I heard that, and that I just saw that. I have less than zero interest in the Bassetts' marital relations, although I can't help hoping she gets her wish and they buzz off to Miami sooner rather than later."

When they reached Nina's cottage, she smeared on another layer of sunscreen and grabbed her new machete, which she took out into the front yard facing the street. The morning sun had moved across the sky and dropped behind the roofline, so part of the front yard was now in shadow. Danish went around the side of the house and came back with two plastic chairs. He sat in one and put his feet up on the other. He opened the knapsack he'd put on the ground within arm's reach and pulled out a can of beer.

"Brew?" he asked.

"No, thanks," said Nina as she started slashing away at the tall grass with her machete, trying to avoid slicing open her shins.

"So, I've got the scuttlebutt on who's going to be at Kiki Savage's party tomorrow night," he said.

"Oh?" said Nina.

"Yeah. Jules and Kiki, Barry and Tiffany, you and me, the Minister of Cultural Heritage and Antiquities, and Alice. Plus, Blue Roker in his capacity as local big shot. The rest of the guests are members of the museum's board of governors: Ted, Pansy, and Michel, my boss at the inn; the school principal and her husband; Reverend Anderson and his wife; Delmont Samuels and his glamorous wife, Lana. He's a local boy who made good as a big-time music producer. They live next door to the Savages. Also, Derek and Cecilia Rathbone, artists and former hippies. Apparently it's a candlelit dinner for twenty, in honor of Tiffany Bassett, who Kiki generally has no use for. The word is Mrs. Bassett wasn't happy with the lack of fanfare accompanying her husband's generous donation to the museum, so Kiki stepped in to smooth ruffled feathers in the interests of local harmony. Jules is roasting a pig in a pit he's dug in his backyard. A new obsession."

Nina had finished cutting about half the grass and had made a big heap of clippings in a corner by the fence. It was starting to look less abandoned. Danish drained his beer and threw the empty in his knapsack.

"It's looking good," he said. "Keep up the good work." He stood up. "I think I'll pass on the watching-the-paint-dry part of this afternoon's entertainment and maybe head down to The Redoubt to scare up a game of darts. Come by for a drink later, if you feel like it. I'll be there." He gave her a little salute and struck off down the sidewalk.

Nina finished cutting the grass down to a height of three inches and then spent another hour pulling weeds from the overgrown flower beds on either side of the walkway and along the picket fence. She found a watering can under the kitchen sink and soaked the beds using the outside tap. Maybe some dormant flowers would come up now that they had some breathing space. As she stood with her hands on her hips, arching her aching back, Ted Matthews drove by in a khaki-colored Jeep with MATTHEWS BONEFISH LODGE on the side. There was a couple in the backseat dressed in fishing gear. He slowed the truck in front of her yard and stuck his head out the window.

"How are things, Nina?" he asked.

"Fine, no problems, thanks," she replied.

"Glad to hear it," he said. "See you later." He touched his fingers to the brim of his hat and drove on toward his place on the point.

He's a cowboy, she thought. *It's like having the lone ranger living next door. Not so bad.*

Nina's muscles were sore. She'd done way more manual labor than she did on an average day sitting at her computer. She decided to call it a day and cool off with a dip in the sea. She shed her sweaty clothes on the bedroom floor and slipped into her bikini. After months of wearing heavy sweaters, coats, socks, and boots, she felt practically naked padding down to the beach in her bare feet, but the water was exquisitely refreshing.

What a life, she thought, floating on her back looking back at her very own cottage on the beach. *I should hang a hammock between those two palm trees.*

Her eyes drifted up the beach to the point. A group of people sat on the covered deck at the very tip of the rocky point, all with drinks in hand.

Must be time for sundowners after a busy day in paradise. What a great idea.

She took a few more strokes through the silky water and then headed back up the sandy path to the veranda, drying herself off with a towel as she went. She put on her cozy sweater and mixed herself a drink using the rum-cocktail recipe book Louise had given her as a going-away present.

Life is an occasion, she reminded herself as she garnished the glass with a little paper umbrella from her own personal stash she'd bought that morning. She sat on the veranda and watched the sunset, then went inside and made herself a salad and grilled cheese and climbed into bed with a new murder mystery. Life could be pretty good.

4

Nina was up early the next morning and had her coffee on the veranda while watching the fishing boats head out at first light. Before getting to work, she composed a quick e-mail to Louise and one to her parents in Maine, describing the sunny little house on the beach, her unusual mailman, and her upcoming dinner at the home of Jules Savage. She did not mention Barry Bassett.

She spent the rest of the morning and early afternoon scraping, priming, and painting the outside of her tiny house. By four o'clock, it had a fresh coat of cheery butter-yellow paint and was looking great. Nina stood on the sidewalk for a couple of minutes, admiring her handiwork and making a plan to tackle the white trim and shutters tomorrow. Then she took a quick dip in the sea and showered, scrubbing drops of paint off her arms and legs.

Pansy and Danish were coming by at five o'clock to pick her up for the Savages' party. Nina stepped into her black silk party dress and zipped it up the back. It had a close-fitting boatneck top with long sleeves and a full, flared knee-length skirt. She slipped on the strappy black heels, swiped on some lipstick, and brushed her long, dark hair. She pinned it up in a smooth chignon and put the mohair shawl over her shoulders. Just as she was finishing, she heard Pansy's cart out front and then her knock at the door. Danish arrived just behind her.

"You ladies look lovely this evening," he said as they came into the house. He cleaned up shockingly well himself. He was wearing a white dinner jacket and black tie. "From my cruise-ship period," he said. They piled into Pansy's cart, Pansy and Nina in front and Danish reclining across the backseat. Pansy headed north past the point and on up the coastal road. A few minutes later, they came to a big concrete sign with **The Enclave** chiseled into it. Pansy turned off and followed a much smoother paved road past a string of widely spaced, outsize multistory villas, each with a pool beside it overlooking the ocean. As they drove, the lots became larger, the houses behind high stucco walls with wrought iron gates across their driveways. Only the rooftops were visible behind the walls, gates, and shrubbery.

The road ended at a narrow point of land where the west coast of the island met the east coast—Caribbean Sea on one side and the Atlantic Ocean on the other. The point itself was enclosed behind a stone wall complete with a gatehouse. The property comprised several acres of landscaped gardens dotted with coconut palms, gently sloping down to a perfect crescent of white-sand beach on one side, rocky cliffs overlooking the Atlantic on the other. A modern, streamlined beach house in putty-gray stucco with red cedar trim around its many windows sat high in the middle of the property, well back from the road.

"Here we are," said Pansy. "Kiki and Jules's place." As they drove up to the gate, it swung open, and a man in a uniform stepped out of the gatehouse and waved them through. After a short distance, they came to a pea-graveled parking area where a dozen carts and cars were already lined up. They parked and made their way up a winding stone staircase lit at ground-level by golden pools of light. Artfully planted shrubs, exotic-looking cacti, and boulders were interspersed with tall, leafy tropical trees strung with white fairy lights on either side of the steps. When they reached the top of the staircase, the parking area was no long visible. They were standing in a flagstone courtyard surrounded by broad-canopied mango trees looming over the long, low facade of the house. In the center of the courtyard was a square koi pond with five or six flat stepping-stones spanning it, just above the level of the water. Bright-orange fish swam lazily around the pond. On the other side of the pond was the front door of the house, standing open.

Pansy, Nina, and Danish skirted the pond rather than attempt the stepping-stones in their party shoes. As they reached the front door, a young woman in a crisp black linen dress stepped forward to meet them.

"Good evening. Mrs. Savage is on the terrace. Right this way, please." They followed her down a long corridor and out onto an expansive stone terrace. It was like standing on the prow of a ship, with a view of the ocean all around. On the far edge of the patio was a curved infinity pool. Scattered about the terrace were palm trees in huge clay pots, strung with white lights winking in the fading light. There were thickly cushioned wicker club chairs and sofas set under the trees and facing the view, as well as a long table set for dinner under the stars. It appeared that most of the other guests had arrived, and they stood chatting in small groups. Kiki Savage saw them and made her way over.

"Hi, Pansy, darling," she said, giving Pansy a kiss on the cheek. "You must be Nina," she said, smiling and holding out her hand to Nina. She gave Nina's hand a little squeeze. "I'm so glad you could make it. We'll have to make some time to talk this week to make sure you get what you need to write your article. Welcome to Pineapple Cay. We'll show you a good time, don't worry. Danish, what a pleasant surprise. Skinny-dipping is not on the program this evening, all right? The Reverend and Mrs. Anderson are here."

Kiki Savage looked just like she did in the numerous photographs Nina had seen over the years. She was tall and slender, with long light-brown hair and a warm smile, a youthful spring in her step, and an easy manner. She was in her midfifties, with attractive laugh lines in the corners of her eyes.

"Jules is down there cooking his pig," she said, gesturing over the side of the terrace. "He'll be up in a bit. Tara, could you please get these folks a drink? Thank you very much. Let me go see to a few things, and I'll see you in a bit." She stepped away with a smile, and the crisp young woman reappeared at their side to take their order, then melted away again.

They walked over to the edge of the terrace and looked down the slope to a flat patch of grass where their host, a man who had spent the 1980s trashing hotel rooms, playing his guitar in sold-out soccer stadiums, and saying naughty words in live radio interviews, was heaping hot coals around a large pig on a spit. His cream linen trousers were tucked into big black rubber boots. A couple of teenage boys in kitchen uniforms were standing by, presumably to help him lift it out.

Their freshly delivered drinks in hand, Nina, Danish, and Pansy inched closer to the group of guests.

"Is Alice here yet?" Danish asked, although Nina had no idea what she looked like. Danish spotted Alice chatting with a white-haired couple across the patio just as Tara reappeared on the terrace with a tall man in a uniform in tow. He took off his cap and tucked it under his arm as Kiki Savage approached him with her arms outstretched. He bent down and kissed her on both cheeks.

"There is he is. Deputy Superintendent John 'Blue' Roker," said Danish. "'The Black Paul Newman.' Whatever. 'Mr. Charisma.' I am saying that ironically, in case you didn't catch it. The guy never cracks a smile. Now he's making a beeline for my woman."

They watched as the police chief parted with Kiki Savage and walked toward the young woman Danish had indicated was Alice. Nina could see why she had caught Danish's eye. She was petite and elegant in a floor-length black lace dress with a mock turtleneck and short sleeves. Her long, curly black hair was pulled back tightly into a neat ponytail at the nape of her neck. Her eyes were outlined in black kohl, and her lips and nails were painted a dramatic dark plum. The severity of her makeup was offset by her wide, bright smile and shining eyes as she turned to greet John "Blue" Roker.

Pansy turned away for a minute to speak to someone near her, and Nina and Danish stood watching Alice and Roker across the terrace. Roker placed his hand on Alice's shoulder and left it there as he said something to the older white-haired gentleman, and then he looked down again into Alice's smiling face.

"Physical contact! Physical contact! Not cool." Danish took an agitated step forward and then back again.

"Gee, Danish. Are you sure they're an item?" Nina said. "I think he's just being friendly. And he must be close to twenty years older than she is."

Danish swung his head around to look at her. "And your point is?"

Pansy rejoined them. Roker had turned away from Alice and was now walking directly toward them across the patio. He moved with the slow, stately gait perfected in the islands. The sun was low on the horizon, and as he walked, he took off his shades and tucked them in the pocket of his shirt. In an instant, Nina saw where he got his nickname. His eyes were an intense icy blue, a startling contrast against his rich brown skin. She had never seen Paul Newman in the flesh, but she thought Blue Roker might out-blue even him.

"Good evening, ladies. Danish."

Pansy jumped in to make the introductions. "Blue, this is Nina Spark. She just bought Miss Rose's place. Nina, may I introduce John Roker, Pineapple Cay's chief of police. We all call him Blue."

"It's a pleasure to meet you, Nina. Are you settling in all right?" He reached out his hand, and she took it. His grasp was firm and warm. She struggled to find her voice as he looked directly into her eyes. His gaze was blinding, like staring into the sun.

"Hello. I haven't done much settling so far, but your island is beautiful." *Very lame, Nina. Very lame.* Despite Danish's declaration that he never did so, Blue Roker smiled.

"Glad to hear you've decided to call it home." There was a brief, awkward silence while Danish glared at Blue, and Nina, momentarily incapacitated, could not speak. Pansy jumped in again.

"So, are you working tonight, Blue?"

"Yes, there's some valuable property on display tonight, so I thought it would be a good idea to keep an eye on things. I've got a corporal in the Jeep down by the gate." He glanced over his shoulder at Tiffany Bassett, who was holding court on a sofa at the far corner of the patio. The emerald necklace was prominently displayed above the plunging neckline of her clinging green silk dress.

"Valuable property. Do you mean Tiffany's new boobs or the necklace?" Danish asked, laughing at his own little joke. Pansy winced. Blue glared at him.

The chief of police turned slightly toward Nina and Pansy. "Well, nice to see you as usual, Pansy, and nice to meet you, Nina. I'll see you ladies at dinner." He shifted his gaze back to Danish. As he took a few backward steps away from them, Blue put two fingers to his beautiful eyes, swiveled his hand, and pointed at Danish. Then he turned away to greet a man in a charcoal-gray suit and tie. Pansy broke the silence again.

"Well, Danish, that was an unfortunate remark to make to your beloved's uncle, who also happens to be the chief of police. Particularly given your reputation with the ladies, of which I'm sure he is aware."

"Her uncle!" exclaimed Danish.

Pansy shrugged. "I thought it was common knowledge. Blue's oldest sister is Alice's mother. She left Pineapple Cay to go to college thirty years ago, married a guy from Nassau, and settled there. Alice has lots of family here. She's staying with her Aunt Agatha, who lives next door to Blue."

"Fantastic!" Danish said. "Let's go say hi to her." He was already making a beeline across the patio toward an unsuspecting Alice, who was still chatting with the elderly couple.

Pansy sighed. "We'd better go give her a buffer from his scorched-earth approach to courting."

"And maybe save him from himself," Nina added. They followed Danish across the patio. They were halfway there when Kiki Savage clapped her hands above her head.

"Hi, everyone," said Kiki. "I'm so glad you're all here to celebrate this occasion. Let's make our way to the table so we can try Jules's pig, and toast the Bassetts."

The speech went over well with Tiffany, who beamed benevolent smiles at everyone as she minced her way to the head of the table in her tight dress, with Kiki on her right and her husband on her left. Jules Savage stood behind the chair at the opposite end of the table. Alice was to his right, and the Minister of Cultural Heritage and Antiquities was on his left. The other guests filled in the seats between, according to place cards on the table. A forlorn Danish found himself next to Barry Bassett, reduced to sending meaningful looks to Alice down the length of the table. Blue Roker was posted across from him.

As Nina was making her way to the table, Tiffany Bassett caught sight of her out of the corner of her eye and changed directions. She tottered over.

"What are you doing here?" she asked loudly, sloshing some white wine on Nina's dress as she leaned in closer, holding her wineglass aloft.

"This a party in my honor, and I don't even know you, except that you cheated my husband out of his land." Nina felt an angry Pansy step up beside her, hands clenched, but before either could say anything, Jules Savage swept in front of Nina and took her elbow, turning his back to Tiffany as he guided Nina to the table.

"Nina, baby! We finally meet! Thank you for making time to attend our little event. I am looking forward to chewing over the old eighteenth century with you one of these days over a few pints. Come sit down. It's a pleasure to have you in our home."

He accompanied her to her seat in the middle of the table. Several guests had been standing by their chairs watching, frozen in awkward silence. Blue Roker and Danish had both taken a couple of steps toward the confrontation. Barry Bassett was leaning back against the terrace rail with his arms crossed and a smirk on his face. He seemed content to let things unfold as they might.

Jules turned back to the table with a smile, playing the charming host, and the guests relaxed. No one paid any attention to Tiffany as she marched to her seat and sat sulking.

Pansy was seated on Nina's left, and she patted her hand under the table. The seat on her right was vacant. She looked at the place card. Ted Matthews. He arrived just as the starter was being served, bending down to kiss Kiki on the cheek and whisper an apology before sliding into his seat next to Nina. He sat back and exhaled before turning to look at her.

"Long day?" she asked.

"We have a full house this weekend, and I was out with a client from Boston until almost sundown. He's been here three days and hasn't hooked a fish yet. Although that's not the be-all and end-all, we try our best to give the sports at least one good story to tell their friends back home," he said. "Some of them come a long way for the experience."

"So, did he get his fish?" asked Nina.

"Yes, he did. I was just about to call it a day, and he hooked a nice one. He was happy, but I think he got more than he bargained for," Ted said, chuckling.

"What do you mean?" asked Pansy.

"Well, I was stowing the gear, and he waded away to answer the call of nature at a discreet distance. I had my head in the cooler when I heard a howl, then a lot of thrashing in the water. I looked up to see him slogging back to the boat as fast as a person in a pair of boots in thigh-high water can. Some sharks are attracted to urine, and a blacktip shark drifting nearby had given him quite a shock. By next week, that will be one of the highlights of his trip to Pineapple Cay." He chuckled again and took a sip of water.

"I apologize, ladies. Maybe that's not appropriate dinner-table talk. I spend most of my days in the company of men. Sometimes the porch talk gets a bit salty, and I start thinking it's normal," Ted said.

"No, that's actually good to know," said Nina. "Not the type of practical knowledge you pick up in Manhattan. So, I guess he didn't get eaten by the shark?"

"Blacktips aren't ordinarily much of a threat to an angler," Ted said. "Now, come across a hammerhead when you're in the water, and that'll put the fear of God into you."

"Makes me think about putting a pool in," said Nina. "Something that blends into the landscape but is shark-free." A factoid about bears and menstruation acquired during her upbringing in Maine popped into Nina's head, but she decided not to share it.

Across the table, the older couple who had been chatting with Alice were now engaged in small talk with the elegant Lana Samuels. When that petered out, Lana turned to her other side to talk to the man in the charcoal-gray suit, and the older lady caught Nina's eye.

"Hello. You must be Nina," she said, smiling. "We haven't had a chance to talk yet. I'm Cecilia Rathbone, and this is my husband, Derek. It's always nice to have a new face in town."

"Very nice to meet you," said Nina. "Danish told me that you're both artists."

"Potters," said Derek. "Self-taught in our misspent youth. You must come by the studio someday so we can give you the grand tour."

Kiki Savage rose to her feet at the head of the table. "It is so nice to have you here tonight to mark this special occasion. Only once every thirty or forty years has a storied wreck like the *Morning Star* been recovered. What a thrilling event. We want to acknowledge Barry and Tiffany Bassett's contribution to preserving the cultural heritage of these islands. May I propose a toast to the Bassetts." She raised her glass and nodded to Barry and Tiffany, and then she sat down.

"Hear, hear!" said Jules Savage from the other end of the table, and other guests echoed the toast. Barry Bassett smiled a tight little smile and took a mouthful of his wine. Tiffany Bassett smiled magnanimously and sprang to her feet.

"Thank you so much, Kiki darling. You are *such* a pal. Barry and I are so happy to be able to donate the multimillion-dollar *Morning Glory* emerald to the Pineapple Cay Museum. Although, personally, I think it looks fabulous right where it is."

She looked down at the emerald, which was nestled in her cleavage, and made a provocative little shimmy with her shoulders. Sitting beside her, Kiki Savage looked down at her plate. Given that the woman was the wife of a rock star, she must have seen worse behavior than that before. *But gawd,* thought Nina, *Tiffany seems tone-deaf to good taste and common courtesy.* Barry sat beside her, his face expressionless. He pulled a wine bottle closer to him and read the label while she spoke, then topped off his glass.

"Anyway," continued Tiffany, "it's our biggest hope that the necklace will become a huge tourist draw and will raise the Pineapple Cay Museum from its second-class status to a world-class tourist attraction. Thanks. Let's have another drink."

There was a smattering of applause. Kiki Savage rose quickly from her seat again as Tiffany dropped into hers.

"And, of course," said Kiki, "we're delighted to have the emerald and the other artifacts from the *Morning Glory* in the museum's permanent collection, where they will be a wonderful way for the children of Pineapple Cay to learn about the fascinating history of their islands. In that project, we are so fortunate that Ms. Alice Rolle has recently accepted the position of curator at the museum. Welcome home, Ms. Rolle." She smiled across the table at Alice, and the guests all clapped their hands. Alice smiled back and nodded slightly. Kiki continued.

"I know that all of you would also like to acknowledge the extremely generous donation of the late Miss Rose Knox, beloved long-time teacher at Pineapple Cay Comprehensive School. Miss Rose's legacy will allow for the development and delivery of educational programs for children and other visitors to the museum for many years to come. To Miss Rose!"

She raised her glass in a toast to Miss Rose, and the other guests followed suit. Beside a now-smiling Kiki, Tiffany Bassett sat with her arms crossed and lips pursed.

"Looks like someone doesn't like being upstaged," said Pansy.

After the dinner plates were cleared and coffee and tea were served by two gangly teenage boys in crisp white shirts, a low murmur of conversation began to build around the long table. Nina saw Tiffany Bassett look at her gold bracelet watch like she was wondering how much longer she had to stay. She took a big gulp of wine and then called loudly to Alice Rolle at the other end of the table.

"Come on, then. Come to the powder room and help me get this off, then I'll let you have it." She rose from her chair, turned her back on the assembled guests, and disappeared into the house without even waiting for Alice. Alice looked taken aback, but she tucked her evening bag under her arm, pushed back her chair, and stepped quickly across the terrace to follow Tiffany, her heels clicking smartly on the stone tiles.

"It's like she actually thinks, 'What would be the most inappropriate, ungracious thing I could say right now?' and then says it," said Pansy.

"You can usually count on Tiffany Bassett to try to ruin an otherwise pleasant evening," said Ted. "On the topic of more inspiring and productive ways to live your life, I ran into an old friend today when I was at the fuel dock on Wreath Cay. Rawson Light. He lives way down in the cays, at the national park headquarters on Turtle Cay." For Nina's benefit, he explained, "There's a chain of mainly uninhabited cays south of Pineapple that the government has protected as a national land-and-sea park. Rawson works there doing park maintenance, cutting hiking trails, fixing the generator, and so on. I've run into him on several occasions supervising a bunch of school kids on some beach or another, or in the park picking up huge piles of plastic and other junk that has washed up onshore. He spent a couple of months cleaning and reassembling the skeleton of an eighty-foot-long sperm whale on the beach at Turtle Cay. The whale swallowed a plastic bag, which blocked its digestive system, and it slowly starved to death. It washed up onshore, and the park interpreter uses it to teach the kids about the fragile ecosystem of the cays. The fragility and the majesty.

"Rawson did a stint in Iraq, although he never talks much about it. He went home to Florida after he left the army and set up an electrical contracting business. He hadn't been home long when he was diagnosed with cancer and given six months to live. His marriage had ended, and his kids had both finished high school. He decided to spend what time he had left sailing in the islands. He bought a boat and was cruising the Caribbean when Hurricane Annie tore through here. Rawson helped at least four other boats get safely tied up in a hurricane hole before the full force of the storm hit. His own boat was torn off its moorings and lost to sea. No insurance. He found himself boatless in the islands. He ended up on Turtle Cay and made a new plan. That was three years ago, and he still looks fitter than a lot of men half his age, although I've never seen him eat or drink anything but diet cola. He's gruff and solitary, but he's always quick to smile and shoot the breeze. A remarkable guy."

"There are certainly a million different ways to live your life," said Pansy.

People began to disperse from the table and settle into comfortable chairs and sofas assembled around several small, cozy fires that had been lit in shallow metal fire bowls. The sky was a canopy of brilliant white stars set in black velvet. Candles floated on the surface of the pool, dancing specks of light in the dark. A man in a tropical flowered shirt took up a position on a stool under a potted palm and picked out a calypso melody on his guitar.

Across the terrace, Nina could see that Barry Bassett had cornered the man in the gray suit and was speaking vehemently at him, stabbing the air with his pointer finger for emphasis. Nina turned away, making a conscious effort to ignore the scene. She, Ted, and Pansy took up their coffee cups and were chatting with the school principal and her husband when Alice Rolle ran out onto the terrace, the staccato of her heels shattering the serenity of the gathering.

"She's gone!" she screamed. "Something's happened to her! There's broken glass everywhere, and she's gone! Uncle John, help!"

Roker sprinted across the terrace, pulling his radio from his belt as he went, speaking rapidly into it.

"Everyone, please stay here," he said over his shoulder as he disappeared inside. Alice stood shaking, clutching her evening bag in front of her. In seconds, Pansy and Kiki were at her side, guiding her to a sofa and sitting on either side of her. Danish hovered beside them with a pained look on his face.

"I'll be damned if I'm waiting here!" said Barry Bassett, and he followed Roker into the house. Nina perched on a chair beside Pansy, Alice, and Kiki while Ted stood behind her. Jules took up a station by the Minister of Culture, and they talked in hushed tones.

"Are you all right, dear? Do you want a glass of water?" asked Kiki.

"No, no. I'm fine," said Alice. "At first I didn't know where she had gone. I checked the powder room by the front door and looked into the living room, but there was nobody there. I could hear people in the kitchen, but I didn't think she would have gone in there. Then I heard the sound of water running. I followed it and waited for her outside the bathroom for several minutes. I figured she was freshening up and would open the door for me when she was ready to remove the necklace. I didn't want to make her cross by knocking. But then I got worried. She had been in there an awfully long time. Maybe she had become ill or something. I knocked and called her name. There was no answer. I was beginning to panic. I knocked again more loudly, and when she didn't answer, I pushed open the door. The room was empty. There was water splashed all over the floor, and the towel rack had been pulled out of the wall."

She took a breath and continued. "I was trying to find her, and I ran down a long hallway and into a bedroom. Maybe a guest room. It was destroyed! Chairs and lamps lying on the floor. Books pulled out of the bookcase. The bed looked like it had been pulled apart. The sliding glass door was open and off its rail. A piece of fabric from her dress was snagged on the handle."

She looked up at them. "And there were drops of blood on the carpet." She covered her mouth with her hand.

Blue Roker reappeared on the terrace and spoke to Jules Savage briefly, then went back into the house.

"May I have your attention, please, everyone," Jules said, projecting his voice across the patio.

"Deputy Superintendent Roker and his officers need to secure the scene and conduct their investigation so that Mrs. Bassett may be found as soon as possible. Therefore, we must call a halt to this evening's festivities. Chief Roker says that you're all free to go now, except for you, Alice dear. He may call on the rest of you in the near future. Thank you all for coming, and I hope we meet again soon under happier circumstances. Good night."

"I'll stay with you, Alice, then I can take you back to your aunt's house. I imagine Blue just needs to talk to you first," said Pansy.

"I'm staying, too," said Danish.

"Ted, can you take Nina home?" asked Pansy.

"Of course," he replied.

"What a horrendous turn of events," said Kiki. "Nina, I wanted to apologize for Tiffany Bassett's dreadful behavior earlier this evening, but now that she's apparently been abducted from my home, I confess, I don't know quite how to feel."

"Is it possible she just took off?" asked Pansy. "Tiffany specializes in making scenes, and maybe she didn't like having to share the spotlight with Alice."

"I guess anything is possible," said Kiki. "We've never even had a break-in here before, let alone any kind of violence. But the blood on the carpet . . ." She was silent for a moment and then turned to Nina.

"Pineapple Cay prides itself on being the kind of place where you can let your kids roam free because everyone looks out for everyone else, where you can leave your keys in the ignition without worrying about your car being stolen." Kiki sighed. "I was going to invite you to come by for a visit on Tuesday. I want to show you that we're a generally hospitable crowd on Pineapple Cay, and also discuss your piece. I'm choosing to believe that Blue will find Tiffany safe and sound very soon, and that you won't have to write the story of the empty display cabinet in the Pineapple Cay Museum—or something worse, God forbid. I hope you can still come."

"That would be very nice, thank you. I'll look forward to it," said Nina.

The guests had lingered uncertainly for a few moments but were now making their way through the house and down to the parking area under the guidance of two uniformed officers. Ted shook hands good night with a few people and then opened the Jeep door for Nina.

They drove in silence for a couple of minutes before he said, "Quite a night."

"Yes," said Nina. "Quite a crime-ridden piece of paradise you've got here."

"Tiffany and Barry Bassett seem to bring the rain with them," he said. "I wouldn't blame you for not believing it, but Pineapple Cay is usually a pretty quiet place. Blue Roker's shop is generally occupied with keeping a lid on small-time smuggling, catching poachers in the national park, and providing security for the annual homecoming parade." He glanced over at her.

"I gather you got a dose of Tiffany Bassett's charm before I arrived," he said.

Nina shrugged. She didn't feel like reviewing the gory details. "Oh, well, I've never understood people like that. Do they enjoy being at odds with everyone?" she asked.

He was quiet for a moment and then glanced over at her again. "Tomorrow is changeover day at the lodge. The current batch of guests is leaving in the morning, and the next group doesn't arrive until tomorrow night. If you're free, maybe you'd let me show you some of the better things Pineapple Cay has to offer."

Nina hesitated. Outside of work, it had been ten years since she'd spent time alone with a man other than her husband. The novelty of the situation made her anxious. But it didn't sound like a date. He was just being friendly.

"Thank you. That would be nice," she said.

"Great. I'll pick you up at nine o'clock. Bring your swimsuit. And with any luck, by sundown tomorrow Tiffany Bassett will be back at home giving Barry a hard time," he said.

They had reached her gate. He got out of the Jeep and walked around to open her door. *His mother raised a gentleman,* thought Nina. She considered herself a feminist, but nice manners were admirable in everyone. They said good night, and she let herself into the cottage. He waited until she'd closed and locked the door before he got into his Jeep and drove away.

5

True to his word, Ted was back at her front gate the next morning at nine o'clock. He had a Boston Whaler with a Bimini top trailered to his Jeep, with a couple of fishing rods, a tackle box, and a cooler stowed inside.

"Good morning," he said. "All set?"

"Yes, great," said Nina. "It's funny. The sun's shining and the birds are singing. It's hard to believe last night really happened."

He nodded. It looked like they were going fishing, and she guessed fish or some other sea creature was on the menu for lunch. That was awkward. She slid into the passenger seat of the Jeep and then watched him go around the front, jump into the driver's seat, and turn the key in the ignition.

"I'm a vegetarian!" she blurted out.

He paused with his hand on the key and looked over at her. "Is that a fact?" He was quiet for a moment as he looked in the rearview mirror, maneuvered the Jeep and attached boat off the shoulder onto the road, and headed south.

"We have a sign hanging in the lodge. It says, 'Vegetarian: old Carib word for lousy fisherman.'" He chuckled. "Don't worry. I won't make you eat any fish."

"Are we going fishing?" she asked.

"I thought you might like to try bonefishing. It'll give you a different perspective on the island." He looked over at her again. "We don't eat them. It's catch and release."

She had never even bothered to try fishing in Maine. Things were off to a rocky start. She wondered what the point was if you just let them go, but she didn't want to offend Ted, who obviously liked it enough to devote his life's work to it and had gone to the trouble to plan a day out.

"Great," she said.

They headed south of town past the airport turnoff. It was another perfect day in paradise. They passed the oceanfront villas she and Pansy had driven by on their way into town a couple of days ago—Bougainvillea Villa, The Flip-Flop, Mermaid House, and a dozen others—and a convenience store and the medical clinic. They passed a whitewashed church gleaming in the sunlight, its doors and windows flung open. The sound of a joyful hymn poured out into the quiet of Sunday morning. Gradually, signs of human habitation petered out, and they were driving through low scrubland with a huge bowl of blue sky above them and the ocean on their right.

The road followed a winding, thin strand of beach along the coast for a couple of miles, then cut inland. A few miles farther on, Ted turned off onto a gravel road. They bumped along for a few minutes, the bush pressing close on both sides of the road. They rolled to a stop in a grassy clearing with the water in front of them again. There were three or four pickup trucks and a couple of trailers parked on a patch of gravel. There was no beach, just an aged concrete boat ramp sloping into the water next to a narrow wooden pier that extended into what looked to Nina like a swamp. Dense clumps of mangrove trees with high, tangled roots grew out of the water. A meandering channel wound its way through the mangroves away from the dock.

Nina got out of the Jeep and stood to the side with her canvas tote over her shoulder while Ted backed the trailer down the boat ramp and slid the boat in the water with the ease of someone who had done it at least a thousand times. He tied the boat to a cleat on the dock, waded back to shore, and parked the truck and trailer out of the way in the shade. His boots and the bottoms of his khaki shorts were soaked, but he didn't seem to mind. He came and stood by Nina with a second pair of boots in his hand.

"Once in a while I see parrots here. They like those red berries." They stood silently, scanning the treetops. There was plenty of raucous birdsong but no parrots in sight.

"Maybe we'll see them next time," he said. He handed her the boots. They were sand-colored with a pair of sand-colored socks inside. "Here. It's probably easiest if you wade out to the boat. These will protect your feet and help keep you upright while you fish."

She leaned against the bumper of the Jeep, slipped off her flip-flops, and put on the boots. They waded out to the boat. Luckily she had worn her bathing suit under her shorts. He jumped into the boat and reached out his hand to help her in over the bow. She sat down, he started the engine, and they began to move slowly away from the dock through the mangrove creek. The vegetation was high on either side of the boat, and they were in shade. It was a different world from the turquoise water, white sand, and brilliant sunlight she'd seen on her side of the island.

"Keep your eyes on the water," he said. "There are green turtles around here. Huge. Some of them eighty years old." She slid to the edge of the bench and peered over the side. There were little brown fish darting all around.

"There!" he said, pointing ahead of him. He motioned to her to look. She looked where he was pointing and saw a large oval shape glide through the water just below the surface. He grinned at her, and she grinned back. The mangroves began to thin out, and the channel opened up. They emerged into a wide sunlit bay. The color of the water changed from olive green to jade, turquoise, and sapphire blue. He cut the engine.

"Are we going to fish here?" she asked.

"The fish around here are fished so hard that if they see a fly, they can tell you who tied it. We've got to go farther down," he said. "I just thought we'd soak up the silence for a few minutes."

They sat there quietly, looking out to the horizon. The only sound was the soft lapping of the water against the hull of the boat. The shallow water was transparent, the grains of sand visible on the bottom. Ted handed her a bottle of orange juice from the cooler, and they drank in silence. He looked over at her, then started the engine again.

"Hang on," he said. The boat gathered speed, and the bow lifted. They skimmed over the surface of the water. Nina felt the ocean spray on her face. They flew along, cutting wide arcs around sandbars until they rounded a point of land and drifted into a shallow, sheltered bay. Swirls of white sand rose above shallow pools and channels of sapphire and green. Ted cut the engine and threw out the anchor.

"Let's try it here," he said. He opened the tackle box to reveal several cascading trays filled with flies and lures. He picked out a cotton-candy-pink-and-silver bundle with shiny metal eyeballs and a hook protruding from it.

"This is a Crazy Charlie. They seem to like them," he said.

"They must be pretty dumb if they think that's a fly. It looks just like a piece of thread and a feather," said Nina.

"Yes, well. It's supposed to be a shrimp. They are not rocket scientists. But they are savvy. Let's see how dumb you think they are at the end of the day," said Ted. He put the fly on her line and handed the long rod to her. They slipped over the side of the boat into knee-deep water and started wading out onto the flats.

"Wait a second," said Nina. "Are there sharks around here?"

"Don't worry about them," said Ted. "They'll be long gone before you even know they were here. They're more afraid of you than you are of them."

"Yeah, right. I'm from Maine. That's what we used to tell the tourists about the black bears. The summer I worked at the state park office, the staff bulletin board was full of pictures of flattened tents and cars with the doors ripped off by bears looking for peanut-butter sandwiches," she said.

"I haven't lost a customer to a shark yet," he said. "See all those circles in the sand with the holes in the center?" He pointed down into the shallow water. "That's where bonefish have been feeding. One way to find them is to look for tailing fish—their tails poking out of the water while they suck small shrimp and crabs out of the sand. Otherwise, they are nearly invisible and very quick. You have to look for their shadows on the sandy bottom rather than for the fish themselves. They sometimes travel alone and sometimes in schools."

He spent several long minutes patiently trying to teach her how to cast; then they stood scanning the flats for signs of the fish.

"There! Cast your line at nine o'clock!" he said. She made a clumsy attempt to throw the line in the direction he was pointing. It landed a few feet in front of her. He deftly took the rod from her and cast the line like a lariat far out in front of them. He handed it back to her.

"Now strip the line. Pull it in with your hand a foot at a time. Strip it. Strip it. You're trying to make the fish think you're a shrimp," he said. They did that several times. Nina could understand the appeal on a certain level. The setting was spectacular, and the peace was enveloping. A sweeping empty vista of blue and white. But after the tenth time pulling the long line in foot by foot, she was feeling ready to move on.

Suddenly she felt the line pull tight.

"OK! You've got one on the hook," he said. She felt a tug through the rod and the movement of the fish in the water. A few seconds passed, and nothing much else happened.

"So, is this what it's all about?" she asked. "Is this what people travel thousands of miles and spend thousands of dollars to do?"

"That fish doesn't know it's hooked yet. Just wait," he said. As the words left his mouth, the line started ripping off her reel, and the handle spun wildly.

"*Ahhhh!*" screamed Nina. For a millisecond, she thought of dropping the rod, but instead, she hung on for dear life.

"OK. Keep the rod up. Let him run. Don't touch the line or the reel while the fish is running. That's it. There's drag on the reel, and that'll tire the fish out." He put his hand over hers on the rod for a second and then removed it. The fish was racing like a missile straight out to sea.

"Wait until it stops running, then start reeling in the line. Keep the rod tip up. Keep the rod tip up so it can't snap the line. Good," he said. The fish finished his run. "OK, start reeling it in. You don't want any slack on the line."

Nina reeled the line in.

"OK. Now watch out. It's going to run again when it sees us." All of a sudden there was a violent pull on the line. The line tore off the reel, and the fish was off running again.

The fish ran three times before Nina was able to reel it in to where they were standing. Ted reached down and gently cradled the fish in two hands just below the surface of the water. He looked up at Nina and smiled.

"Congratulations. You've caught your first bonefish. I wish you many more to come." It was long and slender, with gorgeous silver scales. It was so closely camouflaged to the water and sand that it appeared almost translucent. With one hand, Ted reached into the pocket of his shorts and pulled out a pair of forceps. He clamped them on the hook protruding from the fish's mouth and, with an expert motion, gave them a twist. The hook came out, and the fish shot away. Nina was unexpectedly exhilarated.

They fished awhile longer. Nina did not hook another one, but she did get caught up in scanning the surface for signs of fish and practicing her casting. Eventually, she went back to the boat and sat in the shade of the Bimini top, drinking a bottle of ice-cold water from the cooler, watching Ted cast and cast again. He caught two more fish and gently released them. After he let the second one go, he waded back to the boat, grabbed a water bottle from the cooler, and sat beside her. He lifted his hat and wiped the sweat from his brow. A gentle breeze rippled the surface of the water, and then it was smooth again, like polished glass.

"It's about time for lunch, what do you think?" he asked.

"That was fun. But now that you mention it, sure, I'm ready for lunch," she answered.

He pulled up the anchor and started the motor. They flew back the way they had come, skimming over the water. The breeze and mist from the wake of the boat cooled Nina's sun-heated skin. They cruised slowly through the mangroves back to the wharf. Then Ted loaded the boat on the trailer, and they headed back down the potholed gravel road to the main highway.

"There is a little place at the south end of the island called Rosie's. I thought we might stop there for a bite," said Ted.

"Sounds great," said Nina.

They drove for a couple of miles on a straight road through scrubland devoid of any development, the ocean coming close to the edge of the highway, then moving away again. Gradually, the island narrowed until they could see the water glittering in the distance on both sides of the road through a fringe of palms and casuarina pines. As they crested a low hill, suddenly spread out before them was a sweeping vista of turquoise water, white sand, and patches of green-and-gold grass. At the end of the island, an arm of land curved around in the water, enclosing a bowlful of the Caribbean Sea. Off its very tip, a scattered line of low-lying sandy cays trailed off over the horizon. Immediately in front of Nina and Ted at the bottom of the hill, two ponds rimmed in brilliant white flanked the road. The white was even brighter than the sand.

"Those are salt ponds," said Ted. "There's a small company here that produces and exports Pineapple Cay sea salt."

Beyond the salt ponds, the terrain climbed gently again until it reached the sea. A small village clustered on either side of the road. There was a gas station and a tiny telephone company office dwarfed by a telephone tower and a forest of antennas penned up in a yard surrounded by a chain-link fence. Three goats stood in the shade on the front step of the telephone office, their heads swiveling to watch Ted and Nina as they slowly drove by. There were a dozen or so small cement-block houses, the fishing boats in some driveways taller than the houses. Nina heard a rooster crow and saw a hen and some chicks pecking in the yard of a yellow house with a big red-hibiscus blossom painted on its side. There was no other sign of life in the heat of mid-day. As they drove slowly past the lone gas pump, Nina read the hand-lettered sign taped to it: **BLOW HORN FOR SERVICE.**

Ted followed the narrow road through the village and out onto the arm of land to the very southern tip of Pineapple Cay. There, just below the narrow, rocky point, sat a wooden building painted all the colors of the rainbow. A covered veranda faced the cays, and a beer sign and a giant ice cream cone were nailed to the wall next to the door. **ROSIE'S** was painted in giant white letters on the rainbow-striped wall next to the beer sign.

Ted parked the Jeep, and he and Nina climbed the three steps up to the veranda. The view was amazing: the blue sky, the turquoise water, and the white sails of a sailboat drifting back and forth. A couple of sailboats were moored in the sheltered cove below the restaurant, and an aluminum motorboat and an inflatable Zodiac were pulled up on the sand. Nina surmised that they belonged to the laughing, tanned vacationers sitting at two picnic tables littered with sweating beer bottles and half-eaten plates of food.

Nina and Ted gravitated to a table on the edge of the covered deck, facing the cays. Ted took off his hat and ran his fingers through his damp hair.

A matronly woman in an apron greeted Ted warmly and brought them coleslaw, toasted sandwiches, and cool drinks.

"Apart from the Bassetts, how are you finding life on Pineapple Cay?" Ted asked Nina as they ate.

"Apart from the Bassetts, I like it very much. If you could dream up the perfect little town on the perfect tropical island, I think it would look a lot like this," replied Nina.

"Agreed," said Ted. "With any luck, thirty or forty years from now, I'll be one of those old guys fishing off the town wharf every afternoon, with a good supply of stories about the old days to tell on the porch in the evenings."

She smiled. They ate in silence for a moment, enjoying the view.

"Of course, sunshine and blue skies doesn't work for everyone," he said. "We get all kinds of people who come here to fish some of the best water anywhere. They include some very successful people who, you can tell, really want to excel at having a good time. They've bought all the best gear and are up and ready to go the first morning. Then they get frustrated when they don't achieve perfection with their first cast. They stand in the water with paradise all around them, cursing. Scaring the fish. I always think of that quotation: 'The mind is its own place, and in itself can make a heaven of hell, a hell of heaven.'"

"Mmm," said Nina, "that's very true. Danish said something like that the other day."

"Danish," said Ted, looking out at the water again and then back at her. "I never had him down as a philosopher. More as a fly-by-the-seat-of-his-pants kind of guy."

"Oh, well . . . ," said Nina. Then she decided to change the topic. "So, how did you come to be living on Pineapple Cay?"

"It probably would have been surprising if it had gone any other way," he said. "I grew up in Florida and spent a lot of time fishing with my father. I love it. Always have. I couldn't believe it when I learned you could make a job out of it. I spent about ten years guiding sports in the Florida Keys before the coast got a bit overdeveloped for my taste. I built the lodge eight years ago, and I've been here ever since. The lodge takes up most of my time, but I have no complaints. I'm a lucky guy. I earned a business degree after high school, mostly to please my mother. Most of the guys I went to college with are muscling their way through their office jobs, just looking forward to the couple of weeks a year they get a chance to do what I do every day."

Nina had a hard time imagining the rangy, bronzed outdoorsman across from her folded into a desk taking notes on accounting procedures. It was a bit easier if she imagined him as a youth of nineteen with all those big decisions—like what to do with his life—still ahead of him.

"I grew up at the other end of Route 1," she volunteered, skipping over her New York interlude and its messy ending. "Near Brunswick, Maine. In fact, it's very possible my mother sewed that very belt you're wearing. She worked at the L.L. Bean factory there until just last year, and I think your belt has at least a few years under it."

He smiled. "That's a nice thought," he said. "You're very observant."

"Yes, I am," she replied.

Ted went inside to pay the bill while Nina fretted about whether or not she should have let him. A short while later, they were passing through the green tunnel of tall trees and dappled sunlight on the route back to Coconut Cove. There was no other traffic. At the foot of the driveway of a small white house with weather-beaten shutters, an older man sat in a lawn chair in the shade of a tall tree and a golf umbrella. A rickety wooden shelf stood next to him, filled with glass bottles. Ted pulled the Jeep over to the side of the road.

"Let's go say hi. You'll like Joe," he said to Nina. They got out and walked over to the man.

"Hi, Joe," said Ted. "How've you been keeping?"

"Well, hello, Ted. I can't complain. My daughter has come down from the main island to see me and brought the young fella, so I'm happy. She's up there cooking my favorite chicken foot souse for dinner.

The young fella's watching some noisy shoot-'em-up on the satellite. Who's this, now?" asked the man, looking at Nina.

"Hi. I'm Nina," she said.

"Well, pleased to meet you, Nina. You fishin'?" asked Joe.

"First time today," she said.

Joe laughed. "Well, I hope you like it. You gonna keep company with Ted here, you gotta like fishing."

"I'm running out of hot sauce at the lodge, Joe," said Ted. "What do you have?" he asked, moving over to look at Joe's display case. Joe shifted sideways in his chair and lifted a bottle off the shelf.

"This is my new recipe. More lime. Mmm, mmm. Make your hairdo steam," said Joe.

"Sounds good. I'll take a couple," said Ted, taking out his wallet. "Joe makes the best hot sauce on the island," he said to Nina.

"Old family recipe," said Joe. "Got it off the Internet." He laughed loud and hard. "No, I grow the peppers myself. That's the secret," he said.

"Thanks, Joe. See you soon," said Ted. They walked back to the Jeep. They drove around the bend, and Ted pulled the Jeep over to the side of the road again.

"I'm going to let you in on a local secret," he said. He grabbed a couple of towels off the backseat and led the way up a narrow, sandy path between the bushes on the side of the road. If she hadn't been with Ted, Nina would not have noticed it. The path climbed up and over a low rise and emerged on a pristine curve of powder-soft white-sand beach. A wild fringe of cocoplum bushes and graceful palms ensured complete privacy. Nina could see waves crashing against a reef at the mouth of the cove. The waves lapped the white-sand beach only gently.

"On a windy day, the water here is still as calm as a swimming pool," said Ted, dropping the towels onto the sand. "Care for a swim?" The jewel-colored water looked very inviting.

"You bet," said Nina. She had her bikini on under her clothes, so she kicked off her flip-flops, unbuttoned her shorts, and let them fall, then pulled off her T-shirt and dropped it on top of the towels, trying not to feel self-conscious about her nearly naked body. Out of the corner of her eye, she saw Ted start to unbutton his shirt. She tiptoed down to the water's edge and walked into the surf. After hours in the sun, the water felt delicious on her skin. When the water was waist deep, she dove under, then floated on her back facing the beach, her hair streaming out like seaweed. Ted was standing waist deep in the water in front of her, hair plastered to his head, water droplets in his eyelashes, smiling. His glistening torso was bronzed and well muscled. She tried not to notice.

"That hits the spot, doesn't it?" he asked.

"Magical," said Nina. They swam for a while, then lay side by side on the towels on the sand with their hands clasped behind their heads, looking at the cloudless sky and not talking. Nina flipped over onto her stomach, sighed, and closed her eyes. She must have fallen asleep. When she woke, Ted was sitting up beside her with his shirt on. Her T-shirt was draped across her back.

"I thought you might burn, and I didn't want to wake you. We better get going. It'll be dark by the time we get back to town," he said.

The sun was sinking into the sea as they drove back into Coconut Cove. She wasn't yet accustomed to how quickly the day transformed into night in the tropics, a few spectacular minutes of psychedelic color separating sunlight from darkness.

"Feel like stopping in at The Redoubt for a beer before heading home?" he asked as they entered town.

"Sounds like the perfect end to a perfect day," said Nina. It was Sunday, and the main street was virtually devoid of cars and carts. Ted eased the Jeep and boat to the side of the road in front of the bar. As they pushed open the heavy wooden door that faced the street, the mellow voice of Jimmy Buffett greeted them from the jukebox. Nina was willing to bet that every pale, overworked northerner who booked a holiday to Pineapple Cay popped a quarter in the jukebox to play it, then ordered a margarita. She'd have to ask Veronica sometime how many times a day she heard it.

The bar and restaurant were relatively quiet. Three or four tables of vacationers who didn't have to get up for school or work the next day were enjoying a meal out in paradise. The candles glowed on the tables, casting golden light on the wood-paneled walls. Through the glass doors overlooking the water, Nina saw a bonfire on the beach, the flames leaping up into the now-dark sky as someone threw on a piece of driftwood. She could make out the silhouettes of a circle of people sitting in the sand around it, one of them strumming a guitar. Inside, the backlit bar was a cozy oasis where another half dozen people were gathered.

Veronica was behind the bar drying glasses with a white towel, and Nina spotted Pansy and Danish seated on stools in front of her. She and Ted made their way over. As they approached, all three turned to look at them and said hi. Nina could see both Danish and Pansy's eyes flit from her to Ted and back, but if they were wondering what was up, they didn't say anything. Veronica didn't seem to notice anything remarkable and greeted them warmly, saying, "Good evening! You're just in time!"

"Hi, Nina and Ted," said Pansy. "You just missed Andrew and the kids, Nina. We thought we'd treat ourselves to Sunday dinner out. I'm just finishing my coffee. I wanted to show Veronica the new earrings I made, and then I've got to head out."

Pansy unfurled a roll of flannel on the bar. Hooked to the fabric were a half dozen pairs of earrings made from silver wire wrapped around pieces of sea glass of various sizes and colors. Nina and Veronica bent over to look at them.

"I collect the sea glass myself and make them at home," said Pansy, looking at Nina. "I've got a little boutique with jewelry and other things attached to the real estate office. I give workshops for tourists, and once a year I run one for the kids at the school. Maybe you can go with me sometime looking for glass, and I can show you how to make them."

"That would be fun," said Nina. "They're beautiful!"

"Very nice," said Veronica.

"I thought these might be your style, Veronica," said Pansy, holding up a long, dangling pair made from large pieces of sand-rubbed, cobalt-blue glass with tendrils of silver wire coiled around and cascading down from the glass.

"Cobalt glass is quite rare to find. It is mostly green and white," Pansy said to Nina.

"They're gorgeous, Pansy," said Veronica, holding them up to her ears and looking in a pocket mirror.

"I made them for you, Veronica. Happy birthday," said Pansy.

"Why, thank you, girl," said Veronica. She leaned across the bar to give Pansy a hug. "You're sweet."

"Happy birthday, boss!" said Danish. "Many happy returns!"

"Happy birthday, Veronica," said Ted. He leaned across the bar to kiss her on the cheek.

"It's tomorrow," said Veronica with a smile, "but thank you very much. My son is coming down from the main island, and we're going to have a little family reunion at the farm tomorrow night."

"These are for you, Nina," said Pansy, slipping a pair of earrings made with blue-green glass into Nina's palm and folding her fingers over them. "A welcome present."

Nina was touched. Three days ago, all these people were strangers to her. Now it seemed the most natural thing in the world to be with them in a cozy bar on a quiet Sunday night.

"Thank you, Pansy. You're so thoughtful," she said.

There was a slow flurry of activity while bottles of beer, more coffee for Pansy, and a margarita for Nina were distributed.

Ted's cell phone rang. He glanced at the screen, then said, "A client. Excuse me."

He stood and headed outside onto the deck. Nina watched him lean against the railing and look out at the dark water as he spoke to some obsessed fisherman a thousand miles away. Veronica moved down the bar to serve a couple of customers. Danish watched Nina intently.

"I've got to run to the loo. Be right back," said Pansy.

Danish waited until she was out of earshot, then leaned in close to Nina. "Busted. You were checking out his ass! I saw you. You like Ted! Damn, I'm right, aren't I? That's funny, because I could have sworn you had a thing for Roker, like half the other women on this island. Oh, Nina! The plot thickens! Just a warning. Old Ted has always been kind of a lone wolf. I mean, he enjoys the company of the ladies, but he generally doesn't let them on the premises long enough to make a lasting impression. That's Fortress Matthews up there." He gestured up the beach to the point.

"Listen, Danish," Nina hissed, "I don't have a thing for anybody. Didn't I mention? I'm technically still married."

"You didn't mention it. But I already knew that. Everybody does. You bought a house off the Internet in the middle of the night, left the husband in New York, and moved down here lickety-split. Carrie told me."

"Who's Carrie?!"

"She owns the beauty salon on Seagarden Street," said Danish. "She heard it from her cousin Bernadette who works at the bank. Bernadette saw the paperwork Pansy brought in, with the e-mails from ninaanddarren@whatever.com sent at two o'clock in the morning. Pansy tore a strip off her when she got wind that Bernadette was talking about your business, but really, no one cares what time you bought your house." He took a pull of his beer and watched Nina in silence for a moment, then continued in a slightly gentler tone.

"Really. A lot of people around here ended up on Pineapple Cay at the end of some wild and crazy ride. Some of them have some pretty hideous skeletons in the closet. Your broken marriage slash Internet shopping spree doesn't even make the list of finalists for the most far-out story."

"Maybe not, but the whole point was to turn the page and start fresh," Nina said as Pansy returned from the washroom.

"Oh, Nina. I apologize for the lack of discretion on the part of some people around here," Pansy said, giving Danish a hard look. "We specialize in fresh starts on Pineapple Cay. Live and let live. You know Derek and Cecilia Rathbone, that nice older couple with the pottery studio on Banyan Lane? Derek was heir to a huge crumpet fortune or something. He and Cecilia met at Woodstock in 1968. He was supposed to go back to England and run the family crumpet factory, but instead they decided possessions were chains and moved to a commune in Vermont. He gave away most of his money, and when the commune went feral, they moved down here and bought that old farm for three thousand dollars. I can tell you, it's worth considerably more than that now. Now they make clay pots and serve tea and crumpets to tourists on their front porch."

"That generation got a pretty sweet deal," said Danish. "They spent all their time smoking weed, philosophizing, and sleeping with one another's girlfriends, and they still ended up millionaires in their golden years, living on a tropical island. Do you want to know how I landed here?" he asked.

"Yes, I do," said Nina. She felt Ted slide back into the seat beside her as Veronica rejoined them, leaning forward with her elbows resting on the polished wood.

"Well, I had just graduated from the Boulder College of the Healing Arts, and I got a job as a yoga instructor for the Supersun Cruise Line, now defunct. I was on my first trip down through the islands—Antigua, Barbados, Martinique, Grenada. Yoga classes at seven in the morning and five in the afternoon, exploring the islands all day, and being charming for the old dolls at dinner. I was having a blast. We were on our way back up to Fort Lauderdale when my supervisor knocked on the door of my cabin one night. Unfortunately, I was entertaining the grown-up granddaughter of one of our passengers at the time. Fraternizing with the guests was not allowed, so I was canned immediately. I was put off the ship the next morning in Nassau. Best thing that ever happened to me. I hung around town for a few days, soaking up the sun and showing up every evening for the harbormaster's sundown cocktail party at the marina, where they serve free drinks and conch fritters. I got to talking to some people there who told me that Michel was looking to start offering yoga classes at the Plantation Inn on Pineapple Cay. I bummed a ride down here on that rusted tub of a mail boat. I could probably have swum here faster. Anyway, I took the gig for room and board, and Veronica here gave me a few shifts at The Redoubt. When Mr. Jones retired last year, I got the mail route. The rest is history."

"Wow," said Nina. Ted took a long draught of his beer.

"I'd say Veronica wins hands down any contest for the most spectacular arrival on Pineapple Cay," said Pansy. "Tell Nina the story, Veronica. It's amazing."

Veronica took a sip of her mineral water and a deep breath. "Well. My grandmother always said that her great-grandmother on her father's side was a captive onboard a slaving ship on its way to a plantation somewhere in the Caribbean when it was seized by the British off Pineapple Cay. It was still legal to own slaves in the islands until 1834, but the British outlawed the transatlantic trade in slaves from Africa in 1807. So, the ship was seized. But instead of taking the captives back home to Africa, the British unloaded them on Pineapple Cay and left them here to fend for themselves. I don't know if any of them ever made it back home. My great-great-great-grandmother spent the rest of her life here. My family has fished and farmed out of Smooth Harbour down island for as long as anyone can remember.

"On the day of the night I was born, fifty-five years ago tomorrow, my parents had taken the boat out to fish lobster off the Diamond Cays. My mother was about eight and a half months pregnant, but she was young and strong. She baited the traps for my father after he hauled them in and emptied the catch. The sky darkened ominously midafternoon, and they quickly stowed their gear and headed for home. Of course, there was no Weather Channel in those days. They hadn't been expecting a storm. It hit with its full force as they made for Smooth Harbour in the little wooden boat. My mother went into labor, and she delivered me herself in the rain on the floor of the rocking boat while my father tried desperately to steer us into shore. She cut the umbilical cord with a gutting knife and held me against her bare chest under her sweater for two hours."

Veronica took another drink of her water. The others waited in silence for her to continue.

"Two hundred years ago, wreckers used to go down to the shore at night and wave a lantern to lure a ship onto the rocks so that they could steal its cargo when the boat ran aground or broke apart. Rum, silver candlesticks, timber, whatever. The sailors would think they were seeing a lighthouse on a point and head directly for the rocks.

"On the night I was born, my parents' friends and neighbors ran up and down the beach waving their lanterns to guide my father into the harbor. When the little boat was close enough, the men waded out into the sea and threw ropes to him until he could grab hold of one. Then they pulled the boat up on the sand. So, I arrived on Pineapple Cay when I was two hours old, and the whole village turned out to meet me."

Veronica threw her head back and laughed, then leaned closer to Nina and looked her directly in the eye.

"Let us drink to new beginnings," she said. She reached under the bar and pulled out five glasses and a bottle of rum. Nina raised her glass with the others and downed the burning gold elixir in one go.

"Has anyone heard anything about Tiffany Bassett?" asked Pansy.

"Blue was in here for a few minutes midafternoon," said Veronica. "He said he'd been with Barry Bassett in the station all morning going over events, trying to come up with a lead. His officers were out at the Savages' gathering evidence. He had a few bites of a sandwich, then headed out to The Enclave to supervise a door-to-door search late this afternoon. He didn't say, but I think they're headed down into the cays tomorrow looking for her. Late this afternoon, a Defence Force boat tied up at the police wharf. They're usually stationed at the national park headquarters on Turtle Cay."

They were all silent for a long moment.

"Well, I'd better get back to the lodge, say hello to the new bunch, and get ready for tomorrow," said Ted. "Nina, are you ready to call it a night?"

"Sure, thanks," she replied. They said their good-byes and went out into the warm night. The sky was studded with stars again.

"Well, I think I can understand why you love bonefishing," she said on the short drive to her cottage. "I guess I never really thought about the islands as wilderness, but they're spectacular. Thank you for a wonderful day."

"My pleasure," he replied with a smile. "Maybe another day, we can take a boat down through the Diamond Cays National Park. No fishing, but fantastic snorkeling. There's a colony of giant rock iguanas on Stick Cay that are worth a trip. I mean, two or three feet long."

He walked her to her gate and said good night. As he had the night before, he waited while she let herself in, only getting back into the car and driving away when she waved good-bye through the window in the door.

Nina had a long, hot shower and curled up on the sofa with a cup of soup and her mystery novel. She could hear the steady, gentle roll and hiss of the waves on the beach.

By the tail end of the day, when most of Pineapple Cay was tucked up in bed, Tiffany Bassett still had not been found.

6

Nina spent the morning of her fifth day on Pineapple Cay prying off, scraping, and sanding four pairs of shutters. Then she took a refreshing swim in the ocean. Chips of paint floated off her skin as she lay in the water, soaking the sweat from her hair and feeling the sun on her face.

Shortly before noon, she dressed for yoga and headed over to the Plantation Inn for Danish's class. The ladies on the platform were buzzing with the news of Tiffany Bassett's abduction.

"I heard they were having money problems," said a reed-thin woman in black leggings. "Barry's been having trouble attracting backers for his big condo project. He asked Simon and me to buy in, but we said *no thank you*. It's too risky an investment until the runway extension is approved. Barry's capital is tied up in the land, and he's running out of time."

"I wonder if he has a big life-insurance policy on Tiffany?" quipped a woman sporting a thick gold necklace, bulging gold hoop earrings, and a gold watch against her deeply tanned flesh. "That and a big fat emerald might solve his cash-flow problem."

"Well, I heard that Barry's been making the rounds in Miami to drum up financing. He's trying to solve his cash-flow problem by making a deal with some questionable characters in Little Moscow. Maybe they aren't pleased with the results of their investment so far and decided to teach him a lesson," said another woman in a peacock-blue leotard and white-blonde ponytail.

So, Barry's feeling the financial pinch, thought Nina. *Love, hate, or money. That's the root of every violent crime, isn't it? The runway extension. What's that all about?*

Danish bounded up onto the platform, and the session began. When it ended, he was cornered by a short woman pointing to her hamstring, so Nina waved good-bye and headed across the lawn to the main building of the inn. A long veranda wrapped around the side of the building.

Stepping up onto it, Nina was enticed by the sweet scent of flowering vines and the inviting shade. Halfway down the porch, a parrot squawked in a cage. A wicker sofa sat against the wall at the end where Nina stood, and a row of wrought iron café tables ran the rest of the length of the porch. At the far end, she saw the man in the gray suit from Kiki Savage's party whom Danish had pointed out as his boss at the inn. He was chatting with the elderly couple from the airplane. They were once again dressed in their matching khaki outfits, their bird field guides open in front of them on the table. The inn's owner was now dressed in sandals, a navy-blue golf shirt, and a pair of khaki shorts that revealed a pair of tanned legs. His receding silver hair was cut close to his scalp. They were all smiling politely.

Nina decided to linger for a cup of coffee and indulge in some people-watching, a favorite pastime of sociologists and almost everyone else. She sat down on the wicker sofa to wait for a waiter to take her order. She looked up to see the man from the Savages' party coming toward her.

"Hello, Mademoiselle. May I introduce myself? I am Michel Poitras, the owner of the inn. I saw you from a distance at Kiki's soiree the other night, but we did not have the opportunity to speak. Things got rather dramatic." He actually kissed her hand.

"Very nice to meet you. Nina Spark," said Nina.

"May I offer you a cool drink?" asked Michel. Without waiting for an answer, he looked around and raised two fingers. A passing waiter hurried over and stood attentively, waiting for his orders.

"What would you like, Mademoiselle Spark? May I suggest grapefruit juice in mineral water at this time of day? Very refreshing, I think."

"That would be lovely. Thank you," said Nina.

Michel settled himself comfortably into the corner of the sofa, his arm stretched along the backrest spanning the distance between them. He crossed one leg over the other and studied her unabashedly for several seconds. The drinks arrived, served on a bamboo tray with two lavender-scented cookies on a small plate.

Nina felt compelled to speak. "Mrs. Bassett's disappearance must be quite a shock to the community. I saw her here the day before she was abducted. Do you know her at all?"

He lit a cigarette and inhaled, then blew the smoke over his shoulder, up and away from her.

"You must forgive me. I smoke. She was a poisonous bitch. I hated her." Halfway down the porch, the parrot squawked loudly in its cage.

"Yes, all right! I hear you. I hate you, too, don't worry!" he yelled at the bird. "Stupid bird. It was here when I bought the inn. If I had known that they live to be seventy years old, I would have insisted the previous owners take it with them. It galls me to think that when I am dead and in my grave, it will still be here."

Over his shoulder, Nina could see the tiny bird-watching couple looking at him in horror, their mouths gaping. Nina quietly sipped her beverage, hoping he would return to the subject of Tiffany Bassett. He did not disappoint.

"Yes, Madame Bassett. She took such pleasure in creating situations. Passing on hurtful comments made by one friend about another and delighting in the consequences. On constant guard for alleged transgressions of her presumed rights," he said. "I have spent many enjoyable hours smoking on this terrace, imagining how I would kill her. Run her down in my Jaguar as she hobbled out to her car one evening, a bit tipsy as usual; an appealing salad of chopped snakeroot and moonseed, served as she lunched with the ladies on the veranda; a splash of polonium 210 in her favorite cocktail, the vulgarly named—but immensely popular—'Sex on the Beach.' However, it appears that someone has saved me the trouble."

Perhaps he just has a dark sense of humor, thought Nina, *but it does seem as though he has given Tiffany's death a disturbing degree of prior thought.*

"So, you think she's dead?" asked Nina.

"Oh, well, one can always hope," replied Michel. "She adopted the inn as her second home. A dubious honor. One day, a manicure at the spa. The next, tennis lessons. Happy hour in the bar with and without her obnoxious husband. A dollar is a dollar, whatever the source. I am not fussy about that. But the inn's rating lost two stars every time she crossed the threshold. We have worked diligently to establish a certain atmosphere that appeals to our clientele. That is what we sell. She was extremely rude to my staff, she was loud, and she arrived for dinner dressed like a street prostitute. She once sent gazpacho back to the kitchen, complaining that her soup was cold. She flirted with other women's husbands in the lounge and argued loudly with her own. Her behavior was such that it even earned mention in a review of the inn. 'An obnoxious woman ruined our romantic dinner. Lovely historic inn, but the atmosphere left something to be desired.'"

"May I ask why you didn't just refuse her business?" asked Nina.

"A fair question," replied Michel. "Perhaps I should have. She contravened every tenet of good taste and propriety, but she broke no actual hotel rules or the law. Please, Miss Spark, will you have a biscuit? They have the most delicate lemon and lavender flavor." He passed the plate to her, and she took a cookie to oblige him.

"Thank you. It's lovely," she said after a small bite. He returned the plate to the tray without taking one himself and drew again on the cigarette wedged elegantly between two fingers. Nina remained silent, waiting for him to speak again. It was one of the skills she had learned to interview subjects for her sociological research: resisting the urge to jump into the silence, allowing the subject time to bring forth his or her information. This time, he went off on a tangent.

"Yes, the Internet reviews. A dissatisfied housewife from Milwaukee whose dream holiday with her boring husband did not live up to expectations can scare off a hundred potential reservations with a few sour sentences." He imitated anonymous chatroom critics in a whiny, nasal voice. "'The mint on my pillow was dark chocolate, and I prefer milk chocolate. No one bothered to ask me—three out of five stars.' 'The sheets on the bed where we consummated our marriage were only six hundred thread count, and I really expected one thousand thread count.' 'The food was exquisite, but I did not care for the color of the drapes—four out of five stars.'"

Nina attempted to guide him back to the subject of the Bassetts. She wondered if getting Tiffany out of his hair was enough motive for Michel Poitras to make her disappear. Or perhaps there was a deeper reason for his antipathy. He was quite willing to talk openly about his disdain for her with someone he'd just met.

"I saw you speaking with Barry Bassett at Kiki Savage's party. He didn't look very happy," said Nina.

"Mr. Bassett applied to the local district administration to lengthen the runway at Pineapple Cay airport to accommodate jumbo jets. He hopes to bring in large package tours to stay at his imaginary hotel. I opposed his application. It runs completely contrary to our business model at the inn. We have just thirty rooms and aim at the higher end of the market: fewer guests willing to pay higher prices for the experience we offer. People come here for the intimate setting and the charming small town. Not so charming with a thousand other holiday-makers cluttering up the picturesque bougainvillea-draped lanes and drag-racing Sea-Doos in the cove."

He put his cigarette to his lips again and inhaled the smoke, exhaling it slowly through his nostrils.

"He called me a snob. Yes, so what?" Michel said. "A socialist, too, if I'm not mistaken. Although I would have thought it difficult to be both an elitist and an advocate for the redistribution of wealth from the rich to the poor, but never mind. He accused me of pissing all over the free-market values that made America great. I think he has forgotten that Pineapple Cay is not part of the United States of America, and like many of us here, he is a guest in this country at the pleasure of the government." He smiled at Nina.

"Ah, yes," he said. "The hotel business is very entertaining. A new adventure every day. I had this romantic notion of being an innkeeper on a tropical isle when I retired from publishing in France. Freshly squeezed orange juice followed by tennis in the mornings and glamorous ladies to chat with at dinner. Very Noel Coward. Sometimes it is like that. Other times the glamour must be found in locating someone to fix the sluggish plumbing or finessing women like Tiffany Bassett." His eyes were on the horizon while he spoke. He languidly turned his head to meet Nina's eyes, then glanced away again, eyes roaming the terrace as he continued.

"Yes, there is a whole genre of literature devoted to such tales. The hapless expatriates who move to a charming village full of delightful characters to run a hotel. Have you read Herman Wouk's *Don't Stop the Carnival*? *Hotel Pastis*? *Chateau Bon Vivant*? I have a whole shelf of such books in my library. My friends find it humorous to ferret them out and send them to me as birthday gifts. There is also the subgenre of memoirs by hapless expatriates who move to a charming village full of delightful characters to renovate an old house."

He paused and glanced at her. "Yes, I eschewed retirement to a villa in the south of France for the life of an innkeeper on Pineapple Cay. And what about you, Dr. Spark?" he asked, turning his full attention to her. "What brings you to our island?"

What *had* she been thinking, she wondered. She also observed that he had accorded her the title of doctor for the first time, although she hadn't referred to herself in that way. How did he know that much about her?

"A similar daydream," she replied. "A little cottage on the beach far from the trials and tribulations of daily life. It is certainly lovely here, but I can't say it has been all that peaceful thus far."

"Well, I do hope it will live up to your expectations," he said with a little smile as he rose. She stood as well.

"It has been delightful to meet you, Mademoiselle Spark. Have a pleasant day, and please come again." She was Mademoiselle again. He bowed his head slightly and strolled off down the length of the terrace, nodding and smiling at guests sitting at the wrought iron café tables with their elegant lunch plates and glasses of iced tea. As he passed the parrot's cage, it squawked again loudly and said in a clear voice with a British accent, "Rubbish! Just rubbish!"

"Shut up, you stupid bird!" said Michel. "Didn't I tell you? I found a new recipe for roast parrot in a mango reduction. Mind yourself!"

The bird-watching couple turned their heads in unison to follow his progress down the steps and across the lawn to the tennis courts, their mouths still gaping in shock.

Surely, an obnoxious guest and a business disagreement with her husband would not provoke a person to murder, thought Nina. *What a ridiculous idea. Of course, murder is not exactly a rational act. It is the result of an all-consuming emotion—hatred, jealousy, greed.* She'd noticed that he had continually referred to Tiffany Bassett in the past tense.

And then what about the yoga ladies' theories that either some Russian mobsters were teaching Barry a lesson, or Barry killed Tiffany because he needed money to keep his condo project alive? But if Barry's money problems are due to Michel holding up the airport-runway extension, shouldn't it be Michel who's dead, not Tiffany?

With a sigh, Nina gathered her things and walked through the arched doorway from the porch into the lobby. On a sofa in a corner, Lance the tennis pro was sitting in his tennis whites knee to knee with a pretty young woman in a sundress. They were laughing and talking. Lance didn't look particularly concerned or upset, considering the woman he was having some kind of an affair with had been violently abducted.

On an impulse, Nina went over to the reception desk. "Is it possible to take a lesson with the tennis pro?" she asked the young woman working there.

"Yes, of course, Madame." The young woman looked at her computer screen and typed furiously for a few seconds. "Lance is available tomorrow morning at nine o'clock, if that is suitable," she said.

"Thank you. That would be fine," said Nina.

She walked slowly home down the long tree-lined drive and through town. There, she made a sandwich and took it out on the veranda. After lunch, she took a long, lazy swim in the sea, constantly scanning the depths for the dark shape of a shark. Fatigued from the scraping, sanding, and yoga, she decided to give home renovation a pass for the afternoon and see what she could learn about the *Morning Glory* at the Pineapple Cay Museum.

The Pineapple Cay Museum was located on Seagarden Street, one block from the waterfront main drag, Water Street. The building and grounds of the museum occupied a large lot. The museum itself was relatively small in terms of museums—more the size of a large house—but it was the grandest building in town. The two-story, whitewashed stucco building had a covered portico in front, which was supported by a row of columns. It was situated in the middle of a lawn shaded by ancient banyan and sweet-smelling frangipani trees. Three or four pieces of stone and metal sculpture stood on concrete plinths scattered around the grounds. A low stone wall ran around the entire property. Nina noticed that the diminutive public library was right next door to the museum, housed in a cheerily painted converted clapboard cottage with window boxes overflowing with vibrant blooms.

Nina went through the front gate and up the path to the door of the museum, which stood open. The wooden floor creaked as she stepped through the vestibule, where a few forlorn umbrellas leaned in a stand made from a giant antique-brass shell casing. Directly ahead of her, in the lobby, she could see Alice seated behind a desk and Danish in a chair that had been pulled up to it. He was leaning toward her with his elbows on the desk. Alice was sitting back in her chair with her hands folded in front of her, listening to Danish with an inscrutable expression on her face. There was a cardboard tray with two cups of coffee in it on the desk in front of them, a half-eaten Danish pastry and an untouched cinnamon roll resting on two paper napkins beside it.

"Oh, boy," said Nina to herself as she pulled open the glass air-sealed doors and entered the cool, climate-controlled interior of the museum. Inside the lobby, large paintings hung on all sides. To the left and right, wide archways led into what Nina assumed were the galleries. A set of stairs climbed out of sight behind the desk.

Alice looked up and smiled at Nina. Danish followed Alice's eyes to where Nina stood. He looked slightly put out to see her but also a bit desperate, like a quietly drowning man. Although Nina did not know him very well or for very long, she had already seen a number of instances of his indifference to the numerous small attentions and batted eyelashes of young ladies around town. It was interesting to see him under the sway of this serious-looking wisp of a girl.

Alice stood up and walked toward Nina, smiling. "Hello, Dr. Spark. Kiki said you might come in for some information on the *Morning Glory*. Would you like to see some of the artifacts? I can tell you what we've learned."

"That would be wonderful. Call me Nina. How are you doing after Saturday night?" she asked.

"I'm OK," said Alice. "I just keep going over it in my mind, wondering why I didn't see anything or hear anything other than the tap running. I followed Tiffany into the house right away." She sighed. "Anyway, I know my uncle is working as hard as he can to find her. We're in the process of preparing the exhibit upstairs, if you want to follow me." She headed toward the staircase, and Nina followed.

Danish hung back, unsure what to do.

Alice looked back at him over her shoulder. "You can come see them, too, if you like," she said.

His face lit up like he'd won the lottery rather than the chance to look at some barnacle-encrusted artifacts.

At the top of the stairs was a long hallway. There were a couple of offices and a meeting room on the side facing the street. Large windows filled these areas with sunlight, filtered by the mature trees on the lawn. On the other side of the corridor was a glass air-sealed door. Alice took a key from her pocket and unlocked it, then stood aside to allow them to enter. They walked into a large open space with two long worktables running down its center, and canvases and boxes stacked against the walls and in corners. High transom windows let in the daylight. At one end of the room stood a large putty-green metal floor safe.

Alice walked over to the worktable and switched on a task light. "These are some of the pieces recovered from the *Morning Glory*," she said.

A handful of gold coins, a tortoiseshell comb, a rusted knife, and some tin plates were laid out on a tray. A box of white cotton gloves sat next to it. Alice put on a pair and lifted the coins for them to see.

"The *Morning Glory* was owned by Robert Sifton of Charleston, South Carolina. His wife was Mary. They had been married eight years but had no children. They were loyalists from South Carolina, loyal to the British Crown. After the American Revolution, several thousand British loyalists came to the islands to start a new life, many as plantation owners. As you can see, some of the artifacts look more like lumps of rust than anything else," said Alice.

"I was going to say—" said Danish.

"One of our challenges with the exhibit is to bring them to life for the visiting kids and everyone else," continued Alice. "These are some things we've collected to go with the emerald."

She carefully picked up a photograph. "This is a photograph of a portrait of Mary Sifton that hangs in the National Portrait Gallery in London." She took a magnifying glass off the table and held it over the photograph for them to see.

"See—she's wearing the emerald in the painting. She grew up in England and was the daughter of a wealthy wool merchant. He paid to have this portrait of her painted by Sir Joshua Reynolds the month before she set sail for America with her new husband, Robert Sifton. She met Robert in 1772 when he came to London on business with his father. They were married at Mary's family estate six months later, and they departed for America shortly thereafter. I think her parents must have loved her very much and wanted something to remember her by. That's what I imagine, anyway. As it happens, they never saw each other again. The Revolution broke out, and then the *Morning Glory* sank in the cut between Wreath and Lizard Cays in a storm. It stayed there until Mr. Bassett's crew brought it up."

Nina studied the photograph. Mary Sifton looked very young. There was a little smile playing on her lips and a twinkle in her dark eyes. Her dark hair was piled high on her head. Not for the first time, Nina observed how shockingly low the necklines for proper young ladies were in those days. The emerald rested on the snowy-white skin of her bosom. She stood with an ostrich feather in her hand, a blue sky full of fluffy white clouds in the background. It seemed amazing to Nina that the very necklace that had graced the neck of a young English girl in 1772—and was rendered in the brushstrokes of Sir Joshua Reynolds, one of Britain's most celebrated painters—had hung around the neck of Tiffany Bassett at a party Nina had attended at a rock star's ocean hideaway just the other day.

Alice continued. "Of course, the National Portrait Gallery couldn't send the Reynolds painting here. It's far too valuable, and our museum doesn't get enough visitors to make it worth the risk. However, they've offered to send a full-size reproduction of the painting," she said with excitement.

Danish stood with his brow furrowed, nodding as she spoke. Nina assumed it was his *This is fascinating* pose, put on to impress Alice.

"We also have these letters, on loan from the archives at the University of South Carolina," said Alice. She very carefully lifted one sheet, cradling it in her gloved hands. "They are letters between Mary and Robert, and between Robert and various friends and associates, written in the year leading up to their departure from Charleston on the *Morning Glory*."

Nina leaned over Alice's shoulder and read:

*My dearest Robert, please hurry home as soon as you are able.
The atmosphere here is quite changed . . .*

"The emerald is by far the most valuable artifact recovered from the *Morning Glory*," said Alice. "It was appraised at three and a half million dollars, although, given its provenance, its portrayal in the Reynolds painting, and its romantic history, it's very possible it would sell for more at public auction. But I don't really know what the thief could hope to get for it on the black market . . ." She shook her head.

"The records show that the Siftons were traveling with five other families. They were all slave owners. The passenger list also names eight female and ten male domestics and laborers. Unfortunately, we know very little about them, other than their names. However, we can still use the artifacts and the exhibit to explore the history of slavery in these islands, which is the family history of my ancestors and of many of the children on Pineapple Cay. Most, if not all, of the Europeans who settled here brought slaves, or bought them at local slave markets, to work their plantations.

"No one survived the wreck of the *Morning Glory*, but the life stories of at least a hundred people can be told through the emerald necklace. Then there are the slave rebellions, the pirates, the wrecking, and the rum running. The history of local industries, music, and culture. I can't wait to work on all of the exhibits."

Alice's enthusiasm for her work was infectious.

"I can't wait to see it all," said Nina.

"Me, too," chimed in Danish.

Alice peeled off the white cotton gloves and laid them on the table, and they walked toward the door. "I've been trying to come up with ways to stir up some excitement and get more people to visit the museum. This new exhibit is a big opportunity," she said as they went down the stairs.

"Well, the theft of the emerald is definitely front-page news, but it may not be what you had in mind," said Nina.

Alice grimaced and sighed, pausing at the bottom of the stairs. Danish gave Nina a hard look.

"I'm not sure what we'll do if the emerald isn't returned," said Alice quietly. "The entire exhibit is built around the necklace. All this work might be for nothing."

Hearing the history of the emerald and its worth piqued Nina's curiosity. "Do you have any idea who could have taken it? Was there any concern about the emerald being stolen before? Maybe someone read the articles about it and thought it was an easy opportunity."

Alice frowned. "It's always a concern with a valuable museum piece, but it seems strange to have been taken from the Savages' home. There weren't many people who knew about the party, and there was so much security. Really, it would have been easier to steal it from the museum."

They stood in silence for a moment, and then Alice shook her head and perked up again. She smiled at Nina. "I'm sure the emerald and Tiffany will be found. Uncle John is working hard to find the kidnappers, and how far could they get? And Kiki and I came up with a great idea. It's going to be so much fun! A community treasure hunt to celebrate the finding of the long-lost treasure of the *Morning Glory*! I hope you'll come."

She handed Nina and Danish each a leaflet from a stack on the desk. It said *Community Treasure Hunt* in bold letters with a drawing of an open treasure chest and a few paragraphs of information.

"It's a two-day event, next Saturday and Sunday. There's an article about it in today's paper. Teams will meet in front of the museum Saturday afternoon at one o'clock. There's a children's event in the morning and then a bouncy pirate ship and face painting and all that stuff in the afternoon while the adults and older children do their hunt."

"That sounds great!" said Danish. "I'm in! Why don't the three of us enter as a team?"

Alice looked at him. "Kiki and I wrote the clues, and I know where they're hidden. I'm not allowed to participate," she said, "but I'd be so happy if both of you did. With everything that's happened, I'm so worried no one will show up and it will be a big flop. Kiki and I talked about canceling it when Mrs. Bassett was abducted, but the pirate ship has already been rented and a band has been booked for Saturday night, and we can't get our money back."

"Sure, we'll be there," said Nina. "Maybe we can get Pansy and her husband to be on our team. I'm sure they'll take their kids to the morning hunt, but maybe Pansy can get someone to look after them for the afternoon. It will be fun! What a great idea, Alice."

Alice beamed. "Great! My Uncle John said he'd try to send a team from the police."

Danish's mouth hardened into a straight line.

"Well, if you need any more information about the *Morning Glory*, please just ask, Nina," said Alice. "I thought I'd lock up a bit early today and go hang these flyers around town so we can get a good turnout this weekend."

"I'll help you!" exclaimed Danish, lunging forward to grab the stack of flyers off the desk and then again to grab the stapler.

Alice looked at him sideways for a moment and then said, "OK."

They all walked out together, Alice locking the door behind them. As the door closed, Nina caught sight of the pastries, adrift on two napkins on the desk. Alice and Danish headed for the main street, and Nina decided to make herself scarce by stopping in at the public library before heading home.

The sign on the door read OPEN WEEKDAYS 2:00–4:00 P.M. OR BY CHANCE. She was in luck. The knob on the door turned, and she pushed it open. A small, bent-over woman with a cap of iron-gray hair looked up from the book she was reading as Nina came in and sang out a cheerful hello. The library was one large room, with a small public washroom off the vestibule. Bookshelves lined all four walls, and a polished wooden table with eight chairs around it took up the far end under a mullioned window. Resting on a wooden lectern in one corner was an enormous dictionary, five inches thick. It was an old *Oxford English Dictionary*, the leather cover scuffed and cracked.

Nina browsed the shelves and picked out a couple of novels and a book on the history of Pineapple Cay, then took them to the checkout counter where the librarian sat.

"Found something, dear?" asked the woman with a smile.

"Yes, thanks," said Nina. "May I get a library card, please?"

"Of course!" said the librarian. "Always glad to have a new member." She slowly opened a drawer in the wooden desk and took out a notebook and a blank cardboard membership card. She asked Nina how to spell her name and then wrote in her address without asking for it. Nina smiled—apparently another friend of Miss Rose who'd been kept up to date on Nina's move via the beauty salon. When they were done, she handed Nina a photocopied flyer for the book club.

"Since you're new in town, dear, maybe you'd be interested in joining our book club. We meet here on the first Saturday of every month at ten o'clock. We're choosing the next three selections this week. I should warn you, the discussions can get a little heated, but we've instituted a new rule. You can only speak when you're holding the talking stick."

"Thank you, I'll think about it," said Nina. She looked over the previous year's reading list as she strolled down the gravel walk to the gate. There was *The 7 Habits of Highly Effective People*, *The Girl with the Dragon Tattoo*, *The Lighthouse* by P. D. James, and Agatha Christie's *And Then There Were None*.

Hmm, she thought. *A self-help book and three mysteries set on remote, idyllic islands where horrible murders are committed. What's that all about? Thrills and chills from the safety of the hammock, or some more deep-seated taste for the dark side?*

She looked around. A woman walking her dog down the sidewalk on the opposite side of the street smiled and nodded to her. Nina waved back. With the exception of the Bassetts, people seemed very friendly here, but maybe sunny Pineapple Cay was not quite as sleepy as it seemed.

7

On Tuesday morning, Nina dawdled on the porch with her coffee, leafing through a pile of paint chips she had picked up at the hardware store and sketching plans for her flower beds. Then she sat down and wrote a long e-mail to Louise, providing a description of the tiny yellow house and her white-sand backyard, as well as a slightly giddy recounting of her day with Ted. She paused before adding a brief account of Tiffany's disappearance. She also sent an e-mail to her parents and brothers with much of the same information, but she left out the bits about Ted and about Tiffany's abduction.

She didn't really feel like playing tennis this morning, but when it was time to get ready, she forced herself to get up and change into something appropriate. Although she wasn't particularly interested in the game, she was curious to learn more about Lance and Tiffany's relationship. Could he possibly have abducted her and stolen the necklace? He'd seemed awfully unconcerned about her whereabouts yesterday. After talking to Alice, Nina was increasingly curious about the other guests at the party. Perhaps one of them had something to do with it. As Alice had said, few people knew about the event. Had anyone been missing from the party when Tiffany disappeared?

And regardless of the emerald or Tiffany, Nina was determined to stick to her resolution for her new life: to say yes rather than no when opportunities came along. It was so much easier to stay comfortably put at home, but she was determined not to miss anything else.

When she got to the tennis courts, Lance was already there, finishing up a session with a couple of boys who looked to be about ten years old. Patience clearly was not Lance's strong suit. He was trying to teach them how to serve the ball, showing them again and again how he threw it in the air, reached his arm up, and brought the whole weight of his body down on top of it. Again and again, the boys threw the balls in the air and heaved the rackets, which were almost as big as they were, above their heads to whack the ball across the net. Again and again, the balls went into the net, or sailed high over the fence. Occasionally, one of the boys missed the ball entirely, and it fell to the ground behind or in front of them, and then they both laughed their heads off. Lance was getting increasingly irritated, and it showed in his face and in his curt tone.

Finally, he looked at his watch for the fifth time in five minutes and said, "OK. That's enough. Your mom said to meet her by the pool."

The boys let the rackets fall to the ground with a clatter and took off running in the direction of the pool. Lance wearily reached down to pick up the rackets and placed them on a chair by the side of the court, then took a long drink from his water bottle. Nina walked toward him across the court. The little scene with the boys reminded her why she didn't play tennis. It required a lot of skill and effort, and you had to pay attention because the action was unpredictable. She preferred athletic pursuits that were repetitive and relied on physical strength or endurance, like running and swimming, where she could tune out and think about other things.

Lance saw her coming and wiped his face and hands with a white towel, which he then threw over the back of the chair. He turned toward her with his hand outstretched.

"Nina? Hi, I'm Lance. I'll be your instructor today. Do you play tennis?" he asked, glancing at her running shoes and shorts.

"No," said Nina. "Probably only two or three times in my life."

Lance sighed barely audibly. "No problem. We'll work on the basics," he said.

His manner was professional, if unenthusiastic. If his brain was in turmoil over his missing ladyfriend or from committing a violent crime, he certainly didn't show it.

"Let's start with the serve," he said, and repeated the demonstration he'd given the boys. Nina halfheartedly hit a few balls into the net, then decided to liven things up a bit.

"So, how did you come to be working here at the inn, Lance?" she asked.

"My father's a friend of Barry Bassett's, and he got me the job here. Dad does some legal work for him. I just finished college, and my father was hassling me to do something. Of course, that was before he and Michel started their big feud."

"So, you knew the Bassetts from home," said Nina as she whacked another ball, this time over the net—but out of bounds.

"I met Barry a few times when he came over to see Dad. We live in Connecticut, and Barry was based in Miami and then here. I never met Mrs. Bassett until I came down here." His voice did not give anything away. Nina had an unwelcome flashback to the scene by the equipment shed the other day.

"What's she like?" asked Nina.

Lance looked at her. "She's OK, I guess. I give her tennis lessons. He treats her like garbage," he said, hitting the ball hard over the net.

"You know them both. Do you think he could have had anything to do with her disappearance the other night?" asked Nina. She was being far nosier than she would usually have been. She was reminded of a study she'd read about people's behavior on vacation, how they do things completely out of character, letting their inhibitions run free. She wasn't exactly on vacation, but it would be hard for an observer to tell the difference at this stage.

Lance looked at her sharply this time. He didn't speak for a second. "Maybe. They pretty much hated each other, as far as I could tell." He was silent for a moment, then spoke again, louder and at a higher pitch, as though he was deliberately trying to change the subject.

"Jules Savage sure isn't like I thought he'd be," he said. "There are more books in that house than in the public library. And all of his watercolor paintings of flowers and his kids and Kiki all over the place. But no groupies lounging on water beds. Kind of disappointing."

He pointed at Nina and said, "Do it again, and this time, don't bend your wrist."

Nina endured another twenty minutes of hitting the ball slowly back and forth across the net with Lance, and then a terrifying interlude with a machine firing tennis balls at her like a machine gun while Lance stood on the sidelines shouting ineffectual instructions as she tried to avoid getting hit.

"Enough!" she said. "I've had enough for today, thank you very much."

"OK, it's your dime," he said, and then seemed to switch gears. He sidled up to her and dabbed at her neck with a white towel. She hoped it wasn't the same white towel he'd used to mop up his own sweat before the lesson.

"I've been pretty cruel to you today," he murmured.

She suppressed the urge to gag.

"How about I make it up to you by buying you a drink at the bar later? About seven o'clock?" he said. It was as though he felt it was his duty to put on the moves, like he was on sleaze autopilot. She took a couple of steps away.

"Thanks for the lovely offer, but I'm busy tonight. I actually only met Tiffany once or twice, but I was at the Savages' party when she was abducted, and I find it really upsetting that she's still missing. I'm meeting up with a couple of friends who were there that night, and we're going to see if we can remember anything that might help the police find her," said Nina. She watched his reaction carefully.

Lance regarded her steadily for a long moment and then shrugged. "Yeah, well, that sounds like a blast, but from what I've heard, the police think the kidnappers have taken her to Havana. They think it's Russian-mob stuff Barry was mixed up in, in Miami. That's what my dad told me on the phone last night. Have fun, though. See you around. If you want another lesson, you know where to find me."

He grinned with his mouth but not his eyes, grabbed his tennis bag, and headed toward the main building.

Well, that was very interesting, thought Nina as she walked down the long tree-lined drive to the main road. *So maybe there is something to the Barry-and-the-Russian-mob theory, or maybe Lance had heard that rumor, too. Maybe he'd started it.* She walked slowly on. It was Tuesday, the day Kiki Savage had invited her to stop by and talk about her article. She hadn't given it a lot of thought, in light of the activities of the past few days, but now she wondered how she was going to get there. Just then, she heard the whir of a golf-cart engine and saw Danish, wearing his uniform, driving toward her in his red post-office cart. She waved to flag him down.

"Hello, Nina. How are you on this fine day?"

"Great, thanks. Danish, could I ask you for a favor? I have to go to the Savages' today, ideally pretty soon. Do you think you could give me a ride?"

"No problem. I have a package to deliver in The Enclave anyway. I was just going home for a short health break, then back at it. If you don't mind, I can snooze at your place while you get ready. I'm assuming you want to change clothes. What are you doing out here, anyway?"

"Thanks a lot," she said, hopping into the cart. "I took a tennis lesson from Lance on a whim."

He made a U-turn, and they headed back through town to Nina's place.

"Don't tell me you find that smarmy guy appealing, too," Danish said, glancing at her.

"I was just curious about his reaction—or lack of reaction—to Tiffany's disappearance. He just doesn't seem fazed by it at all," said Nina. She told Danish about Lance's Russian-mob theory. He snorted.

"I suppose it's possible, but why would Blue Roker tell Lance Redmond's father about it? Maybe Lance was trying to throw you off the scent. He must think you're a serious threat, capable of exposing his treachery."

"I guess that's the most logical explanation for his actions," said Nina sarcastically. "Still, it is a valuable piece of jewelry. Who's to say the Russian mob wouldn't want it?"

She showered and dressed while Danish collapsed on the sofa and immediately fell asleep. She could hear him snoring from the bedroom, where she brushed and braided her hair. Then she went into the living room and tapped him on the top of the head.

"Let's go, Danish. I'd like to be there and gone well before lunch-time. I don't want any awkwardness about whether or not we expect lunch," she said.

"Boy, you worry about a lot of stuff that doesn't seem like a prob-lem. If Kiki wants you to stay for lunch, she'll ask you. Otherwise, she'll say, 'Well, thanks for coming,' and show us out. No great mystery," he said, walking toward the door.

They arrived at the Savages' door at eleven o'clock. Kiki opened the door and greeted them in a friendly manner. Nina felt obliged to explain Danish's presence but didn't want to make him feel unwelcome. It was a minefield.

"Danish kindly gave me a lift to your place. I don't have a vehicle yet," she said by way of explanation.

"Come on into the kitchen, both of you. You're in for a taste sensa-tion. I'm going to make you my signature mango lassi," said Kiki.

They followed her into a bright, airy kitchen, which was at the opposite end of the house from the guest room where the evidence suggested Tiffany might have been violently abducted on Saturday night. There was a big gas range and a serious-looking collection of copper-bottomed pots and pans hanging from a rack above a large island in the middle of the room. Kiki opened the stainless-steel fridge and took out the ingredients, pouring some of everything into the blender sitting on the island. When the loud noise of the blender subsided, she poured three glasses of a creamy orange beverage, handed one to each of them, and beckoned them to follow her out onto the terrace.

The view was just as spectacular by daylight. The water glittered all around. Kiki led them to a seating arrangement near the pool, where the view was widest, and they sank into the comfortable cushioned furniture. A potted palm behind them provided just the right amount of shade.

"What do you think?" she asked, smiling as they sipped their drinks.

"It's delicious," said Nina. Danish nodded.

"Hibiscus honey, coconut water, mango, and my homemade yogurt. I keep two goats to keep the grass down," said Kiki. She set her glass down on the table beside her and breathed in and out sharply.

"Well. That was quite a night we had on Saturday," she said.

"Yes," said Nina. "You must have had a late night with the police looking around."

"I stayed up until they let poor Alice go home, and then I went to bed, but I do believe they were here all night and most of the next day. Blue Roker was still here when I got up in the morning. They gathered a lot of pieces of evidence in plastic bags. Cloth from her dress, blood, and fingerprints. They took a lot of pictures down in the garden and along the beach. We have stone staircases and paths running all over the place, and the tide probably washed away any footprints in the sand, so I'm not sure they found anything on the grounds. Maybe they did. I don't know if they could make any sense of it. I certainly can't. Who would kidnap Tiffany Bassett, of all people, and why here? It makes a person feel vulnerable, though. We thought we were pretty well fortified here, with Charlie at the gate and the water all around. Jules is talking about getting a dog. I've never thought of myself as a dog person. I always pitied those people following along after their dogs with blue plastic poop bags in their hands. What a way to live."

"What are you talking about, darling?" Jules Savage wandered out of the house and sat down in a chair next to his wife.

"Tiffany Bassett, Jules."

"Good God. That stupid cow. No manners. No manners at all. Appalling. Why exactly was she here, Kiki, darling? Last time they were 'round was for that bonfire party on the beach"—he turned to look at Danish—"of which I have a vague recollection of your bare arse in my swimming pool. Why is that?" he asked.

"Well," Jules continued without waiting for an answer, "on that occasion, I found her in my study fondling my first editions. Wearing nothing but her bikini bottoms and smelling like a coconut cream pie. Suntan lotion, you know. All over her fingers. Extremely damaging to antique paper. She may have made it to my knicker drawer this time. She has the look of a knicker pincher, if I ever saw one, and I've met a few." He leaned back in the wicker club chair and took a sip of his mineral water, warming to his subject.

"I mean, not to put too fine a point on it, but is that not why we moved camp to this rock?" he asked his wife. She obviously thought it was a rhetorical question and kept silent, sipping her drink.

He continued. "To get away from tossers like that lot. I mean, I got fed up with stepping out to the chemist's to pick up my hemorrhoid medication or whatever and being accosted by the bloody paparazzi, you know? I mean, please do not misunderstand me. I have all the time in the world for the people who bothered to buy my records and turn up at a concert thirty years ago. And for my friends and neighbors. But there is such a thing as common decency and respect for other people, and privacy. In fact, I'm not having it. I'm going to call Charlie at the gate with strict instructions to bar them indefinitely." He fumbled for the walkie-talkie on the table beside him.

"No point, Jules, darling," said Kiki. "She's gone missing. Saturday night at our supper party."

"Oh, right," he said. "Hasn't turned up yet, then? Well, I hope the sharks haven't got her or anything grisly like that, but if she's just buggered off with that necklace, back to Beverly Hills or wherever she was assembled, good riddance. I'm sure she'll turn up." He stood. "I'm in the bog, and then I'm going to look at the hives, if you need me. I think we're getting close to harvest time. Cheerio, Nina. Behave, young man. Ha ha." He strolled into the house.

"Yes, I heard the police have made a breakthrough in the case," said Kiki. "They've narrowed it down to her family, her friends, and everyone who has ever met her." She laughed, and then she covered her mouth with her hand.

"Oh, dear. I'm sorry. That is too bad. Obviously, it's terrible what happened. Unfortunately, she is a difficult person to like. It's sort of sad, really. She tries so hard to succeed, doing the things she thinks successful people do, like buying things and hanging around rich people, but she has never learned basic social graces like courtesy, let alone found any purpose in her life." She paused for another sip of her lassi. Nina took a mouthful of hers.

Kiki continued. "When they first moved here, Tiffany dropped by a few times, looking for a bit of a chin-wag. One of her favorite topics of conversation was her prenuptial agreement, how unfair it was and how it meant Barry didn't love her." She paused again, seeming to weigh whether or not she wanted to say more before she forged on.

"It has crossed my mind, since she disappeared, whether it might be possible she's just done a runner with the necklace. She and Barry weren't happy together, that was obvious. And she told me that if they divorced, under the terms of their prenuptial agreement, she would get nothing. She was a cocktail waitress earning minimum wage when they met, working at an all-night lounge on the low-rent end of the Las Vegas Strip. He'd already amassed his fortune, so it was only fair that he kept what he had before they met if they split up. At least that's how he explained it to her in the first bloom of love, apparently. She complained that the only asset Barry had put in her name were shares in his imaginary condo complex on Pineapple Cay, and she couldn't wait until he tired of it and they could move back to Miami."

"It's a plausible explanation," said Nina. "She probably could have gotten her hands on what most people would consider a healthy nest egg by just making a withdrawal from their joint account and drawing against her credit card before he could shut off the tap. But to not have to get a job at some point in the near future, she would need more money. Selling the necklace would solve that problem."

"She's as lazy as they come," said Kiki. "But he must be a misery to live with. It must have been a hard awakening for her after the novelty of having money wore off. He's one cruel and vicious bastard. Not physically—there's never been any hint of that. He just ignores her, like she doesn't count."

"Maybe he did her in," said Danish.

"I'm sure he's at the top of Blue Roker's list of suspects. He made a big show of it here Saturday night, shouting at Blue about how incompetent the police were and blaming Jules for not providing adequate security for our guests. I guess we can just hope it all ends well—and soon," said Kiki. "In the meantime, how can I help you with your piece on the *Morning Glory*?"

"Well," said Nina, "since the party you hosted was meant to be the hook for the story, it would be interesting to include a few lines about how you got involved with the Pineapple Cay Museum."

"Ah, now that is going back a way. We arrived here fifteen years ago. The kids were both in school and busy with their own activities. Jules was heavy into producing records for other people, and there was a steady stream of musicians through the house. There's a studio down below near the beach on what is now Delmont Samuels's property. It was wonderful, invigorating. But I needed something of my own, too. I was pretty typical of women with half-grown children, I guess. It's a little-known fact that, way back when, I took a first in history at Oxford, so the museum was a natural place to gravitate to," she said with a self-deprecating smile.

"I'm sorry. That's probably far more information than what you were looking for. I met Jules the summer after I graduated, and all that happened. I guess you could say I am finally working in my field. It's very satisfying. These islands have a fascinating history."

Kiki described her role with the museum—a combination of head fund-raiser, associate curator, and office assistant—and provided Nina with much of the same information Alice had given her about the *Morning Glory*.

"The recovery of the artifacts from the wreck sounds like it's been a real boon to the museum," said Nina.

"Yes, it's been fantastic. So exciting," said Kiki. "Not that there haven't been a few bumps on the way. A salvager operating out of Florida has been running around to the news media claiming that everything recovered from the *Morning Glory*—including the emerald—is legally his because he filed a permit to search the waters off Wreath Cay twenty-five years ago, and that Barry was poaching his claim when he brought up the *Morning Glory*."

"If the other salvager is awarded the artifacts, that would be bad news for the Pineapple Cay Museum," said Nina.

"Yes, it would," Kiki said with a nod. "But, record keeping here left something to be desired twenty-five years ago, so things are rather at a standstill on that front. Barry maintains that he was unaware of any prior claim, and the ministry can't find the paperwork." She took a sip of her drink, then continued.

"On another front, the director of the National Museum on the main island has been making noises about how the proper home for the artifacts from the wreck is there in the capital, not here. He's lobbying members of Parliament to have the collection moved."

"Oh," said Nina.

Yes," said Kiki. "The National Museum would also be a good home for the exhibit, but it is very important that the children of the less-developed islands get a chance to learn something about the history of their home. To be proud that they come from an interesting place, and to know that it's not the middle of nowhere. I feel very strongly about that. That's not what he's thinking about. He's attracted by the enhanced profile staging the exhibit would give his museum. He's one of those puffed-up bureaucrats who only think about feathering their own nests and making themselves look good. I call him The Bowerbird. He rather looks like one. All bulging eyes and nervous movements." She snickered wickedly.

"This national guy sounds like a jerk," said Danish. "I didn't know that people who worked in museums were so cutthroat. I always assumed they liked things nice and boring."

Kiki glanced at him and gave him a vague smile, then focused on Nina again.

"Unfortunately, the theft of the emerald will bolster the director's argument. Fortunately, he's due to step down in six months, so we are playing beat the clock. I'm doing my part. I can lobby politicians with the best of them."

Nina had no doubt she could. She imagined Kiki's people skills were pretty finely honed from the life she'd led thus far, and that her name would open doors. And she was obviously very smart.

"But no need to dwell on that," said Kiki. "We have every expecta-tion of success. In the meantime, we are proceeding full steam ahead with the exhibit and the educational programs. It is fantastic!" She sat back in her seat with a serene smile.

"Well, thanks so much, that's very interesting, really," said Nina as she closed her notebook and stuffed it in her bag.

"My pleasure," said Kiki. "So, how are you settling in thus far, Nina?" she asked. "I hope you're not regretting your decision to move to Pineapple Cay in light of recent events. It really is a wonderful place to live. Are you doing anything interesting besides witnessing kidnappings?"

Nina laughed. "Oh, no, no regrets. I'm fixing up the house, I tried bonefishing, and I actually took a tennis lesson this morning at the Plantation Inn."

"Good for you. Tennis was never really my game, but I heard they hired a new instructor. Bonefishing with Ted? Sounds delightful," said Kiki. "I was very fond of Miss Rose. She was very kind to me when we arrived. I spent many hours drinking tea with her on that veranda, talking about life. She had a flair for it. One of the most content people I have ever met, and the kindest. A life well lived. She had no idea what Jules did for a living. She reminded me a lot of my gran. Always telling him to quit smoking and to get a haircut. I miss her and those afternoons on her porch. It's nice to see her place come back to life and not be mowed down to make way for Barry Bassett's WaveRunner concession."

"Well, it would be my pleasure to give you tea on her veranda anytime you're passing by," said Nina.

Kiki smiled. "Thank you, I'll do that."

They all stood, and Kiki walked them to the door. As Nina and Danish walked down the hill to the golf cart, Danish said, "Just curious. Is that woman-speak for 'Yes, I'll definitely visit' or 'No, thank you, I've got better things to do'?"

"You're hurting my head, Danish. I want to go home and have a swim."

They waved good-bye to Charlie in the gatehouse and headed off. The ocean sparkled in the midday sunlight. Nina smiled to herself and plunked the wide-brimmed sun hat she'd bought at the straw market on her head.

"Well, that was very productive, from an investigative point of view," said Danish. "We've identified several viable suspects. Number one, Kiki gave us the motive for Tiffany Bassett to steal the necklace herself: the prenup combined with a toxic marriage and chronic laziness. All the signs of a struggle in the guest room could easily have been staged by her in the minutes between the time she went into the house alone and when Alice gave up waiting outside the bathroom door and went looking for her. The question is, did she do it alone, or did she have an accomplice? Maybe lover-boy Lance was in on it."

"I'm not sure who you think is investigating this," Nina said, but she couldn't help but be intrigued by the mystery. "I guess it could have happened that way. But I don't think you can dismiss the possibility that she was abducted. Based on what I've seen of them in the short time I've been here, I think it is probably safe to say neither she nor her husband would have any shortage of enemies between here and Las Vegas. Maybe someone they crossed paths with in Miami wanted revenge and zipped down by boat and took her. It wouldn't be impossible. It really could be any one of a thousand people we don't even know."

"Yeah," said Danish. "It could also be someone with an obvious motive and reasonable opportunity. Like the salvager from Florida Kiki mentioned. Some guys might find it hard to turn their backs on a jewel worth several million dollars, and dealing with government bureaucracy could send a sane man right over the edge."

He was right, thought Nina.

"I've got to deliver a package to the Davises," said Danish. He turned in at a large white villa, hopped out, and pushed the buzzer on the gate. A moment later it swung open slowly. Danish drove down the long gravel drive, parked, and reached into the backseat for a bundle of mail, which he started to shuffle, looking at the addresses on the envelopes and apparently putting them in some kind of order.

"What are you doing?" asked Nina.

"Mrs. Davis waits for her mail every day. I feel bad when all I have to give her is junk mail. Flyers for two-for-one burgers and her electricity bill. So, when there's something good, like a card from her daughter or a letter from one of her old friends in Dallas, I put it on top."

He hopped out of the cart, grabbed the package from the backseat, and bounded up the front steps two at a time. He rang the bell, and seconds later an elderly lady with freshly sculpted white hair wearing a sweater set and tan pants opened the door. She smiled when she saw Danish. He handed her the package and the bundle of letters, waved good-bye, and bounded back to the cart.

Nina turned to face him. "Kiki said Tiffany complained about Barry putting the condo company shares in her name," she said. "Tiffany didn't care about them. To her, it was just a piece of vacant land and a pipe dream. But it's his obsession. He couldn't divorce her without losing his stake in the project. Maybe she was in the way of both his personal life and his business, so he got rid of her."

"Yeah," said Danish. "I can see that. He's probably more capable of planning and executing a serious crime than Tiffany. She generally doesn't do anything more strenuous than drive into town to get her hair done, which from what I can tell, involves sitting for two hours with tinfoil on your head, cucumber slices on your eyes, and your feet in a tankful of little fish who eat the dead skin off the bottoms of your feet. I'm serious. You should come by the inn and check it out. It's hilarious."

"I'm sure," said Nina, who decided not to mention she'd perhaps done similar things in the name of beauty.

They drove back to Nina's house.

"I've got a few more deliveries to make," said Danish. "I'm working at The Redoubt later if you're thinking of stopping in. See ya."

"Thanks, Danish," said Nina, jumping out.

117

She poured herself a glass of iced tea, mulling over the morning's events. She wandered out onto the veranda and sat down, looking out at the horizon, replaying the scenes with Lance and Jules and Kiki in her head.

Nina had been sitting on her veranda for a while, she didn't know how long, when she heard a loud knock on the door followed by Danish's voice hollering, "Hey, Nina!" He appeared on the veranda before she could get up from her chair.

"Guess what?" he said as he threw himself into a chair beside her. He continued without waiting for her to reply. "I just went to the beauty salon in town to deliver their hair-products shipment, and Carrie told me that this morning Barry got a ransom note from Tiffany's kidnappers. It said they wanted three million dollars or he'd never see her again. Carrie heard it from her cousin Danielle, who's a data-entry clerk at the police station."

That put a twist in things. "Wow. So, does she know what Barry's going to do? I've really go to meet this Carrie sometime," said Nina.

"Carrie's sister-in-law Loretta cleans the Bassetts' house, and she's there now. Carrie said that Loretta called a while ago to tell her that when she got there this afternoon to work, the police were pulling out of the driveway. We probably went right by them this morning and didn't see it because of the hedge." He paused for a moment. "We probably drove right by the kidnappers! Do you remember passing anyone on the road out there?"

"No," said Nina.

"So, anyway," said Danish, "Carrie said Loretta went in the kitchen, and Barry was pouring himself a glass of champagne. He even offered her some. She said no. He took a sandwich and a bag of potato chips and went into his study, and then she could hear the football game he recorded last night playing on the television. Loretta called back a half hour later to say she could hear him snoring through the door. Apparently, he has a comfy sofa and a big-screen TV in there."

"So, at least we know he doesn't care about his wife," said Nina.

"He's not exactly rushing right down to the bank to withdraw the ransom or sitting by the phone waiting for the kidnappers to call," said Danish. "I think he did it, and he knows her body is somewhere the police will never find it. Like in Shark Alley."

"Danish. What a gruesome thought. I'm going to have nightmares now. Maybe I'll see you tomorrow, OK?" she said, and then she walked him to the door.

8

The next morning Nina was lying in bed reading with a cup of coffee in her hand when she was startled by the sound of someone pounding on her veranda door.

"Hey, Nina! Rise and shine!" It was Danish's voice. Nina wiped the spilled coffee off her arm, quickly pulled on a pair of shorts and her sweater, and padded out into the front room. Danish's face was pressed against the window, and he was peering into the room. She opened the door to let him in.

"I chartered a boat to take us into the cays so we can look for Tiffany. Let's go," he said. Nina poured herself another cup of coffee and sat down at the kitchen table.

"That sounds like a very bad idea, Danish," she said. "Aren't the police on the case? I have other plans for today. I'm going to paint my living room."

Danish rolled his eyes and sighed loudly. "What is wrong with you people? You move down here to the islands for a new life and then proceed to do exactly the same things you did up north. Where's your sense of adventure? Let's shake things up a little! We're going to find that emerald necklace and restore it to my lady. You heard her, the whole exhibit is going to fall apart without it. When I find it, she'll know my true worth, and we'll live happily ever after."

"I thought last night you said you thought Barry did it, and that he's killed Tiffany and fed her to the sharks," said Nina.

"Yeah, but what if he didn't? Or what if he has a partner camped out somewhere in the cays with Tiffany tied up, waiting for some tax-free ransom money he's going to pay to himself?" asked Danish.

"I don't know if ransom money is a tax write-off," said Nina. "You might want to look into that."

She took a sip of her coffee and glanced around the room. She was looking forward to whipping the cottage into shape. But Danish was right, it could wait. The chances of running across Tiffany's kidnappers were nil, and she was keen to explore the nearby cays. She looked out at the water. It was mirror smooth, not a whisper of a breeze wrinkling the surface. A beautiful, sunny day. A few hours tooling around the tiny islands trailing off the south end of Pineapple Cay like stepping-stones was beginning to sound like a great way to spend a morning. Let Danish amuse himself. She'd just enjoy the sights. She took another sip of coffee. Plus, on the off chance he did find Tiffany, he might need help avoiding getting killed.

"OK, Danish. Let's go." She gulped the rest of her coffee, slipped on her two-piece swimsuit under her cutoff shorts, and pulled a white T-shirt over the top. She brushed her teeth, splashed some water on her face, and smeared on some sunscreen. She threw a water bottle and a towel into her tote and put on her sunglasses. They went out the back door onto the veranda, the screen door slamming behind them. Danish started off down the beach a few steps ahead of her.

"It's Ted's boat," he said over his shoulder. "He wasn't going to do it; then I told him it was for you and me, and he said all right."

Nina stopped in her tracks. About a hundred yards away at the water's edge, she could see Ted Matthews leaning against his Boston Whaler, watching their progress across the sand. She suddenly felt ridiculous. Humoring Danish was one thing, but she didn't want anyone else to think she was part of his nutty scheme to find the kidnappers and the necklace. Then again, she *wasn't* part of Danish's nutty plan, so what did she care what Ted Matthews or anyone else thought of her decision to take a boat ride through the cays on a lovely day? In five seconds, she had rationalized the whole thing and continued walking toward the boat, which was really all she could do at this point.

"Hi, Ted," she said when she got close to him.

"Morning, Nina," he said.

"Um, I didn't realize you'd been roped into this expedition. I imagine you have more important things to do than go on a sightseeing cruise through the cays today," she said.

"We are not going sightseeing, Nina," said Danish as he loaded his knapsack into the boat. "I see you wore your bikini, but this is serious. We're looking for the kidnappers' hideaway, OK? I have to teach my yoga class at noon, so maybe we could get going now, eh, team?"

"Danish, really," said Nina in a gently pleading tone, "why do you think we can find Tiffany Bassett when the police haven't been able to locate her?"

"Maybe we won't," he said, turning around to look at her over his shoulder, "but maybe we will. The more people looking for her, the better, I say. Anyway, the police boats went north this morning, with scuba tanks. My guess is they are searching below the cliffs at Kiki and Jules's place. So, we'll go the other way."

He and Ted pushed the boat out until it was floating free above the sandy bottom. Nina waded out and stood beside it. She sighed.

"Well, how about this. We go down to the park, and if we see anything suspicious, we'll call the police, OK?" she said to Danish's back as she glanced at Ted, who stood on the other side of the boat wearing his gold-rimmed aviator sunglasses.

"It's OK," said Ted. "I've got a couple of free hours, and it's a beautiful day to be on the water. Let's go."

They all climbed in the boat, and Ted steered it away from shore and south toward Diamond Cays National Park. They flew along, and

Nina gradually relaxed, leaning back in the seat and watching the coast-line go by. They passed a string of pastel-colored vacation houses of various sizes and designs spread out along the beach south of Coconut Cove village, and then the shoreline was alternatively covered in vegetation or backed by sand dunes. They rounded the southern tip of Pineapple Cay, and the Diamond Cays lay spread out before them. Ted slowed down and followed the red-and-green channel markers, threading a course between the cays.

Danish sat cross-legged on the bow of the boat, looking through a pair of binoculars at the small islands as they motored slowly by them. Within the park, they were all uninhabited, their white-sand beaches devoid of any human activity, their interiors covered in dense vegetation. Tall coconut palms towered above the underbrush on some islands. The only litter on the beaches that Nina could see were fallen coconuts and brown palm fronds shed by the trees along the edges of the beaches. Some of the cays were just small lumps of sand and coral rock a few hundred feet long, with low-growing cacti and ground vines the only vegetation. The water was shallow, clear, and inviting. After they had been meandering around for about a half hour, Ted slowed and cut the engine.

"Why don't we take a break," he said. "It's a hot day, and there isn't a leaf stirring out here."

He opened the cooler and handed Nina and Danish each a bottle of water, then took one for himself. They sat in the shade of the Bimini top and drank.

"The snorkeling here is good," he said, looking at Nina. "Care for a dip?"

"Sounds great," said Nina.

Ted opened a bench and took out three sets of fins and three masks with pipes attached.

"I'm going to stay topside and look out for suspicious activity," said Danish.

"Suit yourself," said Ted, handing Nina a set of snorkel gear.

"While you're looking for bad guys, could you also please keep an eye out for big sharks in the area," said Nina.

"I suppose," said Danish, "although we're not on vacation here. This is business."

"Well, you've got to keep the troops fresh, right?" said Ted, unbuttoning his shirt. Nina turned away and slipped off her shorts, leaving her T-shirt on over her bathing suit to protect her shoulders and back from the strong sun. Ted had stripped down to his all-purpose khaki fishing shorts. She tried not to stare at his tanned torso as he also pulled on a T-shirt. She put on her fins and mask and sat up on the gunwale, ready to jump into the water, which was crystal clear and looked to be only about ten feet deep. The bottom was studded with big round clumps of brain coral and waving purple sea fans.

"If you're scared of sharks, you might want to take off those earrings, Nina," said Danish. "They like shiny things. I heard about a lady once, just got married on the beach at some fancy hotel. Got up the next morning and went for a swim wearing her shiny new wedding ring. Shark took her hand right off."

"That is the island equivalent of an urban myth," said Ted.

Nina took her earrings off anyway and threw them into the open top of her bag. She positioned the mask over her eyes and nose, making sure no strands of hair were breaking the air seal, put the mouthpiece in, and slipped over the side into the water. It was bathtub warm. She hadn't snorkeled much, but she loved it. She put her face in the water and breathed in and out through the mouthpiece, kicking gently away from the boat, feeling the fins move the water. She spread her arms out and floated, looking down. A school of tiny striped fish swam by beneath her. She saw a giant red starfish on the sandy bottom. Three curious angelfish, flat as dessert plates with feathery fins waving in the current, swam up to her and lingered for a while.

She felt a hand on her shoulder and looked over. Ted was beside her, pointing at a spot on his other side. Five or six cobalt-blue fish the size of her hand were mooching around the fronds of a clump of coral. Blue tangs. Below them floated a bright yellow-and-blue-striped grunt. Nina was mesmerized. She and Ted floated side by side over a forest of coral alive with multicolored schools of fish. They were everywhere. Reds, blues, greens, yellows, and purples. Some with stripes, some with scales gilded in contrasting colors. Red on blue, yellow on green. The coral was equally otherworldly. Waving fronds of vibrant color; beds of dense, velvety underwater shrubs; and yellow spikes of staghorn coral.

Suddenly, Nina felt a commotion behind her in the water. She spun around to look. She could see a paddle slapping the water next to the boat. She stood upright, treading water, and pulled off her mask and snorkel. Danish was hollering and pointing behind her.

"Shark! Nina! Behind you!" She spun around to look where he was pointing, but she couldn't see anything. She whipped around again and swam as fast as she could toward the boat, legs scissoring hard, arms windmilling through the water. She grabbed the side of the boat and, with superhuman strength fueled by adrenaline, heaved herself over the gunwale and into the boat. She turned around to face the way she'd come.

"Where's Ted?" she asked urgently.

Ted was swimming slowly toward the boat, his mask pushed up on his forehead, snorkel behind his ear. Danish was laughing. He was standing up on the bow of the boat slapping his knees.

"You should have seen yourself. Man, can you move when you want to!" he said with a hoot.

She got it. There was no shark. She pulled off her fins and leaped up on the bow of the boat. "Are you kidding me? You think that's funny?" she hissed.

Danish backed away from her, but she kept advancing on him.

"It was hilarious. Oh, come on, Nina. It was just a joke. It was funny," said Danish.

"Let's see how funny you find this!" she said, pushing him into the water.

He hit the surface with a huge splash, sank, and then bobbed up again, sputtering. "Ah! That is very refreshing! Thank you. Fantastic!" he said, treading water. He dove under and came up on the other side of the boat.

Ted pulled himself up and into the boat. He looked at Nina. "You all right?" he asked, handing her a towel.

"Yes, I'm fine," she said, drying off her face, arms, and legs, her heart still hammering. She sat down on the bench and watched Danish take a few more strokes back and forth beside the boat, then hoist himself up and onto it.

Nina threw her wet towel at him. "That was not funny, Danish. You could give a person a heart attack that way. You remind me of my brother, Eric, and not in a good way," she said angrily.

"You ever pull a stunt like that on my boat again, and you'll be swimming home," said Ted.

"OK, OK. Sorry, man," said Danish, raising his hands in surrender. He got to his feet and sat down next to Nina, putting his arm around her shoulder and squeezing her to his side.

"Aw, come on, Nina. I'm sorry. I really didn't think you'd fall for that one. Really, I'm sorry. Forgive me?" he asked. He dug in the pockets of his dripping shorts and pulled out a sodden packet of Zig Zag rolling papers and two seashells. He slipped the wad of wet paper back into his pocket and held the shells out to her on the palm of his hand.

"Here. These are for you. I found them on the beach at the inn this morning. You have to get up early to beat the shell hounds who stay there. They pick it clean daily."

He held a tiny, perfect pink trivia shell—a smooth, polished oval of delicate pink with a pleated texture. Its edges curled inward to make a cozy home for its onetime resident. Beside it was a tulip shell—furled and marbled, and white and orange, with elegantly tapered ends. Nina looked at him, then picked them up, cradling them in her own hand.

"They're beautiful, Danish. Thank you. They'll be a lovely souvenir of the time you tried to kill me with a very lame practical joke," she said.

"I think it's time we head back," said Ted, starting the engine. They zigzagged through the cays and then back along the coast of Pineapple Cay to the Plantation Inn. Ted pointed the whaler toward the beach and drifted into the sand. They all hopped out into the knee-high water and pulled the boat up onto the sand in front of a row of tastefully landscaped beach bungalows, each with its own screened-in porch steps from the beach.

Danish swung his backpack over his shoulder and turned to face Nina and Ted.

"Thanks a lot, Ted. I'm sorry about the shark thing. It kind of overshadowed the whole looking-for-Tiffany aspect of our mission. She's got to be out there somewhere. Maybe the kidnappers—or Barry—drove her out there in a boat and threw her overboard."

"Well, if Tiffany went into the water, she might have a better-than-average chance of making it to shore," said Nina. "She has her own built-in personal flotation devices." It was a weak attempt to break the tension and defuse residual bad feelings, and she regretted it the moment she said it.

"Whoa, Nina! *Meow*!" Danish made a cat scratch with his hand.

Nina sighed. "You know, Danish," she said, still cringing at her own behavior, "that's sexist. Characterizing any difference of opinion that might exist between two women as a catfight."

"OK, I have no idea what that second part meant, but you think cat talk is sexy? Gee, Nina. You're a bit kinky. I had no idea."

"Not *sexy*, Danish, *sexist*. Do you know there's a difference? Don't you have to take gender-sensitivity training in the postal service?"

"Yes, Nina. As a matter of fact, I am very much in tune with my feminine side, and I must say, I found your remark about Tiffany's perfect fake boobs a bit sexist. In the twenty-first century, a woman should be able to dress the way she wants without being subject to public judgment."

Yes, he's got a point, thought Nina. *It was a low-class joke at someone else's expense.*

"You're right, Danish. That was in bad taste, especially under the circumstances. I apologize." Nina felt her cheeks flush with embarrassment. Ted Matthews was leaning against his boat with his hands in his pockets, watching them. His expression was unreadable behind his aviator shades.

"Apology accepted," Danish said magnanimously.

Ted stood up straight. "Well, if we're done here, I think I'll head out. Nina, can I give you a lift home?" he asked.

"Thanks," she said, putting her bag back in the boat.

"Hey, Ted, man. I owe you some cash for the charter. It's not your fault we found squat," said Danish as he dug into his pocket.

"Consider it my contribution to the cause," said Ted, pushing the boat out from the beach and hopping in. He and Nina sped down the shore, past the town center to the beach below Ted's lodge. He pulled the boat up onshore and threw the anchor into the sand above the waterline.

"Afraid I've got to run," he said, looking at his watch. "I'll see you later, Nina."

"OK. Bye, Ted," she said.

They turned away from each other, he heading up the path to his lodge, and she strolling down the beach to her cottage. The morning had left her discombobulated. The snorkeling had been amazing, and she had enjoyed Ted's quiet, steady company, but Danish's stupid prank and her own faux pas had spoiled the outing. And all that arguing in front of Ted. It was embarrassing. She tried to remember that although she liked Danish, and he was basically a kindhearted, amiable guy, he was still young. He was the same age as some of her students. Some people are grown up when they're twenty-five, and others are not. Her own parents were married, with a child and a mortgage, by that age. She wasn't much older when *she* got married, although that didn't say much about her maturity. Still, it was almost impossible to imagine Danish in that role.

After lunch, Nina decided it was time to get serious about getting her new house in order. She changed into her painting clothes, then found a plastic bucket under the sink and filled it with warm water and a capful of lemon householder cleaner. She put on her headphones so she could listen to music while she worked. Then she pulled on a pair of rubber gloves; dipped a big, thick sponge into the bucket; and started scrubbing the walls in the kitchen. The accumulated grime and dirt washed away, and the walls brightened. It took her a couple of hours and several changes of water to clean every inch of the walls and window frames in the large room that contained the kitchen and living room. The air smelled lemony clean. Now she just had to give it a few hours to dry; then she could give the room a fresh coat of bright-white paint. It was time for a cool glass of iced tea on the veranda and a swim. She stood back and admired her work, pulling the headphones off.

Nina became aware of loud screeching and rumbling noises coming from outside. She could hear the buzz of a chain saw and the beep, beep, beep of a piece of heavy machinery backing up, followed by the nerve-jangling sound of metal scraping on rock.

What on earth is that? she wondered, stepping quickly to her front door and out onto the sidewalk. About a hundred feet away, up the road toward Ted's fishing camp, a big yellow bulldozer was digging a giant hole in the ground next to the road. A man in a yellow safety vest and orange helmet was chainsawing through a tall pine that had been felled on the piece of scrubland between her cottage and the point. Standing beside the big hole in his white shoes and golf shirt was Barry. Nina walked up the sidewalk toward him. He turned to meet her with fake friendliness.

"Hello, Miss Spark. How are you? Lovely day, isn't it?"

"Barry, what is going on?"

"Well, when you told me you didn't wish to sell Sundrift Cottage to me, I was in a real quandary as to what to do with the piece of land I have here between you and Mr. Matthews. I admit, it had me stymied for a few days. What can I do with a piece of roadside scrubland with no water access? Then I had a fabulous idea! I bought a Crispy Fried Chicken franchise, and I am going to build a drive-through on this side, with a miniature golf course on the other side, overlooking the water. Something the kiddies will really enjoy year-round. I can just imagine their screams of delight! Of course, I'm going to need a lot of parking, so I'll put that over there. Very convenient for families with young children, and a nice place for teenagers to get together on weekends—or anytime, really. A good rainy-day activity for the tourists."

"You can't do that. This is a residential neighborhood," said Nina, stepping in front of him with her hands on her hips.

"Oh, please, please. You're trespassing now. Step off my property, please, or I'll have to alert the authorities." He waved her back across a line spray painted in fluorescent orange in the dirt. Nina saw that it ran from the road back about fifty feet toward the water, demarcating a narrow wedge of land abutting both her property and Ted's. Ted owned the wide swath of waterfront next to hers, as well as the point, but not the narrow strip of scrubland along the road behind it, a short distance from her lovely little cottage.

"To answer your question," he said, "I think you'll find that this property was rezoned for commercial development last year. The members of the town planning committee found my arguments in favor of economic development on Pineapple Cay very persuasive."

"What is your problem, Barry? Why don't you just build your big hotel somewhere else? It's a big, wide world," said Nina.

"The problem, girlie, is that nobodies like you and little Miss Sunshine at the Candyland real estate office do not get to decide what people like me can do," he said, sneering at her.

"You're a petty, vindictive little man. I would have thought you'd have more important matters to worry about these days," said Nina, feeling herself losing her temper. "A casual observer might get the impression that you don't care about your wife at all. She's been kidnapped, and you're out shopping for fried-chicken franchises and playing in your big-boy sandbox with your toy bulldozer?"

His face was rigid with anger. "You don't know what you're talking about," he said disdainfully. "You're so smug, with your college education. You and Matthews and Poitras. You and the rest of the local snobs have got the quaint, genteel lifestyle you want, so now no more development allowed. Big, bad Barry with his big, bad hotel. How gauche! What about the jobs the resort will create? Or is no one else allowed to want something better out of life now that you've got your dream house on the beach?"

He took a step closer to her and pointed his finger in her face. "Keep your nose out of my business, or you will regret it," he said menacingly, then turned abruptly and stalked back to his car, which was parked on the side of the road. Nina just stood there, watching him leave and breathing fast. She was rattled. She didn't like confrontation.

All of a sudden, for the first time since she'd arrived on Pineapple Cay, she felt lonesome and homesick. What was she doing here? What kind of nut buys a house off the Internet, gives up a steady job, and moves to a ramshackle hut on an island? Maybe he was right and she *was* being selfish. She wrapped her arms around herself and walked slowly down the sidewalk to her front gate. For a brief moment, she felt a strong urge to go inside and call her mother in Maine. But she wasn't ready to hear the silence on the other end of the phone that meant "I told you not to do it." No, better not worry her parents. She glanced at her watch. Louise would be feeding the girls their supper. It wouldn't be fair to call her in crisis mode yet again. She'd deal with this on her own.

The sun was low, and although she'd been sweating all afternoon while washing the walls, now she felt chilled. A hot shower seemed like a good idea. She went inside, stripped off her clothes, and turned on the shower. She stepped in and let the hot water warm and massage her tired muscles. When she was done, she gently patted herself dry with a towel and smoothed some soothing sesame oil into her skin.

Then she pulled on her soft jersey skirt and a cozy long-sleeve T-shirt with her sweater over top. She grabbed her keys and wallet and pushed herself out the door and down the beach to The Redoubt. She didn't really feel like talking to anyone, but she wanted to be somewhere filled with lively people and happy sounds.

It was just before six o'clock on a Wednesday night, and the restaurant was about half-full. The booth in the back corner was vacant, so Nina slid into it, sinking back into the corner. From there, she had a view of the whole room. Danish was working, delivering an order to a large table of laughing vacationers. He saw her in the corner and ambled over.

"Hey, chum. Why so glum? I hope you're not still upset about this morning," he said, sliding into the booth and pressing up next to her. When Nina felt the warmth of his body next to hers, she started to cry. He looked at her, wide-eyed. Concern, fear, and horror mingled together in the expression on his face.

"Oh, no! Don't cry. Please, don't cry!" He patted her hand like it was possibly radioactive. She sniffled, digging in her pocket for a tissue.

"Hold on! I'll get you a tissue. Don't worry." He jumped up and pulled a napkin out from under some cutlery at an empty table setting. "Here you go, Nina. Don't cry. Everything's going to be all right," he said, although he didn't sound too sure of it.

"How do you know it's going to be all right?" asked Nina, blowing her nose. "Maybe it's just going to get worse and worse. You don't know. Maybe my roof is going to cave in, maybe the toilet is going to back up all over the yard, maybe Barry is going to build a drive-through fried-chicken restaurant and mini golf next to my house. Maybe Tiffany Bassett has been murdered! Maybe my employer will decide I can't work from here after all, and I'll have no job! Maybe my cheating louse of a husband was right. I am no fun, and I should wear more makeup!" The tears were flowing steadily down her cheeks, and she dabbed at them with the soggy, snotty napkin, turning her face to the wall in the hope that no one could see her. Fortunately, the other customers were focused on what was going on at their own tables.

"What *happened*?" asked Danish with his hand on his forehead. "This morning you were so happy. Snorkeling away there with Ted. I'm going to get you a big margarita. Just hold on." He jumped up again and bounded over to the bar. She could feel her tears subsiding. She took a deep breath and wiped her eyes with her fingertips, and her face with the heel of her hand. There.

Danish came back. "Here. Drink this. Eat this cake. It's got chocolate and a pile of ice cream on it. Here are some more tissues." He put a two-inch-thick stack of paper napkins, a large margarita, and a piece of chocolate cake in front of her.

"Where is Pansy when you need her? She lives for stuff like this," he said, looking around the room. "Oh, look. There's Ted, the neighbor you have the hots for. That ought to cheer you up.

"Hey Ted! Over here!" he shouted across the now-noisy room.

"Aw, Danish, no!" she said. That was the last thing she needed.

Several heads turned in their direction, including Ted's. He had just come in with a group of four happy, tanned gentlemen Nina assumed were clients. He motioned for them to sit down at a table near the door, excused himself, and ambled over to where Nina and Danish were sitting. As soon as he saw Nina's face, his own assumed a look of concern. She guessed her eyes and nose must be red, and she looked down at the table for a second, embarrassed.

"Ted, man, praise the lord. Pinch-hit for me here, will you? I'm the only waiter on the floor until six o'clock, and we have a crisis situation. Something about overflowing toilets, a fried-chicken drive-through, and whether or not Nina should wear more makeup. Thanks. Nina, don't worry. Where there's a will, there's a way." He patted her shoulder and took off.

What is that supposed to mean? Nina wondered. She looked up at Ted and rolled her eyes. "I'm fine, really. I'm done, don't worry. Everything is fine." She forced a smile.

He sat down across the table from her and continued to look at her without speaking for a moment. "I have three sisters and fifteen years on Danish Jensen. It takes more than that to scare me," he said. "I don't want to pry, but is there something the matter?"

She shook her head. Over his shoulder, she saw Barry Bassett walk in with three other men she'd never seen before. They looked like out-of-towners. They all seated themselves around a table, and Barry raised his hand, looking around for a waiter. Unconsciously, Nina gave an angry snort.

Ted followed her eyes across the room to where Barry was playing the genial host to his out-of-town guests, smiling his pasted-on smile. Ted turned back to her. "Is this about the new dirt pit next to your house? I saw it on my way home. Don't worry. Barry doesn't have the permits to build anything there," he said. "Has he been bothering you?"

"What if he's right? What if I am being selfish, just wanting to keep my cottage the way it is and standing in the way of people around here who might benefit from the jobs and income a hotel would bring to the island?" she asked.

"Is that what he told you? Listen, the chamber of commerce took a poll six months ago to see how much public support there was for Barry's proposed development. By a wide margin, the residents of Pineapple Cay said no, they don't want it. There's a lot more potential in developing other kinds of businesses here. He's not some great humanitarian, as I'm sure you have discovered by now. He's in partner-ship with an offshore company, which would take most of its profits from the resort out of the country, not spend them here in the commu-nity. His proposed hotel-and-condo development would put all twenty people on my staff at the lodge—including me—out of work, as well as jeopardize the jobs of the hundred people who work at the Plantation Inn. We pay decent wages to keep good staff, and we pay local taxes. Big operations like the one Barry is cooking up don't operate like that. The company will squeeze what it can get in profits out of the resort by building cheap and paying the lowest rate possible for everything, then selling off the carcass. So, please, don't feel bad about wanting to live in your little yellow house by the sea. You're not hurting anyone, and who knows, you may end up making things better around here." He smiled at her reassuringly. "Don't worry. Now, will you excuse me for a moment? I'm afraid I've got a table of guests waiting for me. I'll be back later."

Was he annoyed with her? She watched him walk straight over to Barry's table and say something to him, gesturing for Barry to follow him outside. They went out the front door onto the street together, out of sight. Surely Ted wasn't the type to punch someone in the nose for making a woman cry, like in some Popeye cartoon? Nina poured the rest of her margarita down her throat.

The two men came back in a few minutes later. Ted looked grim but shook it off as he went back to his guests. He put his hands on the shoulders of two of the men as he stood between their chairs; then he pulled up a chair and joined them. He looked around for a server, and a waitress wove her way between the tables toward him. She took Ted's order, and a couple of minutes later came back to the table with a tray full of bottled beer. Ted glanced over at Nina and nodded, then returned his attention to his guests.

Barry had trailed behind Ted into the crowded restaurant, a sour, brooding look on his face. He glared at Nina across the room, then turned his back on her and sat down with his friends again. Their meals arrived, and they all became occupied with cracking and eating the lobsters heaped on a platter in the middle of the table.

"I brought you another margarita," said Danish, reappearing beside her. "Everything OK now?"

"I'm fine, Danish, thanks. Cheers." She raised her glass in his direction.

"Good. I'm off in twenty minutes; then we can talk it out." He hurried off again.

She picked at the chocolate cake he'd brought but didn't have much of an appetite. She dug a few quarters out of her change purse and strolled over to the jukebox. She leafed through the selections and then chose "Sunday Shining" by Finley Quaye, "Easy's Gettin' Harder Every Day" by Iris DeMent, and "Fever" by Peggy Lee. A song to sway to, some good hurtin' music, and something to get her back into fighting form. As she wandered back to her seat, she glanced over at Ted. He was watching her. She slid back into her booth and sipped on her drink, taking a good look at the buoys, nets, and old photographs on the wall as her selections played on the jukebox. When Iris DeMent came on, some guy in the middle of the room yelled, "Oh, come on! Just shoot me already!" There was a smattering of laughter. Nina just sipped her drink and looked out the window by the bar, where Veronica was looking in her direction.

Lance entered the restaurant alone, no Beer Commercial in tow. He looked around, and his eyes stopped on Barry. He walked past Barry's table and out onto the deck, which was now mostly in darkness, just the faint light from inside spilling out onto the wooden picnic tables. A minute later, Nina watched as Barry stood and followed Lance outside. Lance was standing in semidarkness in the corner of the deck against the wall of the restaurant. Only Nina could see him from inside. He didn't glance in her direction, and neither did Barry. She watched as they stood close together, talking angrily. Abruptly, Lance pushed past Barry, bumping him with his shoulder as he went, hurrying down the beach stairs and around the side of the building in the dark. Barry stood for a second, watching him go, and then he spun around with his head down and stalked back inside. He did not look in Nina's direction. He seemed to have forgotten she was there, but even so, she pressed her back into the corner of the booth, out of the circle of warm light cast by the candle flickering on the table.

She looked over at Ted. He seemed engrossed in telling a story, looking from face to face among his companions. He hadn't noticed Lance and Barry's comings and goings.

"Nina. Jeez. What's up with the music? I think we've got John Prine doing 'Angel from Montgomery' and some Tom Waits over there if you want to kill the night completely. We might sell more hard liquor, I suppose," said Danish, sliding in next to her with two more margaritas in his hands.

"Did you see Lance and Barry arguing on the deck?" Nina asked him.

"What? No. Where's Lance?" he asked, looking around.

"They had an argument, and Lance left. Maybe Barry found out about Lance and Tiffany and wanted to have it out with him. Maybe they kidnapped Tiffany together, and they're arguing about what to do now!" whispered Nina. "They knew each other in Connecticut, apparently."

"What about the ransom note?" asked Danish, scratching his head.

Barry and his friends finished their meal and pushed back from the table. Barry picked up his credit-card receipt and tucked his wallet in the inside pocket of his sports jacket. He scanned the room, his head back slightly and his nose up, like he was sniffing the air. When he caught sight of Nina and Danish in the booth, his mouth hardened, and he turned abruptly toward the door, following his companions out.

"Let's follow him," said Nina, grabbing her house keys off the table, surprised at herself. Danish didn't even question her. He took a big gulp of his margarita and then left both glasses on the table and headed for the door. Nina followed. Out of the corner of her eye, she could see Ted's eyes following her as she crossed the room, but she didn't look at him.

Nina and Danish stood in the shadows as Barry shook hands with the three men and they slapped one another on the back with hearty good nights. His friends got in a rented car and headed south, probably toward the Plantation Inn. Barry got in his car and drove past them in the opposite direction, headed north toward The Enclave and, presumably, his house. They sprinted across the street to Danish's red post-office golf cart, hopped in, and followed Barry's taillights out of the village. He turned off into The Enclave. Danish dowsed the headlights and turned off behind him, fifty yards back. The night was clear, and moonlight illuminated the road.

Barry went past his own driveway.

"Maybe he's seen us and is suspicious," said Nina. Barry's taillights disappeared around a curve in the road, and their view of him was suddenly obscured by a bank of tall trees.

"Catch up to him, Danish! Where is he going?"

"I've got the pedal to the metal. This thing only does about fifteen miles an hour. There's nothing else up here but a few big houses. It's a dead-end road, ending at Jules and Kiki's place," said Danish.

He took the curve so fast that Nina had to hang on to the roof. The trees blocked out the light of the moon, and they were orbiting the curve in total darkness.

"Put on the headlights, Danish! We're going to crash!" yelled Nina, giving up on the stealth part of the expedition. Danish flipped on the lights and swerved to avoid the ditch. The road straightened out. There was no sign of Barry ahead. Nina and Danish looked down the gated driveways of the oceanfront estates as they passed, but they saw nothing but darkness punctuated by the faint glow of light from the houses behind their high banks of dense vegetation and berms of pale sand and coral rock.

"How could we lose him on a dead-end road with absolutely no other traffic, and every driveway blocked by an eight-foot-high iron gate!" exclaimed Nina. They had almost reached the end of the road. Ahead of them were just three houses. Behind a wrought iron gate, the facade of the Davises' large white stucco house was lit with floodlights from the lawn. Beside it was the gated driveway into Delmont Samuels's villa. The Savages' beach house lay behind its iron gate straight ahead of them. There was soft light glowing in some of the windows but no signs of movement or of Barry's car anywhere. They could hear the waves crashing against the cliffs a disconcertingly short distance off to their right.

"Wait!" said Danish. "That's the fire service access road to the beach. Maybe he drove down there." He backed up ten feet in the dark and turned down a narrow sandy lane with tall trees and high fences on either side. Danish parked the cart in the shadow of a fragrant frangipani tree a short distance from the road. He took a flashlight out of the box of junk on the floor of the back cargo space, and they proceeded on foot toward the waves crashing against the beach ahead of them. The track was sandy, and Nina skidded and sank into it in her sandals with each step, but she didn't dare take them off in case there was broken glass or sharp-edged shells underfoot. Barry's car was not in the lane.

They reached the water's edge. The tide was high, and the beach was just a narrow sliver of pale sand running in either direction. The black water foamed at their feet, and there was only dark oblivion beyond it. They looked up and down the beach. It was empty. They could see the landscaped lawns of the houses on either side sloping down to the beach, as well as the silhouettes of beach chairs, thatched sun umbrellas, and kayaks in the moonlight.

"Well, he's not here. This is incredible. How did we lose him?" asked Nina.

"Let's go down the beach to his place and see if he's there," said Danish.

"I don't think so," said Nina. "He's got two vicious Doberman pinschers, I happen to know."

Danish had already started walking down the beach. He glanced back at her over his shoulder. "They're kept in the house. Believe me, I know. I deliver Tiffany Bassett's mail-order shopping booty every day. This was your idea, remember?"

He kept walking. She hesitated for a moment and then followed him. They passed about a half dozen large villas perched above the beach. They could see the lights shining out of their floor-to-ceiling windows. Music and laughter wafted down from one of them, but the beach was cloaked in darkness.

"This is it," said Danish. They looked up at a huge, three-story, mint-green villa. Lights shone in every window.

"Either he's home, or he's trying to burn electricity. Unbelievable. He must have gotten home by magic carpet," said Nina.

"Let's go see," said Danish, starting to creep toward the house along the property line. Nina hesitated briefly, then followed. They climbed up beside the house to a sheltered spot along the fence where they could see right into the big, open living area. There was Barry. He sailed into view, two enormous glasses of wine in his hands. A dark-haired woman was seated on the sofa. She looked about forty years old, chic in a black dress, red lipstick, and high stiletto heels. He handed her a glass, then wandered over to the shelves along the back wall. A moment later, horrible improvisational jazz drifted out into the garden. Barry crossed the room toward the woman, snapping his fingers in time with the random, irregular notes of the music. He sat down on the sofa facing her. They both put their glasses of wine on the low table in front of them, wrapped their arms around each other, and started making out.

"I guess he's not missing Tiffany too much," said Nina. "What is wrong with these people?"

"That's Mr. and Mrs. Davis's daughter. She's some kind of corporate hotshot in Dallas. That's where they're from. That must be where we lost him. He must have gone to pick her up at their place."

From inside the house, they heard the muffled barking of two large, barrel-chested dogs.

"Run!" hissed Nina. They stumbled down to the beach as fast they could go, hugging the fence and the cover it provided, the barking of the dogs still audible but mercifully no louder. They hit the beach and kept running. They didn't stop until the only sound Nina could hear was her own labored breath. She bent over and grabbed her knees, feeling her heart pounding in her chest. Danish flopped down on the sand, breathing heavily.

"Whew! That got the old adrenaline going," he said. Nina looked around. They were in front of Delmont Samuels's house. The house itself was invisible behind a hedge at the top of the slope, but there was a single-story building about twenty feet back from the beach. It must have been the recording studio Kiki had mentioned. The front of it was floor-to-ceiling windows, and there was a hot tub beside it.

"Hey. That's Delmont Samuels's studio," said Danish, getting to his feet and heading up the stone path toward it. "What a great place to hide if you were a kidnapper planning to abduct a rich woman wearing an expensive necklace from the house next door."

"Danish! What are you doing? Get back here!" Nina pointed to the spot next to her. Danish kept going.

"If they were here, maybe they left a clue, a matchbook or fingerprints, maybe," he mused, putting his face to a window and peering into the darkened interior. He stepped back and began trying the glass doors, one by one. The one closest to the hot tub opened.

"Come on, Nina, let's take a peek. We won't hurt anything. It's already open," he said, disappearing inside.

"Danish! Get out of there! That's trespassing! Don't you think the police might have already thought of that? I'm staying right here behind the high-water mark. You get back here!" Nina kicked off her sandals and, clutching one in each hand, stepped into the surf. The beaches of Pineapple Cay were public property up to the high-water mark, and she wanted to make sure she wasn't committing a crime as she watched Danish break and enter. She danced back and forth from one foot to the other. Danish reemerged from the studio with a black, rectangular object in one hand and what looked like a roll of scotch tape in the other.

"I saw this on a show once. You can use powdered printer-cartridge ink to dust for fingerprints, then lift them with Scotch tape. I just have to get this cartridge apart," said Danish as he strained to pry it open, putting some muscle into the task. Nina watched in horror as it broke apart and flew through the air into the hot tub. Although it was dark, by the light of the moon she could see a bloom of black ink spreading rapidly in the water.

"Uh-oh," said Danish.

"Please tell me that didn't happen!" Nina covered her face with her hands and then peeked through her fingers at the hot tub. The entire surface was now black.

"Ahhh! We've got to clean it up!" said Nina, dancing above the high-tide mark and then behind it again.

"You can't put that genie back in the bottle," said Danish, still clutching the tape in his hand and breaking into a trot, and then a run, as he pounded down the stone path to the beach.

"Time to scram, Nina. Come on!" he whisper-shouted as he sprinted past her. She hesitated for a second, staring at the hot tub with her hand over her mouth, and then followed him, her feet splashing in the surf. When they reached the fire service access lane, Nina threw her sandals down and stepped into them, her sandy toes rubbing together painfully as she scrambled up the hill in the soft, shifting sand. They threw themselves into the postal-service golf cart, and Danish reversed it up onto the main road, swerving side to side along the narrow path before fishtailing out onto the empty tarmac and gunning it toward town. They didn't speak until they rolled to a stop at Nina's gate. Then Nina turned her whole body toward Danish and stared at him.

"An unfortunate, but relatively minor, accident. No one got hurt," he said.

"That was no accident, Danish! We were skulking around in the dark, peeking in people's windows. You filled the Samuelses' hot tub with black ink! There's no part of that we can justify. Oh, what would my mother say!"

"Come on, Nina," said Danish. "It's not ideal, I agree. But it's not that bad. It's not like we killed anyone. And we've uncovered one very interesting fact. Barry Bassett is getting it on with Cynthia Davis while his wife is allegedly being held captive somewhere by dangerous criminals, waiting for her ransom to be paid."

"We didn't kill anyone. That's setting the bar a bit low, don't you think? I already know more about the Bassetts' love life than I ever wanted to. Danish, I'm not kidding. We are going back to the Samuelses' house first thing in the morning to apologize and make amends. We have to take full responsibility for our actions and do what we can to make it right. Be here tomorrow morning at nine o'clock. Don't be late." She got out of the cart, marched to her door, and went inside without looking back at him.

9

Nina slept fitfully and was up and dressed at dawn. She walked the length of the beach, to town and all the way back to Ted's fishing lodge again, twice. She saw Ted Matthews down near his boats, tinkering with an engine. He looked up both times she came near and raised his hand in greeting. She gave a small wave back but turned around before she got so close she'd have to speak. She wasn't in the mood. She sat down at her kitchen table and tried to read the book on the history of Pineapple Cay that she'd borrowed from the library. Finally, she heard Danish's knock at the door. He had two cups of coffee in his hands.

"A peace offering," he said. She sighed and took one. They drove to Delmont Samuels's house in silence. Danish parked on the road, and Nina buzzed the intercom on the gatepost. She sighed again. She waited for someone to ask for her name and the purpose of their visit, but instead, the gate swung open. She and Danish walked up the long gravel drive to a large white villa. A woman was hanging clothes on a line around the side of the house.

"Good morning," Nina said. "We're here to see Mr. and Mrs. Samuels."

"All right. They're by the pool. This way, please." She led them around the other side of the house and up three steps onto the pool deck. A wide view of the Caribbean Sea lay spread out before them. Nina could see the recording studio tucked into a grove of trees near the beach about a hundred feet down a gentle slope. A couple of little girls were playing in the kidney-shaped pool with a young blonde woman. They were laughing and chattering with each other in French. Delmont Samuels was sitting at a table with papers spread out before him. His wife, Lana, was on the other side of the pool, reclining in a swimsuit on a chaise longue while flipping through a magazine. She glared at Nina and Danish over the top of her sunglasses, then stood and slipped her feet into a pair of high-heeled sandals.

"Isabelle, please take the children inside for their snack," she said, and she sashayed into the house without speaking to Nina or Danish. Isabelle herded the children out of the pool, pulled off their water wings, and wrapped them in thick beach towels. As they went inside, she smiled shyly at Danish and gave him a little wave. Delmont Samuels looked at Danish and Nina in stony silence until the children were gone, then said, "Well, if it isn't Shirley Holmes and Dr. I-Haven't-Got-A-Clue."

"That's a bit harsh, Mr. Samuels," said Danish.

"You threw ink into my hot tub. I had to drain it. It will take a week to clean. Hands where I can see them, please."

Nina wrung her hands with embarrassment but plunged ahead. "Mr. Samuels. We're here to apologize for what happened last night. We trespassed on your land and damaged your property. I'm so very sorry. I can't explain why we did it. We got carried away, I guess. It is ridiculous, I know."

"Yeah. You got that right," he said. "Lana is from Barbados. She's not as easygoing as I am. She was all for throwing the book at you, but Roker talked her down. Apparently, he's convinced her that you two are just a pair of almost-harmless bumblers. Bumblers. Ha ha."

Nina felt another wave of embarrassment wash over her. Of course, Blue Roker had been informed of their activities. She took a deep breath and continued. "We're grateful to you and Mrs. Samuels for overlooking our . . . significant lapse in judgment. I would like to do what I can to make amends. Please send me the bill for fixing your hot tub, at least."

"OK, fine. Never mind about that. I just want my Zodiac back." He leaned back in his chair and fingered the gold chain around his neck as he spoke. Something he did when he was agitated, Nina guessed.

"Someone stole a necklace from you, too?" said Danish. "A zodiac pendant?"

"My boat. My boat. Where is my boat?" said Samuels. "We went to Miami on Sunday for a couple of days, and when I went down to the beach this morning to see what you had done to my hot tub, it was gone. If you bring it back this morning, maybe we can just pretend this never happened. Chalk it up to the full moon or something. You two have proved to be a pain in my ass, but unlike Lana, who is missing her early morning soak in the hot tub very much, I am prepared to give people a second chance. Do unto others as you would have done unto you. All right?"

"We didn't take your boat," said Danish. "We parked our golf cart down the road a way and took the municipal right-of-way down to the beach between the Davis Villa and the big pink rental. We went back up the same way. We didn't see a boat anywhere."

"OK, then. I'd better give Blue Roker a call. Thank you so much for dropping by. Isabelle will see you out." He lifted his cell phone off the table and turned away. The interview was over.

Isabelle, the French au pair, reappeared and walked them to the door, making moon eyes at Danish. He pretended not to notice. Nina walked quickly to the golf cart, with Danish trailing behind.

"I'm mortified," she said. "That was so humiliating. It's all right for you to traipse around doing stupid things, but I'm a grown woman. I know better. I'll see Lana Samuels in the grocery store next week or next year, and she'll glare at me, and we'll both be thinking I'm the pathetic head case who broke into her home looking for kidnappers!" She covered her face with her hands.

"Lana Samuels doesn't do her own grocery shopping," said Danish. "I know that for a fact. She has a French chef. Did you see her manicure? You can't cook with that."

146

"We need to establish some boundaries," said Nina. "I cannot be running around this island playing cops and robbers! I'm done with the Miss Marple. In fact, Miss Marple is a lot more dignified. She doesn't sneak into other people's homes at night. She sits in the parlor or at the captain's table on the luxury ocean liner sipping tea and knitting afghans. She keeps her mouth shut and waits for the clues to come to her. Let's try that approach."

"Who is Miss Marple? Some old lady in Maine?"

"Seriously, Danish. Let's give it a rest. This has gone too far."

Nina wondered what kind of an education he'd had in Colorado that enabled him to quote Ralph Waldo Emerson off the top of his head but didn't include any exposure to Agatha Christie. Maybe it was a generational thing.

"Whatever you say," he said, apparently unfazed by their encounter with Samuels. "What's really important is that the Samuelses' Zodiac boat is missing. It's a major breakthrough in the case. We didn't even have to ask. That clue walked right into the parlor."

They drove on in silence and arrived back at Nina's cottage. "Let's have some tea and maybe knit an afghan," said Danish. He walked right into the house, opened the fridge, and poured them each a glass of iced tea, then carried them out onto the veranda. Nina followed, still not speaking. Danish continued to build his theory.

"So, either Tiffany took the boat, or the person who took her from the Savages' house took the boat. It makes sense. The only getaway route is down by the beach. If they went out the front gate, Charlie would have seen them. There are sheer cliffs on the other side. According to my buddy Sam, who tends bar at the inn and goes out with Doreen, who works in the beauty salon, none of the neighbors recall hearing any vehicles on the road around nine o'clock Saturday night. If the cop parked out on the road had seen something, we would know it by now. The most logical escape route is by water."

"OK, Danish," said Nina. "Since we're sitting here safely sipping tea, why didn't Blue Roker and his officers notice the missing boat on Saturday night? He doesn't strike me as stupid or careless. Quite the opposite. One possible explanation is that it was there Saturday night and was taken sometime between then and last night, before we got there. If the boat had been there last night, we would have seen it. It wasn't. So why would the perpetrator wait to steal the boat?"

"Maybe they kept Tiffany nearby Saturday night, then moved her by boat later when the police were looking in a different place," said Danish.

"OK," said Nina. "Where could the kidnappers have kept Tiffany overnight without the police finding her?"

"Well, the villa next to the Samuelses belongs to the Davises. They're about a hundred years old, and I don't know what beef they could possibly have with Tiffany, except that she gets on everyone's nerves. They hang out with the crowd from the yacht club, not the Plantation Inn, and they have a big sailboat and a tender, so they wouldn't need the Samuelses' boat anyway. I think we can cross Mr. and Mrs. Davis off the list of suspects. Of course, Cynthia Davis's hookup with Barry puts a new twist on things, but I don't know what she would gain from offing Tiffany. Cynthia's already rich, and as far as I know, she only visits her parents a few weekends a year. She probably knows Barry about that well. I don't think she'd risk going to the slammer for him. *But*, the pink villa on the other side of the Davises is the house Lance and the rest of the Beer Commercial are renting for the winter."

"Really. That is very interesting," said Nina. "Especially in light of Lance's argument with Barry last night at The Redoubt. What was that all about? And why would Lance kidnap Tiffany?"

"Lance comes from a well-off family," said Danish, "but he's not rock-star-ruthless-real-estate-developer wealthy. Maybe he's a greedy boy. He's tasted the lifestyle of the very rich and famous, taught them how to whack a tennis ball, laughed at their jokes at the Plantation Inn bar, and shagged their wives. Now he wants to maintain the lifestyle to which he has become accustomed."

"OK, maybe. But the Bassetts' place is only about six or seven houses down the beach from Lance's rental. Also nearby. Barry could have done it and hidden her in his own house. The police would have been unlikely to search there Saturday night," said Nina.

"But if Barry wanted to get rid of Tiffany, why wouldn't he just wait until they got home? Or do it before they went to the party? Or go on a cruise and throw her off the ship one night? Why would anyone plan to commit a crime in a house with at least twenty-five potential witnesses, one of which is the chief of police? That sounds like the dumbest criminal ever," said Danish.

"I don't know," said Nina, "but he seems to have the strongest motive for getting rid of her. They didn't get along, and given the terms of their prenup, it was unlikely she was ever going to leave him. He couldn't have done it himself—he was on the terrace with the rest of us—but he could have hired someone to do it for him."

"Then why the ransom note?" asked Danish. "If he had her abducted and maybe even killed her, why send himself a ransom note?"

"To draw suspicion away from himself, I suppose," said Nina. "Maybe the same reason he staged it during the dinner."

"And how does Lance fit in? I'm confused," said Danish.

"Let's start again at the beginning. Who might have had a motive for kidnapping her, as well as the opportunity and the means?" asked Nina.

"I read that book, too," said Danish. "Motive, means, opportunity."

Nina ticked them off on her fingers. "There's Barry, the dissatisfied husband; Lance, the boy toy who maybe sees an opportunity to cash in on Tiffany's affections and her husband's wealth; there's Tiffany herself, doing a runner with the proceeds from the necklace to tide her over until she meets the next Barry. It's also possible that Tiffany and Lance planned it together so that they can ride off into the sunset, or that Barry and Tiffany cooked it up so that they could sell the necklace and still claim the insurance. What are their finances like, I wonder? A lot of wealthy people saw heaps of virtual money disappear in the recession. Or maybe Barry and Lance were in cahoots to get rid of her. A long shot is your boss, Michel, who hates Tiffany and accused her of damaging his business. Then there's the possibility that it's someone from her past and from Barry's business dealings who we don't know about. Everyone at the party seems to have had the same means and opportunity, but I can't think of anyone else with a motive."

Nina didn't say it, but of all the guests, Alice was the one who most easily could have taken the necklace. She could have slipped it into her evening bag while she was inside and then helped an accomplice abduct Tiffany—or worked with Tiffany to stage the room to look as if something violent had occurred. It seemed inconceivable that sweet, earnest Alice could have done it, but who knows what she had been involved in before she'd moved to Pineapple Cay a month ago? Blue Roker would have a blind spot where Alice was concerned. The neighbors always say, "They seemed so nice, the last person I would have suspected of doing such a thing."

Nina shook her head to shake out the terrible thoughts. She felt two-faced and mean-spirited even thinking them. She was getting carried away.

"OK, Danish. The armchair-detective stuff is entertaining, but seriously, I'm off the case. I'm returning to civilian life. I'm going to paint my kitchen and plant a vegetable garden and write the article I was hired to produce. So, please, drop by for an iced tea when you feel like it, but I'm done with Tiffany Bassett and the mystery of the *Morning Glory* emerald. OK?"

"All right, Nina, if you say so," said Danish. They sat quietly for a few minutes, looking out at the horizon; then Danish hopped to his feet.

"Let me make it up to you," he said. "My buddy Gerry loaned me his boat for the day. I was thinking of going over to Star Cay to do some sun and sand and snorkeling this aft. I asked Alice, but she said no. She didn't even say, 'No, I have to work,' just 'No.'" He looked glum for a moment.

"So, anyway, I've got the boat. Why don't you call Pansy and see if she wants to come along with her kids? We'll have a G-rated beach party. All child-friendly activities. No quasi-criminal behavior or private investigation. OK?"

Nina breathed in deeply and out slowly, releasing the tension that had built up since Barry had shown up with his bulldozer the day before. An afternoon of snorkeling with Pansy and a couple of sweet, innocent children—far from cheating husbands and wives and nasty chatter about the kidnapping—sounded idyllic.

"All right, Danish. That would be nice."

They called Pansy and arranged to meet her and the kids at the municipal dock in an hour, when school let out. Danish went home to get ready while Nina packed a cooler with sandwiches, lemonade, fruit, and coconut cookies. Then she strolled down to the dock to meet the others. Danish was already there, loading jugs of water into the boat.

"I've just got to get some snorkel gear from Gerry's shop, and then I'll be right back," he said as he headed back up the hill to the dive shop. Pansy arrived with her kids. The children were already wearing their life jackets and clutching junior-size snorkel gear in their hands.

"Hi, Nina! This will be fun!" said Pansy, cheerful as ever. The children stood looking up at Nina with big eyes. She smiled down at them. Out of the corner of her eye, she saw movement on the police dock a short distance away. It was Blue Roker, coming down from the police station with another officer. They were both dressed in navy-blue combat pants, dark T-shirts, rugged hiking boots, and shades. Roker had a ship-to-shore radio in his hand. *Where is he going dressed like that?* Nina wondered, hoping he hadn't seen her. She was still smarting from this morning's indignities.

Too late. He spotted them. He changed course and walked over to them.

"Hi, Blue! Beautiful day!" said Pansy, her eyes following her kids, who scampered down onto the beach, looking for interesting creatures under the dock. Blue removed his shades and stood in front of them with his hands on his hips. Danish reappeared, carrying a milk crate full of snorkels, fins, and masks, and stood beside Nina.

"Good afternoon, ladies. Jensen. I had a couple of surprising telephone calls from Lana and Delmont Samuels this morning," said Blue. "Also, a call from Barry Bassett late last night, ranting about prowlers and police incompetence." He looked back and forth from Nina to Danish for a couple of seconds, then spoke again.

"You seem like a nice person, Nina, and I understand that Barry and Tiffany Bassett have been harassing you since you arrived. But, please, both of you, let the police do our job. We're good at it. I assure you that modern policing technology has advanced beyond a reliance on Scotch tape and powdered ink from a printer cartridge." He glared at Danish a full three seconds before continuing.

"We have more resources at our disposal than you do, Mr. Jensen, and more experience catching bad guys. We will find Tiffany Bassett and prosecute whoever is responsible for her disappearance and for the theft of the necklace."

He shifted his gaze back at Nina. "I admire the fact that you braved the wrath of Lana Samuels and went to her place this morning to confess and apologize. That takes nerve and moral fortitude. I think we can attribute what happened last night to a temporary lapse in judgment. I have a pretty good idea who the ringleader of Operation Hot Tub was." He glared at Danish again.

"We've reviewed the surveillance-camera video from the recording studio. Yes, Mr. Jensen. Welcome to the twenty-first century. Also, we only found one set of prints in the studio, apart from those of Delmont

Samuels and his associates." He kept his eyes nailed on Danish for a moment and then shifted his gaze to take in both of them.

"Please, give up the sleuthing. Trespassing is against the law. Interfering with an ongoing investigation is a punishable offense. Kidnapping is a very serious crime. Whoever did this is not a nice person and is unlikely to put their hands up and surrender just because you say, 'Gotcha.' You could get hurt or worse."

Gesturing back and forth between Nina and Danish, Roker said, "I don't really understand this, but it worries me. Take my advice: Go home and relax. Do a bit of gardening. Don't go looking for trouble, OK?" He looked at both of them intently.

"Yes, Deputy Superintendent," said Nina, making a silent vow to do just what he said.

He started to go, then turned back and looked at Nina. "Ted should probably tell you this himself, but in case you're still anxious, he went to see his lawyer first thing this morning and got an injunction prohibiting Barry Bassett from proceeding with construction on the land adjacent to yours." He paused, then continued in a gentler tone. "I don't want to come down on you too hard over last night because I know you were deliberately provoked, and you were a little overwrought at the time, but I would be remiss if I did not point out that Ted accomplished this result by recourse to the legal process and not by tiptoeing around people's backyards."

He looked over at Danish. "You, on the other hand, I can't explain. Before you do something or say the first thing that pops into your head, ask yourself, 'What is the probable outcome of this action?' You might save yourself and the rest of us a lot of aggravation. Enjoy your afternoon, all of you," he said, then turned away. Roker walked back to the police boat in his smooth, stately glide, jumped in, and yanked the cord on the outboard motor. He put on his shades, raised his hand in parting, and peeled away from the wharf, heading out into the channel.

"Oh, my," said Pansy.

Danish threw down the crate in disgust. "What is wrong with you women? Get a grip! All he has to do is stand in front of you and flex his muscles, and you're all, 'Yes, Deputy Superintendent. Whatever you say.' You just set women's rights back twenty years! Pathetic. He sounds like my father." He picked up the crate again and loaded it and their various bags and backpacks into the boat.

"Call the rug rats, Pansy, and let's get over to Star Cay. I need some R & R," Danish said, starting the engine.

He had a point.

What is wrong with me? Nina thought as she watched Blue's boat disappear up the coast, leaving a trail of white froth in its wake. Her marriage had barely gone cold, and already she was checking out the local talent? For the past three months in a city of close to nine million people, she hadn't been aware of a single man she'd passed on the teeming sidewalks. In the midst of forced conversations with the nice-enough and allegedly interesting male acquaintances Louise dredged up for mandatory nights out, all Nina could think about was how soon she could go home, put on her pajamas, and watch Cary Grant movies in bed.

Her hormones seemed to be thawing out rapidly in the tropical sun. Her radar had picked up not one, but two attractive men on Pineapple Cay—population five thousand—in the last week alone.

Yes, get a grip, Nina, she told herself, *before you do something embarrassing. Well, even more embarrassing than being an accomplice to vandalizing a hot tub.* She shook her head to clear it and focused on the other thing that bugged her about that whole exchange.

"Is there no such thing as privacy in this village?" she asked, still smarting over being described as overwrought. "I have a brief crying spell, and the chief of police is notified? In New York, thieves could break into your apartment, be filmed on a security camera stealing everything you own, you could track them down and give the police their address, and *still* the police wouldn't do anything about it because they'd have ten stabbings and a couple of shootings to deal with first that night. I heard about a case like that on NPR."

"Well, you could think of it as a positive attribute of small-town life, rather than a drawback," said Pansy. "At least you know people are looking out for you, even if they're also just watching you . . . Have you been upset?" she asked, putting her arm around Nina. "Are you OK now? What was Blue talking about?"

"I'm fine, Pansy, thanks," said Nina. She filled Pansy in on Barry's fried-chicken drive-through and mini golf project, as well as her argument with him, as they motored across the bay.

"He can't do that. Don't worry," said Pansy. "He has to get approval from the village council first, and they won't give it."

Star Cay was a little island about a mile offshore from Pineapple Cay. It curved around a protected, shallow lagoon. A handful of vacation villas dotted the shore, and a snack bar and some picnic tables occupied one end of the beach. Danish pulled the boat up on the sand near the snack bar. There were maybe a couple of dozen other people on the beach, including a group of teenagers playing beach volleyball.

Nina, Danish, Pansy, and the kids took their picnic and snorkel gear and walked a short distance down the beach to a more secluded spot. Danish lay back on the sand with his head on a life jacket and went to sleep. Pansy spread out her towel, lay on her stomach, and started reading a magazine. Nina played beach-ball soccer with the kids and floated lazily in the water while they chugged around her with their snorkels and fins on. After a while, Nina, Pansy, and the children ate cheese sandwiches and watermelon, and then the kids ran off to chase hermit crabs with several kids they knew from school.

Danish awoke abruptly, sat up, and picked up the conversation where they'd left off before he conked out. "Did you hear what Roker said, Nina?" he asked. "Only one set of prints in the studio, apart from the Samuelses'."

"I'm pretty sure he was referring to yours, Danish," said Nina, lying back on her towel with her eyes closed.

"Duh. Got that," said Danish. "What I'm referring to is the absence of any other prints, i.e., the kidnappers. Unless they wiped off theirs but left the Samuelses', which is impossible, they weren't in there. But if they weren't there, where were they while they waited for the right moment to nab Tiffany, and where were they before they took the boat sometime, which must have been between Saturday night and last night? It had to be somewhere nearby."

"OK, tell me what the two of you were up to last night. Blue was a little bit stern with both of you," interjected Pansy.

"Oh, Pansy, you don't want to hear this," said Nina, but Danish told her anyway.

"Oh, my!" said Pansy. "Well, no surprise Lana Samuels wasn't happy. I sold them that house, and when I was showing it to them, she said she needed a room big enough for a dance studio because she gets up every morning at five o'clock and does two hours of ballet practice, followed by a soak in an outdoor hot tub and an herbal massage. She said it was 'essential.' So, you're trying to find Tiffany's kidnappers?"

"No!" said Nina.

"You bet!" said Danish at the same time.

"Danish," said Nina, "we're monumentally unqualified to be amateur sleuths. Even in mystery novels, the person solving the case is usually an ex-cop or ex-soldier with some useful crime-solving skills, as well as a friend who owes him one in the police department. We, on the other hand, just got told off by the police for vandalizing the hot tub of a nice-ish man who has nothing to do with the recent kidnapping. You're a certified yoga instructor-bartender-mail carrier, and I teach sociology and write travel articles!"

"What about old Miss Marple? I'm not as dumb as you think I am. I have a library card and watch PBS when there's nothing else on. I'm also a certified massage therapist and a nutrition counselor. And I took a course in hypnotism in Boulder. For smoking-cessation therapy, but it's a transferable skill. That could come in handy. And a semester of tai chi," said Danish.

"Tai chi. Isn't that what old people do in the park that looks like they're running in slow motion?" asked Nina.

"It is an ancient martial art. Same as karate," said Danish.

"When did you get a library card?" asked Nina.

"That is insulting!" said Danish. "I went there with Alice last week when she got hers, and I checked out a big stack of books."

Pansy's two children had come back and were standing at the edge of the towels, watching Nina and Danish silently.

Uh-oh, thought Nina.

"I apologize, Danish," she said in a calm voice, smiling at the kids. "Yes, reading is a wonderful pastime. Once you learn to read, the whole world opens up to you. Hours of adventure await. I'm just commenting on the fact that we've been . . . conducting surveillance. We have stumbled upon two . . . romantic encounters, an argument, and a missing boat, and I still don't have a clue what's going on. Tiffany Bassett could be on the moon or floating down the Yangtze River on a raft, for all we know."

The kids lost interest and wandered away to build a sand castle.

Pansy tapped her finger on her lips. "*Hmm.* It does seem strange that Barry should be trying to build a fried-chicken restaurant, taking people out to dinner, and then going to see his mistress, all just the day after he gets a threatening ransom note from his wife's kidnappers. Even if he doesn't care who took her, or if he *did* do it, you'd think he'd at least try to look innocent."

"What really puzzles me is Lance," said Nina. "He and Tiffany seemed really . . . enamored of each other. Could a person really behave like that and then act like he doesn't care when she's kidnapped? Or even kidnap and kill her himself, just for the money? And what were he and Barry arguing about? Maybe Lance killed her for Barry, and they're fighting over money. Or maybe he found out that Barry killed her—or Barry found out Lance took her."

"OK. What've we got?" said Danish, springing to his feet and pacing back and forth in front of Nina and Pansy.

"There's Barry, Lance, and Tiffany. Each of whom could have organized the whole thing themselves with hired help or by working together in some combo. Then there's the rival salvager and the Russian mob, both with access to boats to land undetected on the beach at the Savages'. Motive for all the above: money. Anyone else?"

"Well, there's Michel . . . His feud with Barry about the runway could be motivation, and he definitely hates Tiffany, but how could abducting her really help his cause other than to keep Tiffany out of the inn?" said Nina.

"I can't see it," said Danish. "The whole thing is way too undignified for Michel. I say we take him off the list."

Pansy nodded. "OK, well where does that leave us?"

"The conclusion is . . . people do some crazy, messed-up stuff," said Danish.

"Yeah," said Nina. "Well, as a wise woman once said, the sun is shining and the birds are singing, so let's enjoy it! Anyone want an ice cream cone?" she called to the kids. They jumped up and down enthusiastically and they all walked over to the snack bar.

~

The next day, Nina woke up early, had her coffee on the veranda, as had become her morning routine, and then spent a couple of hours painting her living room walls a nice bright white. It was very satisfying. She scrubbed the floors, thinking she might paint them white, blue, or a nice soft green rather than sand and varnish them. She'd have to think about it. She was thinking about tackling the cupboards when, for the first time since she'd moved in, her phone rang. It took her a moment to find it, following the old-fashioned ring to a vintage black rotary telephone on the floor beside the bed. She picked up the heavy handset and said hello.

"Hello, Nina? It's Pansy. I've found a clue!" Pansy squealed.

"What do you mean? Where are you?" asked Nina.

"I'm in The Enclave. I was showing rentals to a client who's looking for a long-term lease beginning in May. We were in that big pink villa that's being rented by Lance Redmond and his friends. I'd arranged with one of the girls to come by this morning while they were all out. There are three bedrooms upstairs, which are being used by the three couples—the closets and en suite bathrooms are filled with men's and women's clothing and toiletries. But the bedroom on the bottom floor is just Lance's. All that was in there were tennis rackets, a pile of sweaty athletic wear, *and . . . and* a *pink satin bra, cup size 85F,* on the bathroom floor! That's a French size. I'd bet money that it belongs to Tiffany. I know for a fact that Loretta the cleaning lady does Lance's house on Saturday afternoons. She's very thorough. She would never have left dirty laundry in the middle of the bathroom floor. That means Tiffany must have been there sometime after five o'clock on Saturday! And since we saw her at the Savages' at five o'clock on Saturday, it had to have been after that! After she was abducted! Lance must be involved! She must have spent Saturday night in his room! I'm almost at your place. Hold on."

Nina heard Pansy's cart outside and a knock on the door. She went to let her in. Pansy was breathless, her eyes shining. She was clutching her large purse in front of her.

"I've got it in my purse!" she said.

"Pansy, if you're right, that's evidence!" said Nina.

"I know," said Pansy. "That's why I picked it up with the end of a pencil and put it in a plastic bag. I always carry one in my purse— a habit from when the kids were being toilet trained. I waited until my client went into the next room and grabbed it." She opened her purse and pulled out a resealable bag with a bundle of pink satin in it. She held it up, and they both looked at it like it might have more to tell them.

"Yo! Anybody home?" It was Danish. He knocked once and then walked right into the kitchen where they were standing.

"What is that?" he asked.

"Tiffany's bra, we think," said Pansy. She excitedly recounted her morning's activities.

"This could be proof that Lance abducted her!" said Pansy. "He took her from the Savages' house to his place, which is only three houses away, and kept her there overnight. Maybe he let her have a shower. When he hustled her off to a more secure location on Sunday using Delmont Samuels's boat, her bra was left behind in the rush."

"I can tell you one thing," said Danish. "Tiffany Bassett was not wearing a bra on Saturday night."

"How do you know she wasn't wearing a bra?" asked Pansy. Danish just looked at her.

"You know, he's right," said Nina. "She was wearing that low-cut, halter-neck dress. If she'd been wearing this bra, the straps would have shown. So, how did it get on Lance's floor? Maybe he decided not to wallow in his grief and has moved on, like Barry did. It could belong to someone else."

"I know how we can establish if it's hers!" squealed Pansy. Then she looked at Nina with a suddenly somber expression. "I'm sorry, Nina. I'm afraid I'm going to have to expose you to another seedy aspect of Pineapple Cay. There's a waterfront bar down island a few miles. The Pirate's Wake. They have a rather tacky tradition of decorating the walls with women's underwear. I heard Tiffany in the coffee shop one day, telling how she had gone there on a wild night out with some friends visiting from Miami and nailed one of her bras to the wall. Pure silk from France, she said. We need to compare sizes. Let's go."

She headed for the door.

"Pansy!" said Nina. "If any of that is true, we need to hand it over to the police!"

"I know, I know," said Pansy. "We'll drop it off on the way. I just wanted to show you. We'll just need to look for a French size 85F in silk on the wall."

They piled into Pansy's cart.

"Nina, you drive. I'm too nervous," said Pansy. Nina got behind the wheel of the miniature car and turned the key, which Pansy had left in the ignition. She pressed the accelerator and twisted the steering wheel. The cart lurched out onto the road. It was like driving a fancy go-cart. Fun. She decided to look into getting one.

She rolled to a stop in front of the police station. Pansy hopped out, clutching her purse in front of her. She hurried up the walk and into the police station, glancing over her shoulder as she slipped inside. She was back out in three minutes, walking quickly to the cart and jumping in.

"Go, Nina! Let's get out of here," she said breathlessly.

Nina obeyed her, stepping on the accelerator and speeding down the main street while a couple of people on the sidewalk stopped and turned to watch them whizzing out of town in the golf cart.

"Was Blue angry?" asked Nina, glancing over.

"I don't know," said Pansy. "I didn't stay long. I just put the bag on his desk and told him where I got it and what I told you about Loretta. He just stood there leaning against the front of his desk with his arms crossed, looking at me. He didn't say anything. Then I left."

"So, why are we running away?" asked Nina.

"The bank is right across the street from the police station. I didn't want Andrew to look out and see me coming out of there. He'd ask me what I was doing," said Pansy.

"Take your next right," said Danish from the backseat. Nina turned onto a one-lane paved road and followed it past a few concrete block buildings to the waterfront. There was a blue cement building straight ahead, with a covered patio overlooking the water and a flimsy-looking wooden pier with a boat tied to it. A giant beer sign stood on the roof. Danish pushed open the door, and Nina and Pansy followed him inside.

The interior was cool and dark, a sharp contrast to the brilliant hot sunshine outside. The footing seemed uneven. Nina looked down and realized that the floor was sand. The front of the bar was open to the covered patio. A couple of men were playing a slow-moving game of pool with the turquoise sea behind them. A bar counter ran along the back wall, and a man stood behind it, looking at them. Another man, who sat on a stool at the bar, was also looking at them. There was no one else in the bar. Sure enough, almost every square inch of space on the walls was covered with women's undergarments in various colors and fabrics. They hung from the low ceiling as well. Nina could smell burned vegetable oil in a deep fryer somewhere out back.

"Danish," said Nina, "why don't you go order a drink and talk to those guys while Pansy and I look for the goods. We don't need an audience." As soon as Danish had engaged the men at the bar, Nina and Pansy looked around, wondering where to start. There were hundreds.

"I'll look on that side, and why don't you do this side," said Nina. "Hopefully it's not on the ceiling. She crossed the room and started systematically reviewing the items on the far wall. She was about halfway along it when she heard Pansy squeal.

"I found it! Nina, Danish!"

Nina and Danish hotfooted it over to where she stood pointing at a raspberry silk brassiere that was surely custom-made to fit a figure that nature did not produce. Pansy flipped over the label with the eraser end of a pencil. 85F, La Belle France.

"Bingo," said Danish, taking a drink from his beer. "Exhibit B." He took out his cell phone and snapped a picture of it.

"OK. So now we know that much," said Nina. "Let's get out of here."

"Hey, what're you all doing over there?" called the bartender.

Nina and Pansy froze. Danish walked back to the bar.

"That red . . . undergarment over there on the wall. That belongs to the woman who was kidnapped last Saturday," Danish said.

"Yeah, that's right," said the man at the bar. "She wanted to put it up there herself. Came here with a bunch of crazy drunk women a while back. Started asking me for a pair of my *tighty-whities* to hang up, too. Nobody wants to look at men's shorts. That's unappetizing."

They were all quiet for a moment, wondering where the conversation could possibly go from there.

"Actually, she was here on Friday night, the day before she was kidnapped. With a young fella. Hands all over each other, sitting here at the bar. He came by boat. She was driving that big Mercedes of hers. She had a little pink suitcase with her. When they finished their smoochy smoochy in the parking lot, he left with it in the boat. I didn't ask. People do some strange things. It's generally best not to get involved. But I do know it wasn't her husband. He's the angry rich fella who threw a perfectly good club into a water hazard ahead of me on the golf course one day. She was there then, too."

"What did the young guy look like?" asked Pansy.

"A slick city boy. Living large on Daddy's dime. Bit taller than him, styled hair," said the bartender, pointing at Danish with his chin.

"Sounds like Lance," said Danish.

"Have you seen any of them since Saturday?" asked Nina.

"Nope," said the man. "Good thing, too. We don't need trash like that lowering the tone around here. This is a respectable establishment."

They walked out to the cart.

"We need to tell Blue Roker what he just told us," said Nina. "It sounds like Tiffany and Lance were planning to go away together and didn't want anyone—including Barry—to know about it."

Pansy looked worried. Danish crossed his arms and looked away.

"I'll do it," said Nina. "Just drop me in front of the station." Nothing good could come from putting Danish in front of Blue. Pansy rolled to a stop a half block from the station. Danish and Nina hopped out.

"I'm going to The Redoubt to regroup," said Danish. "I'll be there if you want to debrief after the mission."

"Thanks, Nina," said Pansy. "You're right. The police should know about this. Let me know if you need help. I'll see you later—I've got to go to the grocery store, then pick up my kids from school. If they only knew what Mommy has been up to today! Solving crimes!"

Nina walked up the path and through the arched doorway into the station. She found herself in a small reception area. She approached the long counter, and a young male officer in a crisp khaki uniform got up from his desk and came over to her.

"May I help you?" he asked Nina.

"Um, I was wondering if I might speak to Deputy Superintendent Roker for a moment," she replied.

"May I ask what it concerns?" he asked.

"Thanks, Jackson. I'll take it from here." Roker's deep voice came from directly behind Nina. She turned around to face him. He had just come in the front door. He removed his cap and wiped his brow. He was dressed in navy-blue pants and a navy-blue T-shirt with *POLICE* written in white capital letters on the back.

"Good day to you, Nina. What can I do for you?" he asked. Polite but no smile.

"Well . . . " She hesitated, uncertain of how to begin. He pursed his lips slightly, then opened a metal door in the wall beside the counter and gestured for her to go through it.

"Let's go to my office," he said, leading her through the open office behind the counter, where a couple of officers, including Jackson, sat at metal desks, to the back of the room. Like Ted, he looked slightly out of place indoors—a tall, well-muscled man in a flimsy cage. He opened a door to a cluttered office with a large window that overlooked the water and the police dock. He left the door ajar and gestured for her to sit down in the chair facing his desk. He sat in his chair behind the desk and looked at her patiently, waiting for her to speak.

Nina quickly scanned his office. A neat desk, but ragged piles of papers, file folders, and coil-bound reports on every other flat surface. Dusty stacks of loose paper, edges curled by the sunlight. A couple of vinyl chairs, a low, sagging bookcase under the window. A nautical chart of Pineapple Cay on the wall behind his desk. Two framed diplomas next to it. One from the police academy, the other a bachelor of science degree from the University of the West Indies. No family photos.

"OK, Deputy Superintendent Roker . . . Blue," she began. "I think Pansy was here to see you earlier today and dropped off . . . a piece of evidence she found in the course of her work as a real estate agent."

She paused and looked at him. He silently gazed at her, his eyes searingly blue. She took a deep breath and let it out slowly, then continued.

"This morning, Pansy, Danish, and I were in a bar south of town." That sounded bad, she thought. Who goes to a seedy bar in the middle of a weekday morning? But she plowed on.

"Anyway, the gentleman who runs the bar, The Pirate's Wake, told us that Tiffany Bassett and Lance Redmond, or someone who fits his description, were in the bar together the night before she went missing." She told him about the separate car, the boat, and the small pink suitcase.

"Also, um, I think you will find that the . . . undergarment . . . Pansy brought to you this morning is the same . . . unusual . . . size as a raspberry silk item hanging on the wall at The Pirate's Wake, put there by Tiffany Bassett. Maybe you could run some DNA tests on it or something . . ."

Her voice trailed off, and she looked away, then back at him. She was acutely aware of the ridiculousness of the situation. How did her daydream of easy living in the islands get so far off track? He sat silently looking at her, his expression unreadable. Finally, he sighed.

"So. Operation Hot Tub has been superseded by Operation Ladies' Underwear," he said. "May I ask what line of work you were in, in New York, Nina?"

"I was a college instructor," she mumbled. It seemed a like hundred years ago, back when she was far more mature. "I'm really not actively trying to find Tiffany Bassett. Things just seem to happen in my vicinity. I'm here telling you. Isn't that good?"

"So, you and Pansy and Danish Jensen just decided to drop into The Pirate's Wake for a drink and to admire the interior decor before Pansy went to pick up her kids at school?" he said, with just a hint of exasperation detectable in his voice.

"Well, not exactly," said Nina, squirming a bit in her seat. "But we didn't ask the bartender about Tiffany and Lance being there together," she said, mentally blocking out the fact that Danish had asked the bartender about Tiffany. "He—I think he's the owner—brought up all the stuff about the boat and the suitcase and Tiffany and Lance arriving and leaving separately."

"All right, Nina. I don't know what to say. I can't build a case for fraud, kidnapping, or murder, if that's what we are now dealing with, based on Tiffany Bassett's bra size." Blue Roker paused and leaned forward in his chair, elbows on the desk, looking directly at her. She felt herself falling into the icy blue depths of his eyes. Oh, how she hated to disappoint him. But she thought she saw the ice melt a little.

"I shouldn't tell you this, but I want to impress upon you the importance of not getting involved in this any more than you already have. I want you to understand that we, a team of trained professionals, are working the case 'round the clock." He paused and looked intently at her for a moment.

He must know what effect he has on women, Nina thought. *He definitely puts it to work.*

"We have reason to believe that Barry Bassett may be involved in his wife's disappearance. The ransom note he gave us was a fake, written on paper from his own office. We've been monitoring his calls, and in the past few days since his wife's disappearance, he has made several to the number of a known criminal in Miami. Someone involved in organized crime with a history of violence. So, please, let it go, all right?" Blue said, rising and coming around the desk to stand in front of her.

She stood up to face him. He was in her personal space, but she didn't back away. He didn't, either.

"Look, Blue," said Nina, "I'm embarrassed by the whole Delmont Samuels incident. But I haven't actually done anything since then. Neither has Pansy. She was showing a house. Danish, well, Danish . . . has hopefully moved on. But I was right to tell you about The Pirate's Wake, wasn't I? You didn't know about the rendezvous with Lance, the boat, and the pink suitcase, did you?"

He put his hands in his pockets and leaned back against his desk. "This is a small island, Nina. I imagine a lot of people knew that Tiffany Bassett was carrying on with Lance Redmond. But, no, you are right, I did not know about the suitcase exchange on Friday, so I thank you for coming forward with the information. I'll show you out."

Nina felt his eyes on her back as she walked to the counter. Blue reached forward and opened the door, then stood holding it for her. In the reception area, they stood together for a second, and again he stood close to her. He was several inches taller than she was, and she had to look up to see his face.

"OK, well, bye, Blue," said Nina, turning to leave. He caught her gently by the arm.

"Nina, please take care. This game you are playing is not worth getting hurt over. Surely that's not why you moved here." He held her eyes for a moment, then let her go. He nodded slightly and went back through the metal door. She watched him cross the inner office in smooth, unhurried strides, then disappear behind the closed door of his office.

~

That afternoon, Nina resolved to take Blue Roker's advice and mind her own business. She and Pansy and Danish had gotten carried away that morning, barging into The Pirate's Wake and asking questions, gathering evidence from a possible crime scene, and offering unsolicited advice to the police. Blue was right. Time to take a step back.

Nina made a pitcher of iced tea and dug out the home-renovation magazines she'd bought in the airport on her flight down to Pineapple Cay just over a week ago. She took her tea, the pile of magazines, and a notebook out onto the veranda and spent a very pleasant hour leafing through photographs of inviting living rooms, kitchens, bathrooms, and bedrooms—none of which had piles of unfolded laundry on the bed or dirty dishes stacked on the counter. She sketched her plans and made notes, looking out at the water from time to time. The novelty and surprise of finding herself here, with a backyard filled with palm trees, white sand, and turquoise water, had not worn off.

After her second glass of iced tea, she stood up and stretched her arms above her head. She thought of going over to the inn to see if she could catch an afternoon yoga class, but then she thought better of it. Maybe she could use a Danish-free afternoon. Instead, she checked her e-mail, where she found a message from Louise complaining about the cold, damp weather in New York and asking when she could come stay with Nina, as well as one from her mother asking when Nina was coming home for a visit.

She decided to stroll back into the village and pick up some sand-paper for the floorboards and maybe some seedlings for the flower beds, and then she'd get down to work on the article she'd been hired to write about the *Morning Glory* emerald and the Pineapple Cay Museum.

She walked barefoot into town along the beach, carrying her flip-flops on one finger. A fisherman stood at the wooden table at the end of the municipal wharf, gutting fish and throwing the discarded parts into the water. A flock of seagulls circled above him, diving to the surface of the water to retrieve the bits of fish. The mail boat had come in, so the waterfront was bustling. Nina slipped on her flip-flops when she reached The Redoubt and went up the side of the building to the street.

In front of the hardware store were the trays of bedding plants Nina had remembered from her last shopping trip to town. She didn't know much about tropical flowers, so she spent some time reading the little plastic stakes in each pot, which had descriptions of the plants and information on how to care for them printed in tiny letters. She chose a frangipani in a large tub and a purple hibiscus, then went inside to look for some sandpaper.

"You're back again!" said the older man who shuffled out from the back room when she pushed open the door and set the string of bells hanging on it tinkling.

"Yes. Hi," said Nina. "I just bought a house, and I'm doing some painting and general fixing up."

"You've moved into Miss Rose's house," said the man.

Of course he knows that, thought Nina. She held out her hand. "Hello. I'm Nina."

"I know. Nice to meet you. I'm Harold. Would you believe, I'm seventy-three years old, and Miss Rose was my first-grade teacher. I adored her. We all did. She taught me how to read. I'm dyslexic, and nobody really knew what that was in those days. She figured out how to help me, and she came to my house after dinner to work with me. When I read my first story out loud, my mama cried. It was all thanks to Miss Rose. She was something special. Now how can I help you?"

Nina told him what she needed, then paid for the sandpaper and plants and walked down the sidewalk and across the street, taking the path to the beach beside The Redoubt. As she passed, she glanced up at the deck and saw the young bride from the plane. She was sitting at a table under an umbrella, sipping a top-heavy tropical cocktail and contentedly leafing through a magazine. Nina looked around for the woman's new husband, wondering as she did it why she cared if they were getting along. There he was, standing waist deep in the water, wearing a snorkel and mask and holding a fishing spear in one raised hand, looking down at the water. Good. Everybody was happy doing their own thing together.

Nina walked home along the beach, thinking about the woman whose house she'd bought. Then she spent the rest of the afternoon sitting at her kitchen table with her notes on the *Morning Glory* and the history of Pineapple Cay, writing the magazine article. At about five o'clock, she turned off her laptop; stretched her arms, legs, and back; and got out the drink-recipe book Louise had given her, flipping through the pages for something new to try. She landed on something called navy grog. She topped it with a little paper umbrella and carried it out onto the veranda to watch the sunset.

She sat on the step, with her feet in the warm sand. Out on the point, she could see that Ted's guests had gathered—some sitting, some standing along the rail. She thought she could make out his tall form and broad-brimmed hat. She put down her glass and walked barefoot down to the beach and into the surf. The water curled around her ankles. She watched the waves wash up and back over her feet for a few minutes, dragging the sand back and forth with them. Then she strolled back up to her veranda, rinsing her feet in the dishpan full of water she'd finally gotten around to putting on the step to keep the sand out of her house.

There was a violent pounding on the front door, and she looked through the window into her house to see Danish striding into her living room. She made a mental note to resume locking her door.

"Nina! Where are you?" he called. She tapped on the glass. He came out onto the veranda.

"Something very interesting and potentially alarming happened this afternoon," he said, sinking into a chair. She reluctantly lowered herself into the other one and waited for him to continue.

"I delivered a package to Barry Bassett. A large, heavy box from Miami. What do you think of that?" he said, and sat back, watching her.

"Is that noteworthy?" asked Nina. "Didn't you tell me that Tiffany Bassett ordered from mail-order catalogs all the time?"

"This was addressed to Barry. See, Josie, who works at the front desk at the inn, has a sister named Susan, who works at Island Tel. Susan told Josie—who told me—that Blue requested Barry's phone records, and that he seemed very interested in several calls to a number in Miami. Miami, where it is possible to get a gun without too much hassle. The package could be a gun. It was heavy enough," said Danish.

So, the bush telegraph was up to speed on Barry's contact with a criminal in Miami. Still, chastened by her conversation with Blue, Nina didn't want to encourage Danish to pursue things any further. "Oh, Danish, we let things get out of hand this morning. It was my fault, but let's let it go, OK? Anyway, if it was a gun, wouldn't the customs officials have noticed? Don't you think the police are watching deliveries to his house? He could have ordered a croquet set. Also heavy."

"Only if a croquet set fits in a box six inches wide and three inches tall, because that's how big it was."

"My point is it could be anything," said Nina. "I'm sorry, but I'm rapidly losing interest in the life and times of Tiffany and Barry Bassett. I hardly know them, and I do not like them. I do like Blue Roker, and I intend to do what he asked us to do—which is stay out of his way. I'm sorry."

Danish sat quietly for a moment. "It may surprise you to learn that the post office does not open every package it receives to see what's in it. Maybe tomorrow you'll be more interested. My shift at The Redoubt starts in a half hour, so I'd better get going. See you tomorrow, Nina. Alice's Treasure Hunt, remember?" he said, standing up.

Nina walked him to the door. "I'll be there. 'Night, Danish. See you tomorrow." She smiled at him to show they were still friends.

The sun was huge and orange now, and it was dropping fast. She sat on the step with her eyes focused on the horizon, determined to see the green flash if it was on tap tonight. The last sliver of the sun sank below the horizon and the sky was purple, then blue, then black. No green flash.

As she sat there, the stars came out, first one at a time, then in glittering clusters. She looked at the stars and listened to the waves for a while, and then she went inside, took a long bath with a candle burning on the side of the tub, and crawled into bed with a book.

10

Saturday dawned bright and sunny on Pineapple Cay. The residents of Coconut Cove and other island settlements converged in the town center. The harbor was full of sailboats. Alice and Kiki had succeeded in creating a buzz for the treasure hunt. *One good thing about people in small towns,* thought Nina, *is that they always turn out for events.*

And it wasn't just residents—the yachting set was up for a good time, too. There was a festive atmosphere in the air as Nina strolled downtown to have a cup of coffee at the bakery. She sat and read the paper, watching the village fill up with Saturday-morning shoppers and fun seekers. About ten o'clock, she gathered up her things and strolled over to the museum to see what was going on.

A raised wooden platform had been set up in front of the museum. A children's school choir was on stage warbling the big smash hit from the latest blockbuster kids' movie. It looked like Jules Savage had been recruited to serve as master of ceremonies. As the children finished their song and the crowd applauded politely, he bounded up onto the platform and strutted across the front of the stage—microphone in hand, pink linen shirt open at the neck, mirrored shades glinting in the sunlight. The children, dressed in their best clothes, shuffled nervously on the risers behind him. The girls sported elaborate hairstyles of neat braids tied with brightly colored ribbons and baubles. The boys stood stiff-backed, with their arms straight down at their sides, as if they had been told not to wrinkle their shirts. Some of the children stared straight ahead, ignoring the rock star striding back and forth in front of them and yelling at the crowd, his free arm pointing skyward, then panning across the crowd left to right, then windmilling—in a stylized semaphore that Nina guessed he'd developed to be visible from the cheap seats of a packed stadium. Some of the children tracked his movements with big eyes.

"*Hellooo,* fellow Pineapples! Good citizens of Coconut Cove! Good morning, you hungover and or possibly already juiced-up tourists! Not being too loud for you, am I? Hello, you beautiful fruit salad you! Are you ready to have a good time?" Jules shouted to the crowd from the front of the stage. The throng on the grass in front of the stage hooted and clapped their hands.

"Let's hear it for the band! That was a helluva tune! Well done!" He turned around to face the children and applauded them. The crowd joined in enthusiastically. Some of the children smiled; others continued to stare at him, wide-eyed. Jules turned back to face the crowd.

"All right, people, listen up. Your Pineapple Cay Museum has organized a smashing weekend of hijinks for you to celebrate our island heritage. We've got a treasure hunt for the kiddies starting very shortly, to be followed by games and treats and face painting. And look at that pirate ship, eh? I can't wait to give that a go myself." The small children in the audience began to vibrate in anticipation. Jules could still work a crowd.

He continued. "You big kids get your chance at a treasure hunt this afternoon, and you will not want to miss the fabulous Sundowners performing for your pleasure on the waterfront tonight! Come ready to dance! My man Sammy is setting up the jerk pit over there—hey, Sammy!—and Veronica's serving a special Blackbeard Burger with a side salad of locally grown mixed greens and her secret spicy salad dressing all day at The Redoubt. Buns kindly donated by the gals at the bakery. Good on you, ladies! The libations will be flowing all over town. No comment. Don't drink and drive. Golf-cart owners and dinghies, that includes you lot. And to give you the lowdown on the rules of the game, please welcome to the stage the cur-a-tor of the Pineapple Cay Museum, the lovely Miss Alice *Rollllle!*"

Alice stepped up onto the stage and walked tentatively to the center where Jules stood, clapping his hands. They both stood watching as the children's choir shuffled slowly off the stage, row by row. When they'd gone, he lowered the microphone stand for her and stepped back.

"Good morning, everyone," she said into the microphone, holding her notes with both hands. "I am so glad to see you all here. Thank you for coming. The children's treasure hunt will be starting over by the statue of Pompey in about ten minutes. For everyone else: please enjoy the coffee and cinnamon buns kindly provided to us by the Plantation Inn, and come inside the museum and have a look around. Free admission today. The adults' treasure hunt will start right here at one o'clock sharp. We have thirteen teams registered so far, and it's not too late to get a crew together. Competitors: please identify yourselves when I call out your team name."

The crowd of spectators was beginning to separate into little blocks of color as the families with small children threaded their way through the throng over to the statue of Pompey, and the adult treasure-hunt teams began to group themselves together in distinct units recognizable by their team T-shirts.

Andrew went off with the children; and Nina, Pansy, and Danish stood wearing tie-dyed T-shirts with *Peanut Butter on Toast* written across the chest in spidery black letters. They had been provided by Danish. "Leftover merch from my band in Boulder," he'd said by way of explanation as he'd handed them out.

"OK!" said Alice into the microphone. "Representing our local bank, the Loan Sharks!" A team of five bank employees in crisp, blue corporate T-shirts clapped their hands enthusiastically. The crowd of spectators cheered them loudly.

"From Pineapple Cay Comprehensive School, twelve equally fierce competitors: the High School Girls' Sailing Team and the High School Boys' Sailing Team! Yeah!" The girls and boys hooted at one another from their positions on opposite sides of the lawn. Their teenage supporters shouted and clapped and stamped their feet in an effort to drown the other side out. Alice watched, smiling for a moment, then raised her hand to ask for quiet.

"We also have the Smooth Harbour Raiders, and team Family Business is representing three generations of the Dixon family, from right here in Coconut Cove!" The crowd cheered enthusiastically.

"From Matthews Bonefish Lodge, we welcome the Sole Sisters and Their Token Male." Five middle-aged women and a young man—all in Matthews Bonefish Lodge khaki T-shirts and broad-brimmed sun hats—hooted and laughed. Nina guessed they were the nonfishing spouses of Ted's clients having some fun while their partners were out fishing.

"The God Squad is representing the Saint Mark's Church youth group." Alice continued to shout out the names of the competitors. "From the Pineapple Cay Brewing Company, the Brew Crew! Welcome, also, to Scottie and the Hotties, the Clues Brothers, and the Pleasure Hunters!" Three groups of yachties raised their arms and howled as their team names were called.

"Finally, we have the Wrecking Crew and . . . Peanut Butter on Toast." Alice paused for a second, studying the paper in front of her quizzically, then looked up at the crowd again, smiling broadly.

Lance Redmond and the rest of the too-cool-for-school Beer Commercial howled ironically in their matching black T-shirts when Alice introduced the Wrecking Crew, and then they immediately resumed their poses in the *lying on the grass* tableau they had formed upon slinking casually onto the lawn during the children's perfor-mance. Pansy clapped enthusiastically, and Danish howled without irony, hands clasped in a victory salute above his head, when Alice read their team name. Several members of the Beer Commercial snickered contemptuously.

Like the Wrecking Crew showed any great depth of imagination. What is Lance doing here? Nina wondered. If you were having a torrid affair with a married woman and her kidnappers were threatening to kill her if a ransom wasn't paid, would you be lying back on the grass with your friends, sipping a latte? And if you were the kidnapper, wouldn't you have other things on your to-do list for the day?

"Good luck to all competitors, large and small!" said Alice from the stage. She glanced over to where Kiki was supervising the youngest children, who were now clutching the handles of plastic buckets in their small fists and running around in random directions under the trees, looking for things on their lists.

"Here are the rules of the game," continued Alice. "There are eight clues in all. Each will lead you to the next clue on the list. At each location, you will find a stash of gold coins—not real—and the next clue. Please take one coin only and write down the clue, leaving the original for the next team that comes along. Please refrain from using the Internet to solve the clues. This is all for fun and for a good cause, after all, right?" She paused for a moment, then continued.

"We will do four clues today and four tomorrow. Each team will be timed, so when you have collected the last gold coin for today, hurry back here to get your time recorded. The team that collects all eight gold coins in the shortest time wins. We're grateful to the Plantation Inn for providing our grand prize of dinner in their award-winning dining room. We're also grateful to Joe's Boat and Golf Cart Rentals for providing boats and golf carts for teams who don't have access to them. Please let him know if you need either as soon as I'm finished. You'll be venturing beyond the town limits tomorrow, so be prepared. Without further ado, see you all back here at one o'clock sharp!"

Pansy went off to do the treasure hunt, face painting, and bouncy ship with her kids. Danish followed Alice into the museum, looking over her shoulder at her clipboard and trying to be helpful. Nina strolled around the lawn for a while, then sat down on the stone wall with a complimentary cup of coffee to watch the children run around the lawn, excitedly picking up white stones and seagull feathers and one of the hundred or so pennies that had been conspicuously placed for them to find. A police officer in his khaki uniform and cap stood watch over the proceedings, patiently signing his autograph over and over as one after another of the children approached him, clutching their treasure-hunt clue sheet and a pencil.

The Redoubt and the bakery were packed with people, so Nina walked home and fixed herself a sandwich for lunch. She was back at the museum, slathered in sunblock and ready to begin, at one o'clock. She met up with Andrew, Pansy, and Danish just as Alice was climbing onto the stage with the microphone in her hand.

"All right, everyone." An expectant hush fell over the crowd. "Here is your first clue: 'Cad Empire.' I will spell it out for you: c-a-d-e-m-p-i-r-e. Good luck!"

"What the hell?" said Danish. "What's that supposed to mean?"

Pansy took a pencil and a hardback notebook out of her bag and wrote out the clue. All four of them sat on the grass and stared at it in silence for a moment. They heard a rustle in the crowd and looked up to see the Sole Sisters and Their Token Male hurrying out of the yard and down the street.

"You've got to be kidding me," said Nina.

"We could just follow them," said Danish.

"There's no fun in that!" said Pansy.

"Cad Empire. What could that possibly mean on Pineapple Cay?" said Nina "The government office building?"

"Barry Bassett's development office?" said Danish. "There is a trailer parked on his land on the road into Ted's camp."

"I don't think Alice and Kiki would come up with something like that," said Nina. They all looked at the sheet of paper again.

"I think it's an anagram," said Andrew.

"A what?" said Danish.

"The letters are scrambled. We have to unscramble them to get the clue," said Andrew.

"Oh, for heaven's sake!" said Pansy. "There must be five hundred different possible combinations!"

"I need another coffee if I'm going to strain my brain like that," said Nina. Crossword puzzles and word games of any kind bored her, although she knew they were good for keeping the mind sharp. "Anyone else?" Andrew and Pansy raised their hands, and Nina collected three cups from the smiling woman at the Plantation Inn table.

"Is Michel here?" Nina asked her. "I know he's a member of the museum's board of governors, and I thought he might be around today."

"He was called away on urgent business," said the coffee lady. "He's gone off island."

Nina rejoined the group, wondering what kind of urgent business would make Michel Poitras leave Pineapple Cay suddenly. Could it have something to do with Tiffany Bassett? She watched two other teams hustle out of the museum grounds, heading toward the main street. She focused on the paper again.

"I've got it!" said Andrew. "It's carpe diem!"

"That isn't even English!" said Danish huffily.

"Seize the day," said Pansy.

"Yeah, Andrew! So, what does that have to do with Pineapple Cay or sunken ships?" said Nina. "Seize the day. Somewhere on the east side of the island where you can see the sun rise?"

"Hey!" said Danish, jumping to his feet. "There's a boat at the marina . . . I saw it coming into the harbor yesterday when I stopped in for happy hour. That was the name on the stern! Let's go!" They scrambled to their feet and set off at a trot toward the marina, leaving a number of teams on the grass gazing after them. As they stepped onto the floating docks, they passed The Pleasure Hunters heading the other way, looking rather pleased with themselves as they sang out cheery hellos and hurried off to find the next clue.

There were about thirty boats tied up in the marina. Nina, Pansy, Andrew, and Danish walked quickly up and down the floating docks. On the last dock, they found it. Two couples were sitting in lawn chairs on the deck of the boat, cool beverages in their hands. The sun was well over the yardarm, and they were well into their cups, chuckling away. The ladies wore neon-colored T-shirts and khaki shorts. One man sported a bushy white beard, and the other wore a loud flowered shirt.

"Congratulations!" said one of the women. "Good for you!"

"Now, captain's rules," said the man with the bushy beard from his chair. "You've each got to down an immobilizer made from my own secret recipe before I'll give you the coin." He gestured to an upturned cooler topped with several rows of plastic shooter glasses filled with a bright-red liquid.

"What in nature is that shade of red?" Nina wondered out loud.

"You know, there are high school students in the treasure hunt. And a church youth group," said Pansy.

"Don't worry, dear," said the other woman. "They'll get candy bars instead."

Danish had already downed his drink. He threw back his head and howled at the sun, beating his chest with his fists. "Whoa! That is pure dy-na-mite! Get it in ya, girls, and we'll win for sure!"

Nina and Pansy took glasses and sipped them tentatively. Andrew downed his in one go and gasped quietly. It tasted like cinnamon and wood ashes to Nina.

"Frank's professional-grade f-bomb! All right then, catch!" said the man with the beard, tossing the coin toward them. Pansy caught it and put it in her bag.

"You'd better get a move on, Peanut Butter Sandwiches," he said, half reading their T-shirts. "Four other crews have already been here and gone."

"Now, where are you all from?" asked Pansy, apparently more interested in socializing than winning.

"We're all from Omaha, Nebraska," said the second woman. "The most landlocked state in the union. Two retired insurance salesmen and two retired nurses. We learned to sail on Lake Manawa, and now we're fulfilling a lifelong dream. Living on a sailboat in the Caribbean! Carpe diem!"

"That's wonderful!" said Pansy. "What's been your favorite part so far?" She was in no rush.

"Well, that's hard to say," replied the woman. "Every day is exciting. A new port, new people to talk to. We went scuba diving last week. It was incredible. A lot more exciting than the bottom of the Omaha YMCA swimming pool, where we took our introductory scuba course, let me tell you. From the deck of the boat, you look at the sea, and it looks blue. But when you're underwater, color is everywhere—the coral, the fish. They look like cartoon characters, painted every color of the rainbow."

"Wow," said Pansy. "That's so great."

Danish shuffled his feet impatiently. "OK, Pansy," he said, "let's get going. I don't want to lose to the Beer Commercial."

"Hold it!" said the man in the flowered shirt, making the universal sign for stop with his hand. "You have to answer a skill-testing question before you may leave." He picked a piece of paper out of a straw sun hat on the table in front of him.

"Is this part of the treasure hunt?" asked Pansy.

"It's part of my afternoon entertainment," said the man. "The bulging plain brown envelope required to get your passport stamped, as it were. Here is the question: What is the craziest place you've ever awakened in the morning?"

"That's one of your questions, Marcia," said one woman to the other.

"Are you sure you want me to answer that in mixed company?" asked Danish.

"I'll go first," said Andrew quickly. "I worked at the branch of my bank in Yellowknife—in the Northwest Territories in Canada—for two years before Pansy and I met. One weekend a colleague invited me to go caribou hunting with him and his family. We slept out on the ice in an igloo. That was a unique experience for me. It was also surprisingly warm."

"Continuing with that theme, before Andrew and I met, I spent a night at the ice hotel in Quebec City with a former boyfriend," said Pansy. "Even the bed was made of ice. Sorry, honey. He said 'craziest place,' not 'best place' or 'favorite place.'" Andrew shrugged.

"A clarification, please," said Danish. "How are you defining *craziest*? I need the parameters."

"They mean *strangest*, Danish," said Nina, who was unconsciously holding her breath.

"Well, then, after much deliberation, I would have to say that the strangest, most inexplicable waking experience I have had was in San Francisco, California. I was visiting a friend, and we went out one night. I woke up the next morning in a strange house full of people I didn't know. My friend was nowhere to be seen. The people who owned the house didn't seem to know who I was or why I was there, either. They figured I must have met one of their roommates who'd already left for work, but I had no recollection of meeting anyone or going anywhere but to the bar. They were very nice, and they gave me breakfast. Two of them were artists, and their studio was on the top floor. They were dressed in all white, and although they gave me orange juice and a croissant for breakfast, I noticed that the two of them were eating cauliflower with cottage cheese and drinking milk. All white food. Colorless, if you will.

"We went upstairs after breakfast, and they showed me the piece they were working on. They'd won a big grant from the arts council to do it. The whole floor, except for about three square feet closest to the door, was covered in yellow Post-it Notes with messages scribbled on them in black, blue, or red ink. Things like 'Dentist appointment 2:00 p.m. Tuesday,' and 'I am so happy.'" It looked sort of like a paper wall-to-wall shag carpet.

"I asked them what it meant, and they said, 'What do *you* think it means?' I asked them how they were going to move it to the gallery or whatever, and they said the process was the art and that they were going to take a picture of it before they cleaned up. They were also writing a daily blog to document the process. I said, 'Far out,' and one of them wrote that on a Post-it Note and stuck it on the floor. When I got back to my friend's place, he said he'd gone home early from the bar and didn't know any more than I did. Still one of life's unsolved mysteries."

"And I once spent a night in a Mozambican jail," said Nina. Pansy, Danish, and Andrew all looked at her. "I'll tell you about it sometime," said Nina.

"OK! Very illuminating for all of us, I think," said the man with the bushy beard. "There's another team on deck, so here's your next clue. Ready? Read it to them, Marcia." One of the women lifted a notebook from her lap and read it out slowly, enunciating each word very carefully.

"The only place in the world where Saturday comes before Thursday." She repeated it. They called out their thanks and good-byes and shuffled out of the way to make room for the next team—the girls' high school sailing crew in their neat red shorts and white golf shirts with the school crest on the pocket.

Nina, Danish, Pansy, and Andrew hiked up to the small park in front of the police station and sat in the shade on the steps of the bandstand. Danish immediately hopped up and paced in front of them.

"OK. Let's get cracking. We've got to make up some time here. No more small talk with the locals, Pansy."

"Oh, Danish, it's just for fun and to support the museum. The whole point is to get to know your community. It doesn't matter if we win," said Pansy.

"*Yes,* it does matter," said Danish, stopping in front of her. "Don't you see? This is an opportunity for me to show Alice that I am a potential mate of adequate—no, astonishing—intellect. A worthy companion. That our children could grow up to be astronauts—that I've got the right stuff."

"Well, I guess it depends what you think the right stuff is," said Pansy. "My sweet baboo here is smart, but he's also kind and shows an interest in others. Alice might go for friendly rather than competitive." She kissed Andrew on the cheek.

Nina let her eyes wander across the park to the row of shops on the main street. A shiny, black SUV with tinted windows pulled into a parking spot in front of the post office. Two well-muscled men wearing dark sunglasses got out. They went into the bakery and came out a minute later with cups of coffee in their hands. They sat at a table on the sidewalk under the striped awning and looked around, not talking. One of them looked at Nina and continued to look directly at her until she glanced away.

"Who are those men in front of the bakery?" she asked.

"I've never seen them before," said Pansy.

"Those plates on the SUV are from the main island," said Andrew. "It must have come over on the mail boat, maybe yesterday when it was in."

"What could they be doing here?" asked Nina. "They don't look like tourists."

"OK! Let's focus!" said Danish as the high school girls' sailing team ran by, headed toward the school. "The only place in the world where Saturday comes before Thursday," he repeated.

Pansy took out her notebook and pencil and wrote it down. They were all quiet for a minute.

"It can't be referring to a geographical place name, because you could travel backward or forward in time across the international date line, but not by two days," said Andrew.

"So . . . it refers to a state of mind, maybe . . . ," said Nina, thinking hard but coming up with nothing.

Danish continued to pace back and forth, looking more stressed out than she'd seen him since they met.

Suddenly, Pansy jumped up and did a little jig. "I've got it! I've. Got. It! *Saturday* comes before *Thursday* in the *dictionary*! The letter *s* comes before *t*," she whispered conspiratorially as the Beer Commercial strolled by on their way to the marina, too cool to even walk fast.

"You're a genius, Pansy!" said Nina.

"That makes sense," said Andrew, "but which dictionary on Pineapple Cay? We need a place to go to and get the coin."

"I think I know," said Nina. "There's a big leather-bound edition of the *Oxford English Dictionary* on display in the public library. Let's try that. If it's not there, the girls' sailing team seemed to think it's in their school library."

They looked around them to make sure they weren't being followed, then slipped down the lane next to the bakery onto Seagarden Street, where the library stood next to the museum. Nina noticed that the two men in shades and their SUV had disappeared.

The same tiny, bent-over lady was sitting behind the desk in the miniature library when Nina and the others went in. She smiled at them in greeting, her eyes twinkling. The four of them almost filled the room.

"How are you today, Mrs. Smith?" asked Pansy. "Busy?"

"Oh, yes. It has been hopping. More browsers than borrowers, but I'm counting them as visitors anyway. We need the numbers to keep the pittance the government gives us each year to buy books." She held up the counter in her hand and punched the button four times. "Twenty-five visits today so far," she said.

Nina sidled over to the dictionary and flipped to the *s*'s. Tucked between the pages next to the word *Saturday* was a gold coin. She held it up. "Yeah, team!" she said.

"All right. Here is your next clue," said Mrs. Smith. "A leafy bower; a court of love."

"Oh, come on!" said Danish. "And what exactly is a bower?"

"Well, you are standing right next to a dictionary," said Nina. "Look it up."

He flipped to the page and ran down it with his finger. "A pleasant shady place under trees or climbing plants in a garden or wood," he read.

"Oh! I don't believe it! I think I got one!" said Nina. "The tennis courts at the Plantation Inn! The fences around the courts are covered in climbing vines, and the tall trees provide shade during the day. The grounds of the inn are landscaped, like a flower garden."

"And *love* means no score in tennis," said Andrew. Mrs. Smith sat nodding and smiling at them.

"Good luck, kids!" she sang out as they hurried out the door.

"Oh, no. Look!" said Pansy. "Here comes Lance and his crew. He's going to get that one in a second. He's a tennis pro."

"He may not know what a bower is," said Danish. The Beer Commercial was about a block away and hadn't spotted them. Led by Danish, the team slipped behind the library and across the back lawn from tree to tree until they were behind the museum.

"My cart is parked around the corner," said Pansy. "Let's make a run for it." They scurried in single file over the low stone wall of the house next door, across the backyard, and into the dirt lane that ran beside it, where Pansy's cart was parked. They piled in and she peeled away, taking backstreets to the turnoff to the inn, banging over the potholes.

"Take it easy, Pansy," said Andrew between jolts. "We're going to get a flat."

"Hang on, sweetie," she replied as she made a sweeping turn onto the inn's long driveway.

From her rollicking perch in the backseat, Nina kept looking over her shoulder for Lance and the rest of the Beer Commercial. They were nowhere in sight. Pansy wheeled into the parking area and stopped abruptly, pitching them all forward in their seats. She was out of the cart and across the drive to the tennis courts before any of them could say anything.

"So, who's competitive now?" asked Danish.

"You have no idea," said Andrew. "She prefers talky party games like 'If they made a movie of your life, who would play you?' but challenge her to a game of Go Fish, and she'll pound you into the ground."

Before Nina, Andrew, and Danish reached the tennis courts, Pansy was already headed back toward them, the gold coin in her hand.

"Got it," she said briskly. "The last clue is a quest: 'Bring three pieces of sea glass to the museum to exchange for one gold coin: cobalt, white, and sea green.' They obviously don't know who they are dealing with here." She kept walking briskly toward the cart.

"*They* are Alice and Kiki, not Big Brother," Nina reminded her. "I imagine they thought it would be enjoyable for people to spend an hour or so beachcombing, soaking up the island atmosphere."

"Yes, well. I've got every kind of sea glass possible in my shop, so we can shave a good chunk off our time and maybe move into first place. Alice said no Internet—not that you couldn't go into your office for glass that was, at one time, on the beach," said Pansy as she jumped into the driver's seat and turned the key in the ignition. Nobody else cared enough to argue, so they piled into the cart and headed back down the long driveway.

At the turnoff, they passed the Beer Commercial in a white SUV. The windows were down, and Lance was not in it.

"Did you see that?" Nina said. "Lance bailed on the treasure hunt. So, where has he gone? To feed his captive, or to rescue his lady love?"

Andrew turned around to look at Nina quizzically.

"Oh. News flash. Tiffany and Lance were *up to it* before she disappeared," said Danish. "Nina and I saw them. Right by the tennis courts, in fact." Pansy didn't say anything about Operation Ladies' Underwear.

"So . . . you think Lance Redmond kidnapped her?" Andrew asked.

"Maybe," said Pansy.

"Blue Roker seems to think Barry Bassett had something to do with it," said Nina. She told them what Blue had said about the ransom note being a fake and about Barry's calls to a criminal in Miami.

"Blue isn't stupid. He only let those tidbits out because he wants them circulating on the bush telegraph, maybe to see if he can smoke out the villains," said Nina.

"Oh my heavens!" said Pansy. "This is getting too serious!"

She stopped the cart in front of the Pineapple Cay Real Estate office, which was painted in several bright colors—salmon-pink clapboards, yellow window frames with blue gingerbread trim, and a green roof. The little front garden was bursting with flowers in full bloom. They trooped up the winding front walk and into the tiny building. The front part of the office was set up to display Pansy's jewelry and other crafts and artwork. It was filled with sunlight from the large display windows. Pansy went into the back room, where her desk and computer were located, and lifted an enormous glass jar off the windowsill. It was the kind you store flour in, and it was filled to the brim with pieces of sea glass in various colors. She sank her hand into the slippery, smooth pieces and pulled out rounded chunks of white, green, and cobalt-blue glass. She rejoined the others in the front gallery.

"Got them. Let's go," she said, moving out from behind the counter that divided her office from the gallery.

Four burly, sunburned men came into the shop, blocking out the sun with their broad shoulders. Nina recognized them as the Clues Brothers. They browsed intently over the glass shelving units where Pansy's sea-glass jewelry was displayed. One of the men plucked up two pairs of earrings in blues, greens, and white.

"I'll take these, please," the man said, putting the earrings on the counter in front of Pansy.

"Well, OK," she said. "We're not really open, but since I'm here . . . I'm glad you like them." She rang in the sale and took his money. He immediately took one earring out of the paper bag she'd put them in and began to pry the silver wire away from the sea glass with a Swiss Army Knife.

"What are you doing?" Pansy asked, appalled.

"I'm just taking them apart temporarily. I need the glass for the community treasure hunt," he said, as if he thought it was a perfectly logical explanation.

"Well, that's not really in the spirit of things, is it? Why don't you go look on the beach? I made those. It took me hours," said Pansy. She passed the three pieces of sea glass she'd picked out of her giant glass jar to Andrew under cover of the counter and said, "Go!" Without questioning her, he took off at a slow jog toward the museum.

"They're very pretty. I'll fix them later. I did pay for them," he replied. Nina watched Pansy's expression change abruptly from outraged horror to a welcoming smile as she fixed on a new delaying strategy.

"Yes, I guess you're right. And where are you all from? Is this your first visit to Pineapple Cay?" she asked.

"No, we come here once in a while. We're just down from Atlanta for the weekend. We're brothers, and we try to get together now and then. You have to make a point of it, what with kids and work and all. Never tried a treasure hunt, though. Might be a bit girlie for a guys-only weekend. Seemed like a good idea when we were three sheets to the wind last evening, and that nice young lady from the museum came down to the marina and recruited us. It was kind of a kick to see Jules Savage this morning. I haven't seen him since his 1988 world tour. I got grounded for a month when I got home that night. Those were the days."

"Oh, give the hunt another try tomorrow," said Pansy. "I think there are boats involved. Today is just to prime the pump. Now, do you think your wife would like these earrings?" Pansy lifted a white-and-silver pair up to the light for him to see.

"Did you know what a bower was?" Danish asked another of the brothers, who was standing next to him.

"Well, that was kind of my specialty," answered the man. "I'm a high school English teacher and coach of the tennis team."

The first man bought the white-and-silver earrings for his wife, then the other brothers felt they'd better take something back for their wives, too. Pansy helped them choose three more pairs and wrapped them in tissue paper for them.

"Bye now!" she said as she locked the door behind them ten minutes later.

"Pansy, you are devious! Those are the same stealth moves you pulled on Barry Bassett to keep him from getting Miss Rose's house!" said Nina.

"And aren't you glad I did?" said Pansy as they slipped out the back door and walked over to the museum.

Andrew was waiting for them in the garden, watching his children play tag among the sculptures.

"Did we nab first place?" asked Pansy as her kids swarmed her, hugging her waist as she hugged them back.

"I'm afraid not," said Andrew. "The Sole Sisters and Their Token Male are leading, but we're in second place."

Pansy and Andrew went off with their children, and Danish went to find Alice, saying he'd catch up with Nina at The Redoubt later. Nina walked home along the beach and then took a swim. Afterward, she took a shower, put on jeans and a long-sleeve T-shirt, and had a glass of wine on her veranda looking out at the water. Except for the young officer assigned to community-fun-day detail, there had been no sign of Blue Roker or the rest of the force in town all day. Nina wondered where they all were, and if they were closing in on Tiffany's kidnappers. Lance seemed to be everywhere, but she hadn't seen Barry Bassett since she'd spied on him through his living-room window on Wednesday night. She was relaxed and drowsy after spending the day in the sun, and she could have happily stayed right where she was. But she was looking forward to hearing some live music, so when the sun was waist deep in the ocean, she hoisted herself out of her lounge chair, grabbed her bag and her flip-flops, and headed down the beach to The Redoubt.

As she got closer to the village center, Nina could see some activity on the wharf behind the police station. As she watched, three police boats arrived from the north, cutting their engines and floating in to the dock. Pairs of officers dressed in navy-blue combat pants and T-shirts and heavy boots climbed wearily out of the boats, stretched their legs, and headed up the ramp to the station. Blue Roker was among them. They must have been out looking for Tiffany, Nina thought.

The Redoubt was busy, but most of the crowd was outside on the deck or down around the bonfire on the beach. Veronica smiled at Nina as she came in, shaking her head and laughing as she popped the caps off several bottles of beer and set them in front of what looked like members of a local softball team at the far end of the bar—middle-aged men with a few paunches among them.

Nina slipped into a seat at the corner of the bar nearest the beach entrance and looked around. A harried waitress took her order and put a glass of white wine in front of her. Her eyes snagged the spectacle of Barry Bassett presiding over a table with the same three men she'd seen him with the other night. Barry was smiling his pasted-on smile as he raised his hand to flag down the waitress. A few minutes later, she brought a bottle of wine and stood by while he tasted it. He nodded, and she poured glasses for the other men. Barry raised his glass in a toast, and they all drank.

They're celebrating something, thought Nina as she sipped her wine and watched Barry, thinking of the police boats she'd just seen return to the wharf as the sun set, and the tired officers who'd made their way slowly up the road to the police station carrying bulky equipment.

"Hello, Nina." It was Ted standing beside her with his elbow leaning on the bar. He followed her gaze over to Barry, then looked back at her.

"Hi, Ted," said Nina, thinking about Delmont Samuels and Operation Ladies' Underwear and wondering how much Ted might have heard on the bush telegraph or directly from Blue Roker. Her cheeks burned with embarrassment. He looked at her intently. She hadn't noticed before how long his eyelashes were. She looked down into her wineglass, then took another sip. He turned around to face the room, leaning back and resting his elbows on the bar. He watched Barry Bassett in silence, and so did she, glancing furtively over at him from time to time.

"So, having any fun these days?" he asked without looking at her. She decided to pretend that the ink spill, her visit to The Pirate's Wake, and her discussion with Blue Roker at the police station hadn't occurred.

"Well, I'm having fun painting my house, and I spent yesterday writing an article. Today, Pansy, Andrew, Danish, and I did the museum treasure hunt. It was fun," she said innocently, wondering how she could avoid the topic of hot tubs, tears, and Barry Bassett. "Catch any fish today?" she asked.

He took a drink of his beer, glanced at her, then looked away again before answering. "The guys were out today, but I had meetings with the Department of Tourism on the main island. I just got back." He didn't elaborate.

They were both silent for a moment. *He isn't making it easy for me,* thought Nina. She tried another tack.

"Your team did well in the treasure hunt today," she said. "They're in first place." That got a smile out of him.

"Yeah. It sounded like they had a lot of fun. Cheryl, who manages the lodge, told me they burst in this afternoon, took apart a reading lamp in the club room to get at the sea glass, and took off again," he said.

"Good evening, Nina, Ted." It was Blue Roker, standing next to Ted. He wiped his forehead with the hem of his T-shirt, briefly exposing his stomach muscles.

Nina mumbled hello and quickly looked away.

"Blue, how's it going? Done for the day?" said Ted. "Let me buy you a beer." He raised his hand to catch Veronica's eye, and she strolled over.

"Good evening," she said, looking from them to Nina, laughing and shaking her head again. "How is it, Blue?"

"That is a big ocean out there," he said, not giving much away.

"What can I get for you?" Veronica asked. Blue ordered a beer, and she brought it to him with a glass. He took a long drink straight from the bottle.

Veronica looked at Nina again, grinning. "You come see me at the farm next week, Nina. Tuesday around noon. We'll pick some vegetables in the garden and cook lunch together. I think you're running out of things to do." She threw her head back and laughed again, tapped the bar twice with her knuckles, and then moved off again to the far end.

Ted took a sip of his beer and looked over at Barry again. He didn't look at Nina. Blue looked directly at her with his startling blue eyes, then away again, taking another pull on his beer.

"Excuse me," Blue said, placing his bottle on the bar and heading toward the restroom.

Ted swung his head around to look at Nina. "So, is Veronica right? Are you running out of things to do? I can think of any number of safe, enjoyable things to do on a Tuesday night." He paused and surveyed the room again, then looked back at her. "The yacht club shows movies on a wall in their clubhouse once a week. Usually old ones, but those are some of the best. There are crab races here on the beach. That's on Friday nights, but you get the idea. Then there's bingo at the church hall Wednesday nights." He looked away again. "I could even come up with a few good ideas myself. All perfectly legal. None of which involve a pot-smoking, overgrown-adolescent sidekick. Want to play darts?"

"Pardon?" she asked.

He looked at her again. "There's a dartboard over there. Do you care for a game of darts? My guests have come into town for the concert, so I thought I'd stick around for a while."

"Sure," she said, sliding off her stool. So. He *had* heard about the hot tub and her outing to The Pirate's Wake.

Well, what he didn't know was how many hours Nina had logged in her family's basement rec room honing her dart-throwing skills with her brothers. She'd been Spark family champion at the annual Christmas basement tournament for the last three years running.

Ted walked over to the jukebox and popped in a quarter, and the machine sprang to life. The first chords of Peggy Lee's "Fever" filled the room. He sent her a sly smile. She relaxed. Maybe they were past the awkward part of the evening and moving on to the post–hot-tub incident part. He held out a quarter to her.

"You get the next pick. Just a gentle reminder: It's Saturday night, and people are here looking for a good time," he said.

She flipped through the cards again and pushed the button for the Glenn Miller Orchestra's "In the Mood."

"All right," she said, taking the darts in her hand. "Want to up the ante? Make things a bit more interesting? I'm willing to wager that I will beat you—easily—best three out of five."

"You're a bit of a thrill seeker, it seems," he said. "All right." He stood thinking for a second. "If you do manage to beat me, what do you want?" He was looking into her eyes and standing so close to her she could feel the heat radiating from his body.

Good question, she thought.

"Let me think," she said, looking around the room for inspiration. "Well, actually, I could use some help hanging my shutters, so how about that?"

"OK," he said, circling until he was standing directly behind her. He leaned over her shoulder to throw a practice shot at the dartboard. It landed on the outside edge of the bull's-eye. He spoke directly into her ear. She inhaled deeply and held her breath.

"And what're you putting on the table?" he asked. She was momentarily speechless.

"How about this," he said, retrieving his dart and stepping back to the throwing line. "If I win . . . you'll let me teach you how to cast so that you don't accidentally hook a guy in the face."

"All right, but it sounds like I'm getting a better deal," she said. "You go first, then I'll clobber you." Which she proceeded to do. Just as their game ended, they heard the sound of random musical notes down the street at the bandstand.

"Sounds like the band is cuing up. Should we walk over? Excuse me for one minute. I'll be right back," said Ted.

Nina stood by the jukebox waiting for him. Danish materialized beside her as Ted disappeared into the restroom.

"Jeez, Nina. You guys might as well have been having sex right here on the floor by the jukebox. Look at the windows, all steamed up," he said.

Nina chose to ignore his efforts to provoke her. "I'm just trying to get things back to normal. I know you don't care, but it embarrasses me that Ted knows about the hot tub and the underwear and what idiots we are . . . that I am."

"Look, Nina, if he's into you, he's going to let a lot of crazy stuff slide to stay on target. And in my expert opinion, he's into you. He doesn't usually spend this much time hanging out here," said Danish.

"Thank you, Danish, for that frightening glimpse into the thought processes of the twenty-five-year-old male, but I'm talking about adult relationships," said Nina. She looked around. "Barry's gone."

"Yeah. He left a while ago, while you and Ted were making eyes at each other. Blue Roker was on his tail," said Danish.

"Hi, team!" It was Pansy. "I thought I'd find you here. Are you going over to listen to the band? I saw Alice, Kiki, and Jules over there on my way. There's quite a crowd. Alice should be really pleased."

"Hi, Pansy," said Nina. "I'm so glad you're here! How did you manage to get away?"

"It's eight o'clock, and the kids are asleep. I bribed Andrew with . . . well, never mind. He's coming over in an hour or so when Mrs. Smith gets back from her church-group meeting and can watch the kids. Shall we go? Hi, Ted," Pansy said as he rejoined them. "Coming to the concert?"

"Yes, I thought I'd go for a while," Ted replied. He and Nina fell into step behind Pansy and Danish, heading for the door.

Danish stopped at the bar. "Hey, boss! Thanks for the night off. I'll be in tomorrow morning at the crack of dawn to do brunch as promised."

"If you call ten o'clock the crack of dawn, then all right," Veronica said with a smile. "Have a good time."

"Are you coming over, Veronica?" asked Pansy. "I hear the band's lots of fun."

"Sure, I'll be over when it quiets down in here a little." They were just about to leave when Alice came in carrying a large insulated cooler bag. She smiled at everyone, then put the cooler bag up on the bar.

Danish waved at her from three feet away. "Good evening, Veronica. Thanks so much for the samosas. Everyone loved them."

She smiled shyly again at the group standing by the door. "Well, bye. Thanks again," she said, and hurried out.

Danish threw himself onto a stool and put his head down on the bar. "I might as well be a coatrack. She doesn't even notice me. I bring her coffee and ask her out on a date almost every single day, and she always says no. My heart is broken in seventeen places," he said dramatically.

Veronica threw up her hands. "OK. I can't watch this any longer. It's too painful. Look here, boy. That girl likes you. You don't know anything about how Pineapple girls communicate. Better you hear it from me than from one of those yahoos you play dominoes with all afternoon at the jerk pit. I can guarantee you they do not know how to romance a woman properly.

"Alice goes to church every Sunday with her auntie. If you cannot find Jesus, at least put on a clean shirt and invite her to the church picnic. Go call on her auntie. Take her auntie a present. A bouquet of flowers or some Elizabeth Arden. She likes that. Sit and have a glass of lemonade in the lounge. Once you've met her auntie and she's had a chance to look you over, invite Alice out for a nice meal or to go for a walk on the beach. You have her home by ten o'clock while she's living under her auntie's roof. Agatha goes to bed early, and you won't do yourself any favors if you make her stay up. Alice will not defy her aunt, no matter how adorable she finds you. Like a pet puppy."

Veronica paused. "You should probably steer clear of her Uncle Blue for the moment."

She leaned forward on the bar until her face was six inches from Danish's. "Now you listen to me. You do that girl wrong, get up to your usual tricks, you will be answering to me. Never mind Blue Roker. You got that?"

Danish nodded.

Nina, Ted, Danish, and Pansy walked down to the park together. The Sundowners were just taking the stage, and in no time they had the crowd hooting and clapping their hands to country music. Standing beside Nina, a man with dreadlocks down to his waist whistled and stomped his feet in time to the blistering fiddle. Little kids up way past their bedtimes danced on the grass and fell over laughing. Danish even managed to get Alice to dance with him up near the stage. Andrew showed up partway through. Nina hadn't meant to stay for the whole show, but before she knew it, it was over, and the band was saying good night, safe journeys. Ted was still standing beside her.

"We're just parked over there," said Pansy. "See you tomorrow, Nina. I think we're going to win!" She and Andrew waved good-bye and wandered away, hand in hand.

Ted turned to Nina. "May I walk you home?"

"Thank you. That'd be nice," she said. They strolled slowly up the street past The Redoubt and the dive shop, up past houses and cottages—most of them dark and quiet now, some with a cozy yellow glow in a single window. Nina imagined someone reading in bed or watching a late-night movie. They walked through a swath of soft jasmine-scented air. Nina breathed it in deeply. A breeze ruffled the leaves in the trees, and Nina looked up. The sky was full of stars again. They didn't talk. When they got to Nina's gate, Ted looked in her eyes for a long moment, then looked around.

Nina took a breath. Maybe, in another time and place, she'd spend more time thinking about his long eyelashes, his warm brown eyes, and the attractively capable manner in which he loaded his boat on a trailer. But not now. She was just getting used to being her own boss again, finding out where her edges were, and liking it.

Cool your jets, Nina, she said to herself. Yes, he made her heart beat faster, but that was not what she needed right now.

"I guess I left my truck downtown," he said, looking at her again with a sheepish grin. "I should walk back and get it. Good night, Nina. I'll see you soon."

"Good night, Ted." Nina smiled at him and went in, closing the door behind her. She saw him turn away and walk slowly back into the village with his hands in his pockets, looking down at the sidewalk, then up at the stars.

11

Sunday afternoon, the treasure-hunt competitors reconvened on the lawn of the Pineapple Cay Museum. Some of the crews were looking a bit ragged, like they'd just rolled out of bed—or maybe hadn't even made it to bed on Saturday night. The Clues Brothers did turn up, but they were lying flat on the grass with their hats over their faces when Nina arrived. She found Pansy and Andrew sitting on the stone wall. Danish was sitting on the ground beside them. Pansy handed her a paper cup of coffee.

"'Morning, Nina," Pansy sang out with a big smile.

"Hi, guys. Thanks, Pansy," said Nina, hopping up on the stone wall beside Pansy.

"*Please* don't talk to me. I was up very late last night and had to get up to sling scrambled eggs all morning," said Danish. He had his sunglasses on and a ball cap pulled down low on his forehead. He was leaning up against the wall with his knees up, head in his hands.

Andrew's cell phone rang, and he moved away a few steps to take the call. Nina looked around. The sailing teams were doing warm-up stretching exercises and taking turns shouting out team cheers while the yachtie teams around them winced. The Sole Sisters and Their Token Male had the swagger of first place about them as they clapped their hands in time with the sailing teams' cheers. Most of the Beer

Commercial team was slouched against the stone wall on the other side of the garden, and there was Lance, walking toward his friends.

Andrew walked back to them, slipping his phone in his back pocket. "That was Blue Roker," he said. "Someone just made a withdrawal from Tiffany Bassett's account at the ATM on Water Street. He's down in the cays, but he wants me to let one of his officers into the bank to review the security-camera video. Sorry, guys, I've got to go." He kissed Pansy and left.

Danish's head snapped up. "Did you hear that?" he asked, looking at Nina and Pansy bleary-eyed. He jumped up and ran, bounding over the stone wall and up the lane leading to Water Street. Nina and Pansy watched him go.

"Lance arrived just as Andrew got that phone call," said Nina. She and Pansy turned their heads to scrutinize Lance, who was leaning against the wall, chatting with one of his friends.

"Do you think he made the bank withdrawal?" asked Pansy. "He doesn't look very guilty."

Danish was back. "I didn't see anyone suspicious on Water Street," he said. "No Tiffany, no guys in a shiny black SUV, no Lance."

"Lance is right over there," said Nina.

"Let's keep an eye on him," said Danish. "I think he's up to something."

The microphone crackled to life, and they looked over to see Alice standing there with a sheaf of papers in one hand, the microphone in the other.

"Hello, everyone! Are you ready to play again?" she said, smiling. The assembled crowd cheered and applauded with the level of enthusiasm their physical conditions allowed.

Alice said, "OK! Thank you all for turning out to support your local museum. Get ready for an afternoon of adventure! You are heading into the wild today. We'll start out with an easy one to help you get going! Kiki is distributing your first clue. Please take one per team, and *good luck*! See you all back here later for the barbecue. Bring all your friends and family. Have fun, everyone!"

Kiki handed Pansy a piece of paper, and Nina and Danish looked over Pansy's shoulder at the clue she held in her hand.

"It's a blank piece of paper!" said Danish in the same incredulous, despairing tone a person might use to say, "A space alien just vaporized the entire city!"

"Alice, baby! You're killing me!" he yelled toward the stage. A heavy-set, stern-looking woman in a print dress looked over at him disapprovingly. Aunt Agatha Roker, Nina was willing to bet.

Pansy turned the paper over just to make sure there was nothing written on the other side. It was, indeed, blank.

"Now what?" asked Nina.

"You know, when Kevin and Susan were born, I stopped working for a couple of years," said Pansy, contemplating the paper. "I used to watch enviously as Andrew headed off to work to his grown-up office every day, while I settled down in my rice cereal–spattered sweatpants for a day of peekaboo and coloring, making macaroni and cheese and doing laundry. Then, later, it was all playing princess and going to puppet shows and scavenger hunts at the public library. In theory it was what I wanted, and I loved being with my kids, but I wondered if I had traded the chance at a fascinating career for the joys of motherhood. Maybe we should have scraped together the money and hired a nanny right off the bat. Maybe I should have been using the education my parents paid for to make a useful contribution to the world rather than spending another mind-numbing hour making crafts out of toilet-paper rolls. But now it's all paying off! The clue is written in invisible ink! I made up a treasure hunt for Kevin's seventh birthday party and found instructions for making invisible ink on some mommy blog designed to make me feel inferior."

"Yeah!" said Danish. "My brother and I used to do that when we were kids. Write something in lemon juice, and when you scorch the paper, it becomes visible. I've got a lighter right here." He pulled a lighter out of his pocket, flicked the little wheel to make the flame, and held it close to the bottom edge of the paper. The edge of the paper began to wrinkle and brown; then a corner caught on fire. No words appeared.

"No! Danish! Stop!" said Nina.

Pansy dropped the paper on the ground and gently tapped out the fire with the toe of her sneaker. "OK, I don't think it's written in lemon juice," she said, "but I know from my extensive experience that another way to do it is to write in white crayon and then go over it with a highlighter. Fortunately, I think I have one in my bag." She dug around in her purse and brought out a yellow highlighter. She laid the sheet of paper carefully on top of a notebook, also extracted from her bag, and colored the center of the page. There it was.

"It's a riddle," said Pansy. "'What can travel around the world while staying in a corner?'"

"What does that mean?" asked Nina.

"Is this supposed to be fun?" asked Danish.

"I think Alice and I must have read the same mommy blog," said Pansy. "It's a stamp. You put it in the corner of an envelope, and it can go around the world while staying in the corner."

"Yeah, Pansy! Supermom!" said Nina. "I guess it's off to the post office we go."

They trooped out onto the sidewalk and up the lane to Water Street, where the post office stood in a commanding position in the center of the main block. Danish led the way up the two stone steps and through the arched doorway into the small building. Post-office boxes lined the two side walls, and a counter ran along the back wall, where a woman in a crisp uniform like Danish's stood sorting through folders full of stamps.

"Hello, Doris! How's tricks?" boomed Danish. The woman looked up and rolled her eyes.

"Hi, Doris," said Pansy. "This is Nina. She just moved here." Nina waved to Doris, who smiled and said hello.

"Doris, we're here to collect our gold coin, if you please," said Danish. He strode over to the counter.

Doris reached below the counter then handed him the coin, still without speaking or smiling.

"Now we are ready for our clue, if you don't mind," said Danish. Doris pointed with the end of the pencil she was holding to a bulletin board on the wall. There was a piece of paper pinned up in the middle, between two wanted posters for criminals on the main island. Nina, Pansy, and Danish huddled around to read it. Pansy took out her notebook and copied it down.

"'A watery treasure chest: where emeralds mix with sapphires, and diamonds lie scattered before you.' Now what is that?" she asked.

They went outside and across the street to the bandstand that stood in the middle of the small, grassy park. Nina sat on the step, leaning against a post and looking out at Star Cay across the harbor. It was another beautiful day. The bad weather that had been predicted the night before had bypassed them. Sailboats dotted the bay, and in the sunlight, the sandy beach on Star Cay glowed bright white against the brilliant turquoise water, which deepened into an intense blue before lightening into shades of jade and turquoise as it reached the shore of Coconut Cove.

"I have an idea," said Nina. "Could it be talking about the tip of the island, where the dark, deep, sapphire-blue water of the Atlantic meets the lighter, blue-green water of the shallower Caribbean Sea? The diamonds could be the string of cays in Diamond Cay National Park, off the south end of the island."

"Yes! That makes perfect sense," said Pansy. "There's a historical marker on the southern tip of Pineapple Cay. I bet that's where they put the coins."

Reenergized by the possibility of victory, they hurried over to where Pansy had parked her golf cart and jumped in. They breezed out of town, cruising along at fifteen miles an hour under the canopy of tall trees and dappled sunlight south of the village. Nina leaned back in the front seat beside Pansy, enjoying the ride. It was Sunday again, and there was a wedding at the whitewashed church she and Ted had passed the week before. The bride and groom were just emerging from the church dressed in their finery, the bride's white dress brilliant in the sunlight. Their friends and family, dressed in brightly colored dresses and shirts and ties, were clapping their hands and tossing confetti at the smiling couple as they made their way to a highly polished maroon car festooned with tissue-paper flowers and streamers.

Pansy steered the cart along the coast, where the waves were crashing against the narrow ribbon of seaweed-strewn sand that ran alongside the road; then they drove up and over the hill and between the salt ponds at Sandy Point, passed the restaurant where Ted and Nina had eaten lunch, and rolled to a stop where the road ended at the foot of a sandy track leading up to a high point of land at the very end of the island. They unfolded themselves from the cart, stretching their legs.

"Onward we go," said Nina, putting on her sun hat. They hiked up the track in single file.

At the very tip of the point, there was a commanding panoramic view of the sea and the islands. The scattered string of cays trailed off over the horizon. The water was indeed a darker blue on the Atlantic side of the islands and lighter, more welcoming shades of green and turquoise on the Caribbean side. On the stone monument, there was an inscription:

THIS MONUMENT MARKS THE LOCATION WHERE IT IS BELIEVED CHRISTOPHER COLUMBUS STOOD WHEN HE PASSED THROUGH THESE ISLANDS IN 1492. AT THAT TIME, THESE ISLANDS HAD A POPULATION OF ABOUT 1,000 NATIVE PEOPLE, WHO LIVED IN SETTLEMENTS ALONG THE SHORE AND FISHED THE WATERS YOU SEE BEFORE YOU.

At the base of the monument, there was a piece of paper beneath a large piece of dry white brain coral. The edges of the paper rose and fell in the breeze. Beside it was a small terra-cotta flowerpot full of gold coins.

"I guess we just help ourselves," said Pansy.

Danish pocketed a coin. Pansy lifted the brain coral with both hands, and Nina pulled out the sheet of paper and read it aloud.

"A bark on a barque."

"Hmm," said Pansy, looking at Danish.

"Interesting choice for a community event involving interaction with tourists and sensitive teenage girls," said Danish, looking at Pansy.

"What do you mean?" asked Nina.

"You'll see," said Danish.

"Alice and Kiki wouldn't have chosen him, would they?" Pansy asked Danish.

"Who?" said Nina.

"There's an old guy named Rusty who lives with his dog, also named Rusty, on a sailboat behind The Pirate's Wake bar. Rusty and Rusty. A bark on a barque," said Danish. "In other words, a dog and a grouch on a boat. They let Rusty use the bathrooms in the bar and get water from the tap, and they give him a hot meal now and then. He's a bit of a loner."

"I've always thought he was a bit sweet on Agatha Roker, Alice's aunt," said Pansy. "Maybe that's how he got roped into participating in the treasure hunt," she said. "Although I don't think she's ever given him anything that could be considered encouragement. Just a Christmas basket every year and invitations to the church picnic. Agatha runs a tight ship, but she walks the talk. She's very big on doing the Christian thing, reaching out to the unfortunates in the community."

"I guess it's back to Coconut Cove," said Danish. They stood enjoying the view for a moment, then trooped back down the spine of the hilly point to the cart. They cruised back to Coconut Cove at the cart's maximum speed of fifteen miles an hour, watching a couple of carloads of treasure hunters blow by them in both directions, hooting and waving their arms out of open windows. Pansy sighed. Her dreams of victory were fading.

They reached the outskirts of the village and turned off the main road toward The Pirate's Wake. They walked into the dark interior, and Danish bought a couple of cans of cola from the bartender and ordered a burger to go. It was the same man they'd spoken to the last time.

Nina was pretty sure the customer sitting at the bar was the same man, sitting in the same seat, that they'd seen the other day. She glanced over at the pool table, where two men played a slow, lazy game. They, too, were the same men who'd been playing two days ago.

"OK. Let's do this," said Danish when the burger was ready. He grabbed the cans of cola with one hand and the burger with the other and headed out onto the covered patio and down to the rickety wharf. Nina and Pansy followed.

There was a rough-looking vessel tied up snugly to the dock. Empty fuel cans and tangled piles of thick rope littered the deck. On a small patch of deck where the clutter had been pushed back, a faded lawn chair sat next to an upturned plastic bucket with a cola can sitting on it. The boat's paint was flaking and faded all over, but Nina could make out the name *The Painted Lady* on the stern.

"Yo! Rusty, man! I've brought you some cold colas and a burger. Have you got a stash of gold coins in there to trade for them?" shouted Danish as he strode onto the narrow wharf. It swayed beneath his weight. Nina and Pansy followed tentatively. A dog emerged from the dark hole of the boat cabin, wagging his tail. Pansy rummaged through her bag and brought out some string cheese. She stepped forward, peeling back the cellophane, and threw it onto the deck of the boat.

"There you go, Rusty. Good boy!" said Pansy. The dog gobbled it up eagerly.

A slight, disheveled man with long, gray hair pulled back in a pony-tail and a beard and mustache to match emerged from the cabin of the boat. His face was almost completely obscured by his facial hair, his bushy eyebrows, and the peak of his greasy ball cap, which advertised a brand of motor oil.

"Well, if it isn't the human rainbow and her pet unicorn," he growled. "I should have known you two would be mixed up in this fiasco. Who's the new girl?"

"Hello, Rusty. How are you today?" said Pansy in her singsongy, soothing-small-children voice. "This is Nina Spark. She just moved to Pineapple Cay from New York City."

Rusty ran his eyes slowly over Nina from her shoes to her sun hat and back again. "Uh-huh," he said when he was done. "Well, here is a word of advice for you, missy. I'd stay clear of these two, if I were you. Cherry Kool-Aid here and Bozo the Clown. She's on something, and so is he."

"Here, Rusty. These are for you, man," said Danish, passing him the cans of cola and the burger. Rusty took them without comment and placed them carefully on top of the plastic bucket. He disappeared inside the cabin while they stood there uncertainly, wondering if he was coming back. He reemerged with the gold coin in his hand and held it out to Danish, who stuffed it into his pocket.

"There you go. Now skedaddle," said Rusty, reaching down to stroke his dog, who sat quietly next to him, wagging his tail.

"So, Rusty, have you seen a guy with a pink suitcase around here lately?" asked Danish.

"Again with the pink suitcase!" said Rusty irritably. "Like I told Agatha's brother, the copper, when he came snooping around here the other day: Richie Rich was here about a week ago, cluttering up my dock with his boat and his bloody suitcase, trying to make small talk about sports and the weather. He gave me twenty bucks and said, 'We've never met,' like Robert De Niro or some goddamn thing, then lit out of here in the dark, heading south. It's getting to be like Grand Central station down here. I've had enough. And I told the copper to tell Agatha that this fiasco here pays off that Christmas basket, too, and to bugger off and leave me in peace for a while. Not to bugger off, but the rest of it."

He lowered himself gingerly into the lawn chair. "Now it's time for our nap, so get out of here. People have been bugging me all afternoon, and I'm tired of talking. If I'd known how much work this would be, I'd have said no, even though it was Agatha's niece who asked me."

"So, a lot of people have been to see you already?" asked Pansy.

"That's what I said," said Rusty.

"About how many?" asked Danish.

"Too many!" said Rusty. "A bunch of teenage girls who giggled the whole goddamn time. Wave after wave of bloody tourists. Old man Dixon and his whole goddamn family. Now you with all your questions. Now listen up, I'm only going to say this once!" He read haltingly from a piece of paper he held close to his face. "'Call me Ishmael. Some years ago—never mind how long ago precisely—having little or no money in my purse and nothing particular to interest me on shore, I thought I would sail about a little and see the watery part of the world.' Adios. Have a nice life." He grabbed the burger and a cola off the bucket and heaved himself out of the lawn chair, and Rusty and Rusty disappeared below deck.

"Those are the opening lines of *Moby-Dick* by Herman Melville," said Danish. "Whenever it is a damp, drizzly November in my soul; whenever I find myself involuntarily pausing before coffin ware-houses . . . whenever . . . it requires a strong moral principle to pre-vent me from deliberately stepping into the street, and methodically knocking people's hats off—then, I account it high time to get to sea as soon as I can. This is my substitute for pistol and ball," he recited.

Nina stared at him.

"I stayed with my grandparents a lot when I was a kid," said Danish. "That was my granddad's favorite book. He read it to us at least ten times. He gave me my own copy when I got the job on the cruise ship. I read it again every once in a while. He lived his whole life in Colorado. I don't think he ever saw the ocean."

"Well, good for you, Danish!" said Pansy.

"So, back to the library, I guess," said Nina. They piled into the golf cart and cruised back into town. The ladies' auxiliary was busy decorating the town square with bunting and balloons for the evening's festivities, while the band did its sound check.

Mrs. Smith was still at her desk in the library. She stood when they entered and gave them a mischievous smile but said nothing. Nina went quickly up and down the shelves.

"Melville. Melville. Here it is. Three copies."

She handed one each to Pansy and Danish, and they all riffled through the pages and shook the books out upside down. No coins fell out. They looked at Mrs. Smith. She smiled again and shrugged, palms up.

"I thought librarians were supposed to be helpful," said Danish.

"I'm not supposed to say anything," she said. "Sorry."

They went back outside and sat on the stone wall in the sunshine.

"OK, so it's not in the library," said Pansy. "It's something about sailing and the 'watery part of the world.' Something offshore, in the cays, maybe. Lots of people sail there. Or maybe it's the wreck site where they found the *Morning Glory*."

"Maybe," said Nina. "Or maybe the clue is the whale in *Moby-Dick* . . . That story that Ted told us at the Savages' dinner party the other night. About his friend who had reassembled a whale skeleton on a beach in the Diamond Cays National Park. Where did he say it was?"

"It's on Turtle Cay," said Pansy. "That's pretty far from here. At least a half hour by boat."

"Alice and Kiki wouldn't send people to the wreck site," said Danish. "The cut between Lizard and Wreath Cays is wide-open and rough. That's part of the reason why it took so long for someone to find the *Morning Glory*. And where could you stash a fake gold coin on the open water? Unless someone sat there in a boat all day, which seems unlikely."

"So, should we try Turtle Cay, then?" said Nina. "I'd like to see it, anyway. I don't think we're in any danger of winning, so a little sightseeing couldn't hurt. We'll still finish the hunt and show up for the closing barbecue Alice has planned. What do you think?"

"Sounds good," said Pansy.

"Yeah," said Danish, "but if we aren't in a hurry, how about refueling at The Redoubt before we go? I could use a burger. I skipped brunch, and it's going to take a couple of hours to get there and back. We've got to get the boat from Joe in town anyway."

Nina and Pansy agreed. They drove back into town.

The Redoubt was busy, but not overflowing, and they chose a booth in the cool interior. Most of the action on this sunny Sunday afternoon was out on the deck overlooking the water.

"You three haven't given up, have you?" asked Veronica when she came over to their table to take their order.

"No, just a pit stop," said Pansy. She and Nina asked for iced tea. Danish got his burger and a beer. When he had demolished both and a second beer, he said, "Excuse me for a few minutes, ladies. Some of the guys are out on the deck, and I think I'll go say hello."

Nina and Pansy chatted about house-paint colors for a few minutes. Danish came back with another glass of beer in his hand and slid into the booth beside Nina.

"Hey, look who just came in," he said. Nina and Pansy looked toward the door. Barry Bassett peacock-walked up to the bar and stood with his foot on the rungs of a stool, surveying the room. Before Barry saw the three of them, a waitress came over to take his order. As she went through the swinging doors to the kitchen, he turned toward the bar and hoisted himself up onto the stool.

"Look who else is here," said Danish urgently. It was the two guys from the black SUV they'd seen yesterday. The men strolled up to the bar and sat on either side of Barry. They were big, burly guys with shaved heads, both wearing neatly pressed golf shirts and Bermuda shorts.

"Is that what the Russian mob is wearing these days?" Pansy asked.

"For guys who live in Miami, they're pretty pasty-looking," said Danish.

Barry looked casually from one to the other. They talked for a few minutes. *Calmly, but seriously,* Nina thought. Then the two burly men stood, nodded at Barry, and headed for the door. No smiles or handshakes. They were not friends. The SUV guys swept the room with their eyes as they walked to the door. One of the men looked Nina straight in the eye and held her gaze for a moment. She looked down quickly.

"Look! Barry boy is getting right on the horn to someone," said Danish excitedly. Nina looked up.

They watched Barry pull his cell phone out of his back pocket and answer it. He turned sideways on his stool and hunched forward as he listened to whoever was on the line. His brow knitted, and he reached behind the bar and grabbed a notepad and pen. He scribbled something and hung up, slipping the phone back into his pocket and tearing the page off the notepad. He stuffed it into his shirt pocket as he hurried out the door.

"Rookie mistake," said Danish as he sprang out of his seat and strode quickly across the room. He grabbed the notepad off the bar and came back to the booth. Nina and Pansy looked at him quizzically.

"Pansy, I know you've got a pencil in that gigantic purse. Cough it up, *por favor*," he said.

"It's not really a purse, but yes I do," answered Pansy, rooting through her voluminous satchel and pulling out a yellow rubber-tipped pencil.

"What are you doing, Danish?" asked Nina. He was rubbing the lead of the pencil rapidly but lightly across the notepad. When the whole page was blackened, he studied his handiwork, then held it up for both of them to see. There was a series of numbers visible in white on the notepad, where Barry's pen had pressed down on the sheet of paper beneath the one he'd written on.

"Ta-da!" he said. "The subject of old Barry's serious convo and the reason for his sudden departure. Something to do with Tiffany, I bet. Unless he's making a date with Cynthia, but I think she left. Mrs. Davis was sort of blue when I delivered her mail on Friday because her daughter had gone back to Dallas. I slipped one of my secret-admirer cards into her mail to cheer her up. I always keep a few on hand. Anyway, Barry would have a smile on his face if he was going to rendezvous with Cynthia. He didn't look happy. He looked mad."

"Yes, he did," said Nina. "So what do these numbers mean?" They studied the paper. Nina wrote the series of numbers and markings on a clean sheet of paper.

"I'm pretty sure these are geographical coordinates. Longitude and latitude," she said. "See, the little circles. Degree symbols. He must be headed to this location. Maybe he's found out where Tiffany is, or he's going to take her there and kill her. I don't know."

"If that was a gun I delivered to him Friday, she could be in danger," said Danish.

"Maybe we should tell Blue," said Pansy.

"I really don't think I could do that again," said Nina. "He already thinks we're idiots. What would we say? That Barry scribbled some numbers on a piece of paper, and Danish delivered a heavy box to him on Friday? I can just imagine what he'd say. If we find anything concrete, we'll tell the police."

"I guess you're right," said Pansy.

"Quick, Danish, does Veronica keep nautical charts here?" asked Nina.

"I have the charts for the cays in my bag," said Pansy, rummaging in it again. "We bought them for boat trips, and I thought we might need them for the treasure hunt since Alice said we'd need a boat today." She pulled out a chart book with a coil binding and laid it on the table. Nina turned the pages quickly, looking for the coordinates Barry had written on the notepad.

"Here it is," she said, flipping the book around for them to see. "Love Cay. Halfway between here and Turtle Cay, inside the park boundaries. It's tiny."

"I've never even heard of it, let alone been there. Have you, Danish?" asked Pansy.

"Nope. We can at least check it out on our way to Turtle Cay. Let's go. I'll go get the keys to the boat from Joe. Barry doesn't keep his boat at the marina, so he'll have to go home first. Maybe we can beat him there." He started to stand up, then sat down again quickly.

"Sorry, ladies. I'm afraid I accidentally got somewhat hammered. I can't drive the boat. Maybe I could give Ted a call and see if he's around to take us down there."

"Listen, Danish. Get the keys to the boat and meet us at the wharf in five minutes. We don't need Ted to chauffeur us. I'm from Maine. I can drive a damn boat," said Nina. She quickly tucked some money under her iced-tea glass, and they hurried outside.

"Look!" said Pansy. "Barry is still here." He was coming out of the grocery store with a jug of water and a sagging plastic bag. He threw them into the backseat of his convertible and walked quickly around to the driver's seat. They hung back behind the cover of a leafy shrub as he sped past them. He was definitely in a hurry. Danish took off walking in the direction of Joe's rentals down by the marina while Nina and Pansy hustled across the street.

"Pansy, could you go get a few jugs of water? I need to get some supplies at the hardware store," said Nina. She glanced up and down the sidewalk.

"Hey!" she half shouted, grabbing Pansy's arm. "There are those guys again!" Halfway down the block, the two strangers in dark shades were getting into their shiny black SUV with its main-island license plates. Nina and Pansy watched as they backed out of their parking space and headed north on the road that ran past Nina's house. But there was no time to investigate if there was any chance of them reaching Love Cay before Barry. Nina turned her back on the disappearing SUV, and she and Pansy jogged away to do their errands. In the hardware store, Nina spun around in the aisle, wondering what they might need. She grabbed a coil of rope, a roll of duct tape, and some protein bars made for backpackers, just in case, and paid Harold for it all in a rush.

"Rope, tape, and rations. Does this have something to do with the treasure hunt?" he asked Nina.

"Sort of," she replied. "Thanks, Harold. Bye!"

Nina and Pansy met on the sidewalk a minute later and jogged down to the dock. Danish was in the boat with the engine running. They hurried into life jackets and untied the ropes, and then Nina eased the boat away from the dock. Once they were clear of the no-wake zone, she opened the throttle and headed south. They had been flying over the water along the coast of Pineapple Cay for about ten minutes and had just passed the southern tip of the island and begun to thread their way among the string of cays in the national park when Pansy stomped her foot on the bottom of the boat.

"Oh, that Kevin! He is going to get the time-out to end all time-outs when I get home! The battery just died on my phone. I charged it last night. He must have snuck it out of my bag to play video games again!" she said with exasperation. "I don't have GPS anymore."

"Danish, did you bring your cell phone?" asked Nina.

"Nope. I left it at home because Alice said no electronic devices," he said.

"We've got the charts," said Nina. Although she was from Maine and could drive a powerboat, Nina had never bothered to learn to read a nautical chart with a compass. Neither had Danish or Pansy. So they went by sight, with the chart spread out on the seat in the middle of the boat for visual reference.

"We're looking for a croissant-shaped island with a sheltered cove about six islands down from Pineapple Cay in a clump with two other small cays!" Nina yelled above the sound of the engine. "That one looks more like an apple turnover, and it's too small. It's not that one."

"Are you hungry?" asked Danish. "Try to focus."

She slowed down as the water became very shallow in places, not more than a couple of feet deep in some spots. They all scanned the horizon and assessed the low humps of land on either side of them, looking for Love Cay. There were about forty cays of various sizes in the park. They could look for days before finding the one where Tiffany was, if she was here at all. Then Nina saw a brief flash of light some distance ahead of them. She waited a couple of seconds, looking at the same spot on the horizon. It flashed again.

"Did you see that?" she asked the others, pointing in the direction where she'd seen the flash. Just then, it happened again.

"It came from that island over there. Someone must be there," said Pansy. Nina pointed the boat in that direction and accelerated. As they got closer, the island's croissant shape became clear.

"That's it!" said Pansy.

"Go to the lee of the long, thin island this side of it," said Danish. "That way, they won't be able to see us against the vegetation along the shore. If we come directly at it across the water, they'll see us coming a mile away."

Nina maneuvered the boat into the cover provided by the neighboring island. They motored slowly to its tip and looked across the narrow channel of water separating it from Love Cay. There was no sign of anyone. The beach was empty and smooth. No footprints, and no sign of Delmont Samuels's Zodiac. The vegetation beyond the beach was dense and dark.

"Well, what're we waiting for? Let's go look!" said Danish with the bravado of someone with at least three beers in him on a hot day. Nina pointed the boat toward the backside of Love Cay and motored over slowly, trying to minimize the noise as much as possible. About halfway down the island, a tall palm tree had fallen over onto the beach, its leafy, fronded top resting in the sand at the water's edge. Nina pointed the boat toward the beach.

"Here. We can hide the boat on the south side of this tree and cover it with palm fronds. That way at least it won't be immediately visible when Barry comes from Pineapple Cay," said Nina.

They pulled the boat up onto the sand next to the fallen tree, tied a rope from the boat around the tree trunk, and covered the boat with palm fronds they found along the forested edge of the beach.

"Let's head inland," said Danish. "If the kidnappers have a hideout here, it must be in there."

They walked along the beach, looking for a break in the trees. A few hundred yards from the fallen tree, they found a narrow leaf-covered path leading into the woods. They followed it in single file, not speaking. The island was small, and Nina was beginning to think they were going to reach the other side without finding any explanation for the flashing light, when the dark shape of a hut became visible in a clearing ahead of them.

"Look!" said Danish. They all crouched down and inched forward slowly. There was no sign of movement around the hut. It looked like an abandoned shelter, the thin wooden poles that comprised the walls well weathered, and the palm-thatched roof thin and dusty. In a small clearing beside the hut was a blackened fire ring surrounded by chunks of limestone. There was a pot sitting in the ashes, which had gone cold.

A small mirror hung from a tree trunk at eye level, with a flowered toiletry bag hanging from a branch beside it. *If someone was holding the mirror and it caught the sun, it could have caused the flashes we saw,* thought Nina. A clothesline was strung between two trees, and Tiffany Bassett's green party dress was draped over it. Pansy gasped.

They crept closer and stopped, listening for signs of life inside. A woman's whining moans were suddenly audible inside the hut, and they increased in volume. She sounded like she was in pain. They could hear the sounds of a struggle, and some random thrashing and banging inside. They looked at one another, wide-eyed, and scurried up to the hut, crouching below a glassless window. Side by side, they raised their heads above the windowsill and peeked inside. In an instant, Nina took in a hot-pink suitcase, its multicolored contents spilling out on the floor, and a startling tangle of naked flesh writhing on an air mattress. Tiffany Bassett was grinning down at Lance, who was pinned beneath her. The emerald necklace swung from her neck.

Nina, Pansy, and Danish dropped to the ground and scrambled noiselessly back down the path, not stopping until they reached the boat. They threw themselves down on the sand and sat side by side with their backs against it.

"They were doing it! Lance and Tiffany!" said Pansy.

"I could have lived a long and fulfilling life without that scene burned onto my retinas," said Nina.

"Uh-huh," said Danish.

"They're fake, Danish," said Nina.

"What kind of kidnapper–kidnappee relationship is that?" asked Pansy.

"I knew it! She wasn't kidnapped!" said Nina. "They're in it together. I should have known it was Lance! He told me all about Kiki and Jules's house like he'd been a guest there, but when I mentioned taking tennis lessons to Kiki, she acted like she didn't know who he was. He must have snuck in and trashed the bathroom and guest room while we were eating dinner. I remember Tiffany looking at her watch while we were all sitting at the table, like she had somewhere more important to be. I thought she was just being rude, but I guess she really did have somewhere else to be—a rendezvous with Lance!"

"They must be shacked up in their little love nest here waiting for Barry to come through with the ransom money," said Danish.

"It's kind of sweet, actually," said Pansy. "They chose Love Cay for their hideout. A love nest on Love Cay."

"I'm not feeling the sweetness," said Nina. "Just the nausea."

"Barry's taking his time with the ransom. It's been a week since she disappeared!" said Nina. "Speaking of Barry, where is he? He should be turning up any minute."

"So, how does Barry fit in? Why is he coming here?" asked Pansy.

"Maybe the call was from Lance, and Barry's coming to deliver the ransom money and get Tiffany back," said Danish. They could hear the faint growl of a motorboat growing louder. They peeked over the top of the fallen palm tree and saw a powerboat quickly closing the gap between it and the beach. There was only one person in it. Barry.

"Well, it looks like we're about to find out," Danish said. They watched Barry nose his boat close to shore, throw out an anchor, jump up onto the bow of the boat, and hop from there onto the sand without getting his feet wet.

"He's got a gun!" whispered Nina. Barry was walking quickly toward the tree line, with a hunting rifle clearly visible in his hands.

"And unless he's giving Lance a check, I don't think he's got the ransom with him. Three million dollars doesn't fit in your pockets, and he isn't carrying a bag," said Danish.

"Oh! Oh! Oh!" whispered Pansy, squirming as she knelt in the sand. "He's going to kill Lance! Or Tiffany! Or both of them! We've got to stop him!"

Barry had almost reached the edge of the forest and was nearing the path. His back was to them. Danish rose soundlessly and sprinted across the sand, tackling Barry and sending him face-first into the sand before Barry even knew he wasn't alone. The impact of the tackle sent the gun flying out of Barry's hand and into the sand. Nina and Pansy raced across the beach to where Danish and Barry lay in a heap. Barry was struggling to get himself free of Danish, who sat on top of him with his knee in the small of Barry's back, struggling to hold both of Barry's arms behind his back. Pansy grabbed the gun and backed away, holding it gingerly, pointing down at her side.

Nina whipped her daypack off her back and tore it open, yanking out the duct tape. Together, she and Danish taped Barry's hands together behind his back, wrapping the silver tape around and around several times. She moved quickly down to his feet and sat on his legs while she taped his ankles together in the same way, moving her head back and forth to avoid Barry's attempts to kick her in the face.

"Heavy-duty duct tape on your hairy legs. That is going to hurt coming off, Barry boy," said Danish. Barry gave another angry kick, grunting and swearing at them as he struggled. Nina ran back to the boat and grabbed the coil of thin, strong rope she'd bought at the hardware store. Danish got off Barry's back. They quickly tied Barry's hands and feet together. He was trussed up like a Thanksgiving turkey. Danish flipped him on his side. Barry's eyes burned with fury as they darted from Danish to Nina to Pansy and back again.

"You idiots! You'll pay for this for the rest of your lives! Who do you think you are?" he said, his facial features distorted with anger.

"The question, Barry, my friend, is what do you think *you're* doing here on lovely Love Cay on a sunny Sunday afternoon with a gun in your hand?" asked Danish, pacing back and forth in front of Barry, his hands clasped behind his back like Sherlock Holmes.

"This has nothing to do with you losers!" spat Barry, his muscles twitching as he struggled against the restraints. He was vibrating with anger.

"She was a stupid cocktail waitress when I rescued her from her pathetic life, and now she's making a fool of me with her boy toy! They're both going to pay for it!"

"And just how do you know Lance and Tiffany are in on it together?" asked Nina.

Barry laughed bitterly. "That moron called me from his *cell phone* to ask for three million dollars for the return of my wife, and he called me on the private phone I keep for business transactions. No one knows about it except for Tiffany, so I knew she had to be involved. I told him she's not worth it. I decided to pass.

"I wrote a fake ransom note and gave it to Roker, saying I found it on my doorstep, to keep him out of my hair while I tracked them down. Pretty good, I thought. Then I called Redmond back and told him I was reconsidering my position, but I wanted to speak to my wife on the phone, to know that she was OK. I called in an old favor from a business connection in Miami, and he tracked that moron's cell-phone location here. I decided to deal with my own personal business myself. What business is it of Roker's? It was a bit of sport, actually. A challenge. I like those. Who would find my treacherous wife and her sniveling boy toy first? Superman Roker or me? Looks like I won. Now untie me, you idiots, or I assure you, you will regret this for the rest of your pathetic lives! A rich man can do anything he wants. That's a life lesson, especially for you, Pollyanna," he said, looking at Pansy.

"Well, Barry, I admire your can-do attitude, but from where I stand, things aren't looking too good," said Nina.

"Barry, is it possible that Tiffany might think you've been making a fool of her with all your lady friends?" asked Pansy, gesturing toward him with the rifle. Barry cringed a little. "Have you considered that maybe your actions drove her into the arms of her tennis pro?"

"Oh my God. Are you for real?" said Barry with disgust, while still keeping a wary eye on the rifle. "You just don't get it. It's different for a man. A romp in the sack is just that. It's not a goddamn fairy tale meaning happily ever after."

"He has a point," said Danish. "Sometimes you think you're both just having fun on a Friday night, but then you get five or six extreme phone messages, and you have to change your phone number."

"Danish!" said Nina and Pansy together.

"Of course, now that I've found true love, I don't see it like that," said Danish, putting his hands up.

"And you," Barry said, looking at Nina with narrowed eyes. "No wonder your husband went looking for a little something extra. He must have realized he was burdened with a tedious shrew with no fashion sense and nothing better to do than interfere in things that have *absolutely nothing to do with you!*"

Nina glared at Barry and then shrugged. "We'll be sure to pass on your interesting account of the story thus far to Deputy Superintendent Roker when we see him. Tie him to that coconut tree over there, Danish, and let's make it snappy. We've got to make sure Tiffany and Lance don't decide to make their getaway with the emerald.

"That is, when they're done making whoopee in their romantic love nest in the woods," she said, still looking at Barry. He lunged at them ineffectually. They grabbed hold of him and dragged him up the sand to the tree line, muffling his angry torrent of words with another piece of duct tape across his mouth.

Once Barry was securely tied to the coconut tree, they regrouped by the boat.

"OK, I guess it's time to call Roker," said Danish. "We'll have to use the ship-to-shore radio." He started rooting around in the storage shelf on the boat. Pansy was still holding the gun gingerly in her hands. Danish glanced over, then stood up and pried her fingers away from the stock, taking the gun from her. He expertly took the shells out of it and lay the gun gently in the bottom of the boat, and then he put the shells in his knapsack. Nina and Pansy looked at him questioningly.

"You're not the only one with a past. I grew up in Colorado," he said. "Well, who wants to give Roker the good news?" He held the radio in his hand.

Nina began pacing back and forth, looking down at the sand as Pansy and Danish stood quietly watching her. She stopped and spun around to face them.

"You know what? I have a few demons to exorcise, and doing yoga and drinking margaritas is not going to cut it. Tiffany is all the snotty bitches who were mean to me in high school *and* the one who screwed my husband on the antique velvet sofa we bought *on our honeymoon* in Vermont *and* every rich, entitled airhead I've had to make way for my whole adult life, rolled into one. Barry is every arrogant bully who walked into a room, looked me up and down, and dismissed me as irrelevant. He deserves everything he's going to get. And Lance is every self-satisfied, inconsiderate jerk I knew in college who let his you-know-what do his thinking for him. He needs to smarten up before acting like an idiot is so ingrained in him that he's a lifer. I'm going to blow them to kingdom come." Danish and Pansy stared at her with their mouths open.

"Relax," Nina said. "No one's going to get hurt. I'll notify the police in a timely fashion so Deputy Superintendent Blue Roker can be on hand to apprehend the criminals and recover the necklace, but first I'm going to give them something to mull over all the days and nights they sit in the slammer. Mr. Calm, Cool, and Collected Ted Matthews told me someone needed to teach Barry Bassett a lesson, but who says it has to be him? I'm the one who Bassett and Bassett have been harassing."

"Whoa, Nina! Rock and roll! Let's do it!" Danish whispered loudly, punching the air with his fist.

"*Shhh!* OK," she said. "But we have to hurry. We need to get back to town and get a few supplies and then burn it back here ASAP. Hopefully Lance can keep her entertained for at least a half hour longer. If they leave before we've told Roker where they are, we'll be guilty of withholding information from the police, and they'll get away with it, just like they've gotten away with everything their whole lives."

She paused and looked at Danish. "I can't believe it's me leading *you* astray."

"I *know*. Far out!" said Danish.

Nina thought for a moment. "Let's find the Zodiac and hide it so they can't leave," she said. She glanced at her watch.

"It's just a little more than an hour until sunset, so they're probably here to stay for the night," she said. "Maybe they're still expecting Barry to call to arrange a drop for the ransom. I'll take Pansy back to town so her kids won't have to visit her in jail if things go off track, and while I'm there, I'll get the supplies I need. You stay here and keep an eye on the motley crew. If things get messy, take the Zodiac or Barry's boat, and call the police right away. I'll be back here in forty-five minutes, tops. As soon as I get back, we'll call the police. Three quarters of an hour isn't going to make that much difference. Barry's certainly not going anywhere."

They looked over at Barry, who was slumped against the trunk of the coconut palm, watching them, quiet for the moment.

Pansy clapped her hands. "This is exciting! And to think I was just going to do the laundry this afternoon if we finished the treasure hunt early!"

They circled the small island at a slow jog, looking along the edge of the forest for the Zodiac. They found it on the other side of the island, facing the channel, under a pile of palm fronds. They dragged it down to the water and then pulled it by a line along the shallows until they figured they were out of earshot of the hut in the woods, and climbed in. Danish started the motor and they made their way slowly to the far side of the island, where they put their boat back in the water and hid the Zodiac beside the fallen palm tree. Danish hunted around on the bottom of the Zodiac for a radio, but there was none.

"Lance and Tiffany must have it with them," he said.

"Barry must have one," said Nina, wading out to his boat. She grabbed it off the seat and handed it to Danish.

"Here. Take his emergency flares, too, just in case," said Nina.

"Kevin is going to get to know the naughty-step very well," said Pansy to no one in particular. "A cell phone is not a toy."

Danish took the rifle out of the boat, put his knapsack over his shoulder, and grabbed a jug of water.

"Drive carefully, ladies. Don't forget where you left me, eh?" he said. Then he trudged up the beach to where Barry sat tied to the tree.

12

Nina started the boat and nosed out from the shallows. Once they were out in the main channel, she opened the throttle, and they zoomed back to Coconut Cove along the coast of Pineapple Cay. Now that they knew where they were going, the trip seemed much shorter. Nina eased the boat into the municipal dock, and Pansy hopped out to secure the rope to a cleat. They walked quickly up the hill to Water Street, trying not to attract attention.

"I'll call you when we get back, Pansy. If you don't hear from Danish or me by eight o'clock, call the police and tell them everything, OK?" said Nina.

Pansy looked uncertain. "I should go with you."

"We need you to stay here to call for help in case something happens. Which it won't," said Nina. "Just one more thing. Do you have a portable stereo or boom box at home?"

"Yes," said Pansy, breathlessly. "We have an old one we use for the beach and pool parties."

"Perfect," said Nina. "May I borrow it for a couple of hours?"

As Pansy took off at a trot, Nina called after her, "And bring the loudest or most annoying music CD you have! Meet me at the dock as soon as you can."

Nina walked quickly down the street to the hardware store. She knew exactly what she was looking for. She pushed open the door and walked into the dark shop, looking around her as her eyes adjusted to the change in lighting. She was looking for the bin filled with fireworks that she had seen on her first visit a week ago. The bin was still there by the counter, but it was now filled with colorful plastic balls and children's sand pails and spades. Nina hurried over to the counter as Harold emerged from the back room.

"Back again! What can I do for you, Nina?" he asked with a smile.

"Hi, Harold. The other day when I was in here, this bin was full of fireworks," said Nina.

"Yes," said the man, nodding. "Mrs. Savage was in here yesterday and bought the lot for the museum barbecue tonight. I didn't think I was ever going to get rid of them. It was supposed to be a surprise, so you'll keep it to yourself, won't you?"

"Yes, of course," said Nina. She was dismayed. Her plan hinged on those fireworks. She stood there for a second, wondering what to do next. Go to the police station, then go get Danish, she decided.

"Now if I could only get rid of the other four boxes out back. Were you looking for some?" he asked.

"Yes!" said Nina. "I'll take them all." She went out back with him and carried them to the counter, where she paid for the fireworks, along with a heavy-duty flashlight, a box of long matches, a hunting knife, and some cord. She borrowed a wheelbarrow to carry it all down to the dock. Out of the corner of her eye she saw Ted's Jeep roll slowly by her, hauling a boat down Water Street, but she didn't look back.

She hopped into the boat, put in the boxes, took a long swig of water from a jug, and lifted the red fuel can to see how much gas she had left. It was more than half-full. Pansy's turquoise golf cart wheeled into the loading area next to the dock, and she ran down onto the dock carrying the biggest boom box Nina had ever seen.

"It's got batteries in it, and here are some CDs. I hope that's what you had in mind. Be careful!" she said as Nina waved and pulled away from the dock.

In another minute, Nina was flying back down the coast, her hair whipping in the wind. She glanced at her watch as she slowed down to approach the back side of Love Cay. Twenty minutes to sundown. She could see Danish sitting on the sand with the rifle across his knees and Barry beside him, still sitting with his back resting against the trunk of the palm tree. Danish stood up as Nina nosed the boat up onto the beach, hopped out, and pulled it up onto the sand. Together they lifted the boxes of fireworks out and hid the second boat next to the Zodiac.

"I just snuck back to the hut to see what Lance and Tiffany were up to," he said. "Lance was starting a fire, and Tiffany was still lounging on the bed in her birthday suit. I don't think they're planning on going anywhere tonight."

"Good. Now we lay the charges," said Nina. Danish looked at her with raised brows.

"Fireworks," said Nina, smiling. "The boom-boom surprise."

They gave Barry a drink of water, ignoring his verbal abuse, and then Nina sat on the sand by the boat bundling up the cakes and tubes of fireworks as quickly as she could. She dug through the boxes to see what types she had to work with, planning the sequence in her mind's eye. Then, with Danish's help, Nina quietly made a couple of loops around the hut with a string of firecrackers and set a ring of rockets and Roman candles alongside those, about thirty feet back from the hut. Lance and Tiffany were back inside, once again otherwise occupied on the air mattress.

"I guess they really do love each another," whispered Nina sarcastically.

Nina and Danish laid another row of charges alongside the narrow path out to the beach to the spot where they had found the Zodiac. Nina made sure to place the rockets about fifteen feet off the track and zigzagged the firecrackers back and forth in the sand along the edge of the forest near—but not too near—where they'd found the Zodiac. Finally, she set up a battery of fireworks behind a boulder near where they'd found the Zodiac. She angled all the rockets away from the island and from any traffic in the boat channel. They walked back to their boat on the opposite side of the island, where Nina picked up the CDs.

"What do you think?" she asked. "Raffi, the Archies, or Nickelback? The Gallaghers certainly have eclectic musical tastes."

"Let's go with the Archies. It's been a while," said Danish. Nina loaded it into the stereo, which she set gently on the sand.

"OK," said Nina. "Time to call the police."

Danish pulled the ship-to-shore radio off his belt and turned it on. He took a deep breath and pressed the "Outgoing" button.

"Calling the Pineapple Cay police detachment. Come in Roker, over." The radio crackled. Two seconds later, they heard Blue Roker's voice coming over the radio.

"This is Roker. Pineapple Cay Police. Is this Jensen? What do you want?"

"Jensen here. Roker switch to channel six eight, over."

Danish switched the knob on the radio to a secure channel so that Lance and Tiffany wouldn't hear if they happened to have their radio on in the hut, and neither would any passing boats. The radio crackled again.

"All right, Jensen. What do you want? I'm busy," said Blue.

"Well, Deputy Superintendent Roker, sir, I just thought you would like to know that my associate and I have located Tiffany Bassett and her abductor. It turns out she abducted herself with the help of her lover, Lance. We also have apprehended Mr. Barry Bassett, who was armed and about to kill them both. The *Morning Glory* necklace is also here. I have had a visual on that. We are here on Love Cay in Diamond Cays National Park, if you would like to come collect all the criminals we have bagged here this afternoon. Over."

"Tell him to approach the island from the channel side, the west side," said Nina quickly. "Otherwise a rocket might fall on them."

Danish pressed the button on the radio again. "Pineapple Cay police, come in. Jensen here. Please approach Love Cay from the west side for your own safety. Just to clarify: that is not a threat, just a safety tip. Over."

There was silence on the other end of the radio for several seconds. Then it crackled to life again. "I am six minutes away. Do not do anything stupid. More stupid. Stupider. Do you hear me?" shouted Blue.

Danish held the radio away from his ear. "Okeydokey. See you soon. We'll put the light on for you. Over," said Danish.

"He said thanks and he's on his way," Danish said to Nina.

"I heard," she said. "We haven't got much time. Let's go."

She handed Danish the stereo and the flashlight and grabbed the long matches and the duct tape. They crept up the sandy path to the ring of firecrackers and fountain fireworks they had placed around the hut. Nina took a deep breath and ran swiftly around the ring, lighting the cakes of rockets and then the fuse on the string of firecrackers.

"I hope this works," she said apprehensively as they watched the cord burn toward the first rocket. The spark reached it, and it shot into the air with a huge bang, exploding into a shower of red and gold above the trees. Nina pushed the "Play" button on the stereo, and she and Danish ducked down in the shadows of the trees to watch. Sparkling fountains of colored sparks sprang up ten feet tall around the hut, lighting up the clearing. The firecrackers sounded a rat-a-tat over the voice of Andy Kim, like a machine gun strafing the forest floor. The rockets shrieked and boomed, one after another. Shriek, boom; shriek, boom; shriek, boom! The sky was full of shimmering, cascading flowers and starbursts in green and gold, red and blue. Just as she expected, Lance came running out of the hut followed by Tiffany. He was dressed in just a pair of shorts, and she in one of his T-shirts and underpants.

"What is that? Someone's shooting at us!" yelled Lance. Nina heard Tiffany scream repeatedly as she hopped up and down in her bare feet. They spun around, looking for their attackers, and then looked up into the sky as the colorful rockets burst into bouquets of pink flowers in the now–midnight-blue sky above them. They were so distracted by the constant hiss and boom of the rockets and the flashing lights that they did not see Nina and Danish crouching in the forest a short distance away.

"Grab the necklace, babe, and let's get out of here!" shouted Lance.

"You get it!" screeched Tiffany. "Why would you even ask me to go back in there when the roof could fall in on my head? Don't you care about me at all?" He disappeared inside the hut and came back with the necklace in his hand.

"Let's go!" he shouted. "To the boat!" He grabbed her hand, and they started down the path to where Delmont Samuels's Zodiac had been hidden. Nina lit the first charge along the path. It exploded with a shower of sand as they passed.

"Ahhh!" shrieked Tiffany. Nina lit the string of firecrackers along the path, and then she and Danish crashed through the undergrowth onto the beach just as Tiffany and Lance emerged from the forest path. They were both yelling, and the sky was full of starbursts, streaks, and flashes of colored light. Lance and Tiffany looked around wildly, pulling fallen palm fronds away from the area where they'd left the Zodiac.

"It's gone!" said Lance incredulously.

"You idiot!" said Tiffany, rounding on him. "I suppose you left the keys in it!"

"It had an outboard motor; you don't use a key, you idiot," he said nastily. The firecrackers near where the boat had been hidden started to pop, and Lance and Tiffany hopped up and down on the sand with their arms shielding their faces.

"OK, Danish, now for the big finale," said Nina. They dashed across the darkened beach and behind the boulder where the battery of fireworks was set. Nina lit the fuse, and five rockets shrieked into the night sky, bursting into a grove of sparkly green-and-gold palm trees above the island, their fronds drooping gracefully into the treetops. Then red chrysanthemums filled the sky. As they faded, multicolored starbursts burst one after another, lighting up the water. Silver spinners whirled, and red-and-yellow comets shot up into the sky, rapid-fire. The show ended with a grand finale of glittering silver-and-gold starbursts trailing down into the sea, a giant emerald nestled among them. The faint chords of "Sugar Sugar" could still be heard from the woods.

As the shrieks and pops of the rockets subsided, Nina heard the steady drone of two boats approaching, one engine with a low whine, the other at a slightly higher pitch. She looked out at the dark water and saw a large dual-engine powerboat racing toward them with three bright floodlights mounted on a frame lighting up the water in front of it and the beach where Tiffany and Lance were cowering in the sand. From where Nina stood, it looked like Lance was trying to shield himself from Tiffany as she slapped at him with both hands. Behind the big boat was a Boston Whaler. As the light landed on them, Tiffany and Lance froze and looked out at the water.

"This is the Pineapple Cay Police. Halt, and put your hands above your head," boomed Blue Roker's voice through a megaphone.

"Oh, no!" shouted Lance. "Quick! To the other side of the island! Whoever did this got here somehow. Maybe there's a boat!" He turned and scrambled up the beach toward the forest path, still clutching the necklace in his hand, not even looking back to see if Tiffany was following him. She stood there for a second, looking after him and then out toward the lighted police boat, the word POLICE now clearly visible in navy-blue capital letters on its white flank. There were the silhouettes of a half dozen officers in it. She turned and started to scramble up the beach after Lance. Nina had a flashing vision of Barry's speedboat anchored in the shallows on the other side and their own rental boat nearby.

"Oh, no, you don't!" she said, breaking out of her crouch behind the boulder on the beach. She pounded across the hardpacked sand along the water's edge with her hands above her head. When she reached Tiffany, she tackled her to the ground. Tiffany went down with a grunt. She struggled wildly, more angry than frightened, trying to see who had flattened her. Nina sat on Tiffany's back, pinning her arms to the sand.

"Hello, Tiffany," she said. "Going somewhere? Everyone's been so worried. Did you enjoy the show?"

"You!" screeched Tiffany, straining to turn her head to glare at Nina.

Nina could see Danish churning up the beach and into the woods after Lance, and then she heard a muffled thump and some grunts. Danish dragged Lance out of the trees and onto the sand by his ankles. Nina quickly duct taped Tiffany's arms together behind her back and threw Danish the roll of tape. She could hear the boats skidding onto the sand directly behind her, and several pairs of feet splashing through the water and up onto the beach.

Blue Roker ran by her to where Danish was struggling with Lance. Lance was taller and stronger than Danish, and now that the element of surprise was a no longer on his side, Danish was having trouble subduing him. Lance threw Danish off and sprang to his feet, which Danish had somehow managed to tape together. Lance hopped around like a pogo stick, hitting at Danish with both fists. Then he lost his balance and tipped over into the sand, where he lay on his side, struggling to right himself as Danish danced around him. Blue grabbed Lance's wrist and flipped him onto his stomach, putting his knee across his back; then he grabbed Lance's other hand and twisted it behind his back, snapping on a pair of handcuffs, all in one smooth motion. He pulled Lance to his feet and stepped back. A second officer moved in, grabbing Lance's bicep in one hand and putting the other hand on the top of his holstered gun.

Nina was still sitting on Tiffany's back. Blue walked toward them, staring at Nina with a look of bewildered amazement on his face. Nina rose from Tiffany's back and took several slow steps back. Blue pulled Tiffany to her feet, cut the duct tape on her wrists with a knife, and cuffed her with a pair of regulation police handcuffs. An officer stepped forward and held her in the same manner as the first officer held Lance. The pair of them stood squirming angrily in the firm grasp of a muscular, uniformed officer.

"You led them right here, didn't you?" said Tiffany angrily to Lance. "Did you even bother to look to see if anyone was following you?"

Blue cut in to read them their rights, but Tiffany couldn't help herself.

"We were so close, you dumb jock! All you had to do was go to Star Cay and collect the money, and we'd be in Rio tomorrow!"

Lance, head poseur in the Beer Commercial, exploded.

"Guess what? Your husband didn't want to pay to get you back. He *thanked* me for taking you off his hands. In fact, he offered me a million dollars to get rid of you permanently! Said he wouldn't tell the police that we'd stolen the necklace if I did it. I told him to go to hell, but I should have taken it!" he yelled.

"Deputy Chief Superintendent Roker, sir," said Danish, brushing the sand off his clothes and sidling up next to Blue. "Barry Bassett, attempted murderer, is currently tied up to a coconut tree on the other side of the island. He has been treated humanely, given water and a granola bar."

Blue sighed loudly and gestured for two other officers to go get Barry. They took off at a synchronized jog, lighting the forest path with flashlights they pulled from their belts.

"Now that I've had to spend so much time with you in that hut, I wouldn't spend another night with you for a million dollars!" Tiffany shouted at Lance. "You snore! And the way you eat spaghetti is revolting!"

"OK, princess," said Lance, "for your information, you get a *subscription* to *Cosmopolitan* magazine, not a *prescription* for it. If you've got a prescription for it, I think you've been overdosing. The hooker look seemed hot, but the novelty has *definitely* worn off."

"Where's the *necklace*?" asked Nina. It suddenly occurred to her that no one was holding it. "The last time I saw it, it was in Lance's hand," she said.

Lance laughed with a sneer. The officer holding Lance searched his captive's pockets with his free hand, but it wasn't there. Tiffany was wearing only a T-shirt and underpants, so it was unlikely she had it. Nina was suddenly aware of Ted standing beside her. He and Blue swept the sand with beams of light from their flashlights. Nina retraced Lance's steps up the beach, trying to imagine how far he might have been able to throw it. Danish grabbed his flashlight out of the sand and disappeared into the woods on the forest track. He reemerged a couple of minutes later with the necklace in his hand. He held it aloft as he walked triumphantly over to Blue and slapped it in his hand. Blue put it in his shirt pocket and buttoned it.

Tiffany seemed to notice Nina's presence again. "You! Are you some kind of sicko wannabe? Always showing up in the middle of my business? Why don't you get your own life?" she snarled at Nina.

"Really, Tiffany. Sleeping with the hunky tennis pro? That's a bit of a cliché, isn't it?" asked Nina. "You don't have much of an imagination, do you?"

"Seriously, bitch. The ruggedly handsome fishing guide? Or is it the strong, silent type in uniform?" asked Tiffany in a needling nasal whine.

Danish nodded his head. "Touché, Nina. She's got you there."

"Shut up, Danish," snapped Nina.

Lance grinned slimily. "Hunky, eh? Thanks, Nancy Drew. I think you're pretty hot, too, for a more mature woman."

"Shut up, Lance. I think you're probably going to prison for extortion, fraud, or something very serious like that. Game over," said Nina, swinging her backhand.

Blue stepped forward, shaking his head. "OK, OK. We'll take over from here. Mandy, put them in the boat. Ted, can you take these two home?" Blue glanced at Nina and Danish. "I'm going to be a while."

"Sure, no problem," said Ted.

Blue scanned the forest edge with his eyes, then turned to Nina and Danish, his hands on his hips.

"I can't think offhand what law you may have broken here, but given the unique sequence of events that has transpired, I'd like to hear the full story tomorrow morning, if it suits you. In the meantime, please give me a break and stay out of trouble. Can you do that?"

Nina nodded emphatically.

As they followed Ted to his boat, Danish paused in front of Blue. "Did you see all that, Blue? Top-grade nephew-in-law material right here." He thumped himself on the chest twice and walked out into the surf.

Blue seemed to hesitate for a moment. He looked first at Danish and then at Nina. "I would be remiss if I didn't thank you for alerting us to the location of the suspects. I can't endorse your methods, but we'll all be glad to see this case closed. See you in the morning."

As Danish pushed the boat out and climbed in, Ted held up a set of keys on a miniature foam flip-flop key ring. "These yours?" asked Ted. "I found them on the municipal dock."

"Oh. Thank you," said Nina, pocketing them. "Don't take this the wrong way, but what are you doing here? After dark in the cays?"

"I might ask you the same thing," he said. "I saw you hauling *explosives* down to the dock this afternoon, then taking off by yourself in a boat less than an hour before sundown. I apologize for following you, but I was concerned. Explosives aside, you haven't been here very long, and you don't know these waters. I turned the truck around and followed you. It wasn't hard to find you, what with the fireworks and all. Blue arrived at the same time. He was already here in the cays, down by Wreath Cay. He bombed back up here like a bat out of hell when Danish radioed him."

"Are you two done with your little tête-à-tête over there?" called Danish from the boat. "I'd like to get back and give Alice the good news."

They drove home slowly in the dark, with the lights on and Ted's fishing sonar beeping out the changes in bottom depth. He kept to the channel, the lights on the red-and-green markers glowing in the night. They let Danish off at the Plantation Inn, tying up at the hotel dock this time. It was lit with tiki torches running in pairs up to the lawn of the inn. People sometimes boated the short distance up the shore from the marina for dinner. The inn glowed invitingly in the dark, and laughter floated down from the veranda, where people had gathered for predinner drinks. Here in Coconut Cove, the evening was unfolding in a civilized manner.

Ted maneuvered the boat away from the inn, and they hummed along in silence until he beached it below the fishing lodge, pulling the motor up and tying the boat up to a fallen tree trunk for the night.

He turned to Nina. "I don't know about you, but I could use a drink about now. Do you want to come up for a glass of wine?" he asked.

"Sure, that sounds good," said Nina. She was coated in dried sweat and sea salt, but she was very curious to see where he lived, and she wasn't ready to call it a night just yet. Adrenaline was still humming in her veins. Ted went ahead of her up the path, lighting the way with his flashlight. Through the tangle of trees and shrubs lining the path, she could see cabins on both sides facing the beach, warm yellow rectangles of light filling the windows. There was movement behind the curtains in one cabin. Nina surmised the guests were dressing for dinner.

"Fortress Matthews," she said under her breath.

"Pardon?" he asked.

"Nothing."

They emerged at the edge of a narrow band of grass surrounding the main lodge. A short flagstone path led to a wraparound veranda. Ted took the stairs two at a time and held the screen door open for her. The interior was a large, open club room furnished with comfortable cushioned chairs and sofas grouped in front of a stone fireplace and along the walls. There were windows all the way around, except on the back wall, where there was a bar. The walls, floor, and ceiling were all varnished hardwood, stained a warm brown. There were low bookshelves under the windows filled with novels and field guides. Along one wall, a long table had been set for dinner with a dozen places.

"It's beautiful," said Nina.

"Thanks," said Ted, looking around. Nina could tell he was proud of it.

A woman in her midfifties wearing a khaki golf shirt with *Matthews Bonefish Lodge* embroidered on the sleeve emerged from the door behind the bar.

"Ted! There you are. Where have you been? Our special guests are arriving at the airport in an hour and a half. I was getting worried," she said.

"Hi, Cheryl. Don't worry. Everything's under control. I'll head out to pick them up shortly. Cheryl, this is Nina Spark, our next-door neighbor. Nina, may I introduce Cheryl Wilson, the brains of the operation," said Ted.

Cheryl looked at Nina with curiosity for a millisecond, then smiled and held out her hand. "How do you do, Nina. Pleased to meet you."

"Nice to meet you," said Nina, shaking her hand and smiling back at her.

"Can I get you anything before you go, Ted?" asked Cheryl.

"No, thanks, we're fine," he said, striding over to the bar and reaching over the polished mahogany top to grab a bottle of red wine, an opener, and two glasses. "I'm going up the hill for a breather before I go. See you shortly." He held the door open for Nina again.

Cheryl now looked at her with open curiosity, a smile playing on her lips as the screen door slapped shut behind them.

"I thought we might get a few minutes of peace up here," said Ted, looking back at Nina over his shoulder as he started up a path through another grove of dense green vegetation. "The guests will be starting dinner in the lodge soon."

The short path through the trees brought them to a clapboard cabin, a little bigger than the guest cottages on the beach. It was perched above the lodge, and it looked down over a short, gentle slope onto the rest of the camp. A covered veranda ran across the front. Behind the cabin was nothing but dense dark-green vegetation. It was very private, hidden from below by the grove of trees.

"My sanctuary," said Ted, leading the way up onto the veranda. "You can't see it in the dark, but the view is something else. I can even see your little yellow cottage from here," he said, looking at her and smiling. The sky was strewn with layers of brilliant white stars. Ted set the wine, opener, and glasses on a weathered wooden crate, pulled up a chair for her, and patted the back of it. She sank into it while he pulled a matchbox from his pocket and lit a candle made from a coconut shell and set it on the crate. He sat down beside her and opened the wine. Then he handed her a glass and held up the other.

"To the end of the Tiffany Bassett affair," he said.

"I'll drink to that," said Nina.

They raised their glasses to the stars and sipped the wine.

"You certainly live up to your name, Nina Spark," he said. "There has been hardly a dull moment since you moved in next door. Rose used to call me to chase her ill-natured cat out from under her veranda every once in a while, but that's about it. Then she'd feed me milk and cookies and give me what she called a *pep talk*."

Nina thought about what Danish had told her about Miss Rose her first day on Pineapple Cay. She wondered what kind of love advice Miss Rose had offered Ted during her kitchen-table pep talks.

"What kind of pep talk?" she asked.

He glanced over at her, then looked down at the lodge with its cozy golden glow. "Oh, you know, she was very concerned with everyone's welfare and happiness, and she had pretty strong opinions on what constituted a good life . . ." His voice trailed off, and he looked over at Nina again.

"She used to cut out articles from Oprah's magazine and flag me down as I was driving by so she could give them to me. I can't remember the particulars, although I did glance at a few over breakfast, because she'd quiz me about them when I saw her. The phrase *work-life balance* sticks in my mind. She once gave me a very detailed article on decluttering your closets because she said my truck was a mess. If you don't mind me saying, it's sort of terrifying to think that a good portion of the women in the English-speaking world are walking around armed with the kind of knowledge they gleaned from that magazine. Kind of makes a man feel unprepared."

"Well, I don't have a cat, and my cooking is probably not up to Miss Rose's caliber, but if you come by and help me hang my shutters someday, as per our arrangement, I'll bake you some cookies. Spark secret recipe," she said.

He smiled again. "Sounds good. That was quite a fireworks display. Did you do that?" he asked.

She told him about the family business and the summers and fall weekends she'd spent traveling with her father and her brothers to state fairs and festivals throughout New England. "I'll have you know that I designed the display the night Miss Whole Milk Cheese was crowned in Swiss Falls, Vermont," she said.

"So, what are you going to do now that there are no dangerous criminals to chase on Pineapple Cay?" he asked, glancing over at her and then back out at the star-filled sky.

"I'm going to fix up my lovely little house, plant a garden, and get back to work. This has been one exhausting two-week-long vacation.

But I must admit, today was sort of exhilarating. And I've met a lot of nice people. I like it here," she said.

He smiled, and then they were both quiet again, looking out at the star-studded sky and listening to the breeze rustling in the leaves of the trees.

"I was married once," he said, breaking the silence. "We met at college in Asheville and moved down to Key West after graduation, thinking we'd start there. She was an artist. Still is. It took us five years to figure out that while we were both aiming at getting far enough ahead so that we could explore the world beyond Key West, she was aiming at New York or Paris, and I was yearning for the middle of nowhere. It happens. She's happier now, and so am I."

Nina didn't say anything. So, he knew about Darren. Well, who didn't? After a few moments, Ted set his glass on the table and stood up.

"I would much rather stay here enjoying the night air with you, but I've got a special charter coming in less than an hour. Let me walk you home. You must be tired after wrestling criminals to the ground today," he said.

"Thanks for the wine. This is a lovely spot. Now I'll have a picture of it when I imagine you talking about the one that got away at dinner, and then sitting out here watching the sun set from your hilltop aerie, cleaning your fishing pole or something," said Nina.

He looked in her eyes with a small smile on his lips, but he didn't say anything.

She stood, and they walked down the hill to the beach and along the surf to her cottage. It was only about eight o'clock, but it felt much later. She was looking forward to a long, hot shower and then bed. At the foot of the stairs to her veranda, they stood facing each other.

"Well, I'd better get back to the lodge and make sure things are organized," said Ted.

He seemed to hesitate for a moment. He turned to look out at the dark water and then turned back to Nina. "I'm headed down into the cays for a few days, taking some clients on a camping fishing trip in a remote part of the chain. Maybe when I get back you'll let me take you out to dinner?"

She realized she'd been half hoping he would do this—and half hoping he wouldn't. She needed to catch her breath. One the other hand, the idea was not unpleasant. She almost asked him if it was her borderline criminal behavior that prompted his invitation. But she didn't.

"That would be very nice," she said.

"Great," he said, and smiled. "I'll give you a call when I get back." He turned away with his hands in his pockets and started back up the beach to his place.

He'd only gone a few steps when he stopped, stood still for a second, then turned around and walked back to where she was still standing, watching him. He looked deeply into her eyes, and then he lifted her chin gently with one hand, bent down, and kissed her tenderly on the mouth. His lips were soft and warm. She kissed him back. She felt his other hand rest lightly on her hip, then slide around to the small of her back and pull her to him. It was a long, intense kiss. She felt her knees buckle slightly. He held her up with both arms and pulled his head back to look at her. Mr. Nice Guy had suddenly transformed into Mr. Extremely Dangerous and Highly Flammable. He closed his eyes and bent down to kiss her neck. She wrapped her arms around him tightly. She could feel his heart pounding in his chest, and her own, too. Finally, he pulled away and rested his forehead against hers, breathing hard, still holding her in his arms.

"I have wanted to do that for a long time," he whispered.

She couldn't resist making a joke. "You mean, ever since we met eleven days ago?" she whispered back.

"Actually, I think it was when you hooked that fish. Nothing is more erotic than a woman reeling in a fish," he said.

She wasn't sure he was joking.

He kissed her again. "Mmm. Lightly salted Nina Spark. Delicious," he said. "For the first time in my life, I don't want to go to work. Tonight of all nights."

Her brain was hormone-addled, and her limbs were rubbery. It was beyond her ability to reply. She licked her lips. He stroked her side gently, then kissed her once more, softly, and let her go. She leaned against the veranda post and looked up at him. He looked down into her eyes but didn't touch her.

He sighed deeply. "I've got to go. Stay out of trouble. I'll be back on Friday. We have a date, don't forget."

"I won't," she murmured.

He smiled and turned away. "Don't blow up my lodge while I'm gone, eh?" he said without turning around.

In a daze, Nina let herself into the cottage and had a long, hot shower. She dressed in clean clothes, pulling her soft wool sweater on over top. About an hour later, she happened to glance out the window of her bedroom and saw Ted's Jeep go by, heading in the direction of his lodge. In the front passenger seat was a man looking straight ahead. Nina thought his profile looked very familiar. A woman and two girls were in the backseat. They were in shadow in the dim light from the street lamp. Behind Ted's Jeep was the shiny black SUV with dark windows and license plates from the main island.

She called Pansy, who said she'd be over later, ate a salad, and then mixed a pitcher of iced tea and took a glass out to the veranda. It was a warm night. She lit a pillar candle and set it down on the edge of the deck. She heard the front door open, and Danish called out a hello. He pushed open the screen door onto the veranda a moment later, a glass of iced tea in his hand.

"Well, I had a shower and went over to Aunt Agatha's house and had a glass of lemonade while I gave Alice the news that we had recovered the emerald for her. I think it went well. Her aunt offered me a digestive biscuit halfway through the visit," he said.

"Danish," said Nina, "is it possible that I saw the president of the United States and his family in Ted's Jeep a half hour ago?"

"Sure," he replied. "Ted's had a few former presidents over there. Politicians are big-time fishermen, I would say. A few movie stars, too. Not too many musicians, I don't think. I wonder why. Mostly doctors, lawyers, businessmen. A few women fishermen, too. Some serious hard-core ones with all the gear."

"Well, that would explain the men in mirrored shades in the black SUV we saw around town over the past few days. They weren't criminals hired to help Barry Bassett! They must be Secret Service agents doing a security check before the president arrived!" said Nina.

They heard a tap on the door. Danish jumped up to let Pansy in.

"Oh, you guys. I can't believe it! You did it! I was on pins and needles, looking out the window every five seconds until I saw the police boat come back," she said. She fell into the chair next to Nina. "So, tell me what happened!"

Nina and Danish filled her in.

"I love fireworks," said Pansy. "We watched the show after the barbecue. It was great, but I wish I'd seen yours."

"I'll create a display just for you sometime," said Nina. "On your birthday."

Pansy smiled and clapped her hands.

"So, who won the treasure hunt?" asked Nina.

"The girls' sailing team. The Clues Brothers never made it out of The Pirate's Wake, apparently."

"Well, we're pretty awesome detectives, I must say," said Danish.

"You were great, Danish," said Nina, "running after Barry when he had that gun! And keeping Lance from getting away. You're very brave."

"Back at you, kid," said Danish, raising his iced-tea glass to her.

"You, too, Pansy," said Nina. "If it wasn't for your insider knowledge of the maid-service schedules of the rich and infamous on Pineapple

Cay and familiarity with French lingerie sizes, we'd never have known about Lance and Tiffany."

"Although, honestly," continued Nina, "I've been going over it in my mind, and until Danish's slick retrieval of the GPS coordinates for Love Cay from Barry today, I couldn't really think of any other point since Tiffany disappeared when we actually had a clue about what was going on. I mean, it was really a complete fluke that we found them."

"I'm taking the win," said Danish.

"I went by the police station on my way here, and Blue was taking Tiffany, Barry, and Lance out to the police van. They were all in handcuffs. I think they're sending them to the main island tonight," said Pansy. "The Pineapple Cay station only has two holding cells, and I can't imagine what pair out of those three you could put together in a confined space after all that's happened." She sighed.

"Why couldn't they just be happy?" she asked. "None of them had to worry about paying the rent or having enough food to eat. In fact, they had enough money to satisfy any whim, and do some good in the world to boot. And, look at this, we all live in a place where the sun shines almost every day."

Danish leaned back in his chair and gazed out to the horizon, where a huge moon was rising out of the sea. "Well, to paraphrase the beloved American troubadour and lifestyle expert Jimmy Buffett, Pineapple Cay is a state of mind, my friend. You can be angry and bitter, or you can be happy. It's usually a choice."

"If you can't be a poet, be the poem," said Nina.

Danish nodded. "Right on."

ACKNOWLEDGMENTS

I am extremely grateful to Miriam Juskowicz for offering me the opportunity to publish this novel with Lake Union Publishing. It is the thrill of a lifetime. My sincere thanks to Kristin Mehus-Roe for her meticulous and thoughtful editing of the manuscript and for her ideas on how it might be improved. She has made me sound much more literate than I am, and it is thanks to her that Nina Spark did not have to pay excess baggage fees for all the stuff that did not fit in her duffel bag en route to Pineapple Cay. Thank you, also, to all the other members of the editorial, design, marketing, and administration team at Lake Union Publishing who contributed their expertise to producing this book. I am honored to have had the opportunity to work with you.

ABOUT THE AUTHOR

Junie Coffey lives with Fisherman Fred and Hurricane Annie in a little town north of forty-five degrees latitude, which got two hundred inches of snow last winter. She has worked as a travel writer and has both lived and vacationed throughout the Bahamas and the Caribbean, spending time in the islands every chance she gets. To learn more about the author and her work, visit www.pineapplecay.com.